A GENTLEMAN OF DUBIOUS REPUTATION

THE LORD JULIAN MYSTERIES

BOOK TWO

GRACE BURROWES

GRACE BURROWES PUBLISHING

DEDICATION

CHAPTER ONE

On my lengthy list of reasons for avoiding the Caldicott family seat, Harry's ghost took top honors. My oldest sibling, Arthur (still extant), came third, and Lady Clarissa Valmond (lively indeed) occupied the spot between them.

Harry haunted me even when I wasn't at Caldicott Hall, appearing in my daydreams and nightmares. Like the good brother he'd been, he did not stand on ceremony in death any more than he had in life. I'd nonetheless been relieved to quit the Hall months ago to finish recuperating at my London town house, though I'd yet to achieve a full return to health.

After parting ways with the military following Waterloo, I'd come home from the Continent in poor health. My eyes still objected to prolonged bright light, my stamina wasn't what it had been on campaign, my hair was nearly white, and my memory...

My memory had been a problem before I'd bought my commission.

And yet, I knew every tree of the lime alley that led to the Hall, forty-eight in all, though two were relative saplings, having been planted in my great-grandfather's day. The other forty-six were nearly four hundred years old, but for a few new recruits necessitated by lightning strikes, Channel storms, and other random misfortunes.

Atlas, my horse, knew the path to the Hall as well as I did and picked up his pace as we turned through the ornate main gate.

"You would not be so eager to complete this journey if His Grace had summoned you," I muttered.

Arthur had signed his summons with an *A*, meaning as a brother, not as the Duke of Waltham and head of the family. He was six years my senior and possessed of worlds more consequence, not merely by virtue of his title. Arthur carried the dignity of his station as naturally as a gunnery sergeant carried a spare powder bag.

He had been born to be a duke, just as Harry had been a natural fit with the role of charming spare. Our father had assured me many times that my lot in life was to be the despair of his waning years.

Atlas marched on, his horsey imagination doubtless filled with visions of lush summer grass and long naps in sunny paddocks. Harry and I had raced up the lime alley more times than I could count, on foot and on horseback and, once when slightly inebriated, running backward.

In earliest boyhood, I'd routinely lost. Harry had had two years on me, and for much of my youth, that had meant size and reach. Then Harry attained his full height, and I kept growing. Had he lived to be an old, old man, I'd have delighted in reminding him that I was the tallest Caldicott son, having an inch on Harry and a half inch on Arthur.

What I would not give to gloat over that inch to him in person.

Harry had been taken captive by the French, and I had followed him into French hands, thinking the two of us could somehow win free where one could not. I am not the smartest of the Caldicotts, clearly. Harry had expired without yielding any information to his captors, while my experience as a prisoner was complicated by...

Many factors.

I'd survived and escaped, and I'd do the same again if need be, but now that I was back in Merry Olde, public opinion castigated me for having the effrontery to outlive my brother. At least one faction of the military gossip brigade concluded that I'd bought my life through dishonorable means—betraying my commission—though the military itself had cleared me of such allegations.

Arthur had welcomed me home with the reserve of a duke. Not until we had been private had he informed me that acts of self-harm on my part would reflect poorly on the family honor. I was not to indulge in foolish histrionics simply because I'd been labeled a traitor, much less because I could barely see, my memory was worse than ever, and I never slept more than two hours at a stretch.

Petty annoyances were no justification for imbecilic stunts, according to Arthur. He'd delivered that scold with characteristic sternness, though I'd never wanted so badly to hug him.

One did not presume on ducal dignity. My time among the French had also left me with a peculiar reluctance to be touched. With few exceptions, I kept my hands to myself and hoped others would do likewise concerning my person.

I emerged from the lime alley to behold the Hall, sitting uphill on the opposite bank of William's Creek. That placid stream was named for a multiple-great-grandfather, who'd no doubt played in its shallows as Harry and I had. Aided by juvenile imagination, that waterway had been the English Channel, where we'd defeated the great Spanish Armada; the Thames; the raging North Atlantic; and the South China Sea.

As Atlas clip-clopped over the arched stone bridge, a pang of longing assailed me, for Harry's voice, for his presence, for even his relentless teasing and boasting. Why did Harry have to die? Why had he left camp that night? Why hadn't the French taken my life as they'd taken his?

I'd asked those questions a thousand times, though I posed them now with more sadness than despair.

Caldicott Hall was sometimes referred to as Chatsworth in miniature, meaning the Hall was merely huge as opposed to gargantuan. Like the Duke of Devonshire's seat up in Derbyshire, the Hall was built around a central open quadrangle. All four exterior approaches presented dignified, symmetric façades of golden limestone, with obligatory pilasters and entablatures adding an appearance of staid antiquity.

I drew Atlas to a halt, giving myself a moment to appreciate my family home and to gather my courage. My mother was off at some seaside gossip fest, thank the merciful powers, but Harry's ghost was doubtless in residence, as was my father's. And if that wasn't enough to give a fellow pause, my godmother, Lady Ophelia Oliphant, had threatened to follow me to the Hall once she'd tended to some social obligations.

Atlas rooted at the reins, suggesting a dutiful steed deserved his bucket of oats sooner rather than later. A slight movement from the window at the corner of the second floor caught my eye.

"We've been sighted," I muttered, letting the beast shuffle forward. "The advance guard should be out in less time than it takes Prinny to down a glass of port."

Half a minute later, a groom jogged up from the direction of the stable and stood at attention by the gents' mounting block. As Atlas plodded on, I nearly fell out of the saddle.

A footman coming forth to take charge of my saddlebags would not have been unusual.

The butler, Cheadle, might have welcomed me home in a fit of sentimentality, or one of my sisters might have bestirred herself to greet me if she were calling on Arthur.

Arthur *himself* sauntered out of the house, checked the time on his watch—which had been Papa's watch—and surveyed the clouds as if a perfectly benign summer sky required minute inspection. He was to all appearances the epitome of the reserved country gentleman. Tall, athletic, his wavy dark hair neatly combed, his aquiline profile the envy of portraitists and sculptors.

To the educated fraternal eye, though, the duke was in the next thing to a panic. His Grace set very great store by decorum. When I had returned from France after escaping from captivity and before the Hundred Days, Arthur had received me in the library and offered me a brandy in Harry's memory.

All quite civilized, though at the time, I'd been barely able to remain upright, my hands had shaken like an old man's, and I'd managed a mere sip of libation. When I'd come home from Waterloo, Arthur had merely greeted me at supper as if I'd been up to Town for a few fittings.

Before my wondering eyes, he came down the terrace steps and joined the groom at the mounting block. I swung from the saddle, taking care to have my balance before I turned loose of Atlas's mane. I'd fallen on my arse a time or two after a hard ride, but I refused to give Arthur the satisfaction of witnessing my humiliation.

"You are a welcome sight, Demming," I said to the towheaded groom as I untied my saddlebags. "Don't bother too much brushing Atlas out. A stop at the water trough, a quick currying, and a shady paddock once he's finished cooling out will be the answer to his prayers. Then he will roll in the first dusty patch he can find."

"Aye, milord," Demming replied. "Does himself get oats for his trouble?"

"A mash tonight wouldn't go amiss, but no oats until tomorrow if there's grass to be had."

"We've plenty of that. Come along, beastie."

Arthur was an accomplished horseman and would not begrudge Atlas good care, but impatience rolled off the ducal person as Demming led Atlas away. Now would come an interrogation. Had my journey been uneventful? How was Lady Ophelia? Was there any particular news from Town, and what did the physicians say about my dodgy eyesight? What exactly had happened at the Make-peace house party, and where were my valet, footman, groom, and coach?

"She's driving me mad," Arthur said, striding off toward the terrace steps. "The damned Valmond woman leaves me no peace, and it's well past time you took a bride."

~

I was supposed to march along beside my older brother like a good little soldier, but that way apparently led straight to the altar.

I would sooner go back to France. "Waltham, get hold of yourself. Harry was not engaged to marry Lady Clarissa, and neither am I. I nominate *you* to assuage the lady's matrimonial inclinations."

I barely had time to duck. For the first time in living memory, Arthur Beresford Cedric DeVere Caldicott took a swing at a family member.

"You missed on purpose," I said, resisting the urge to stick out my tongue. "Offer me something cool to drink, and let's discuss this like gentlemen."

Arthur regarded me as if I'd spouted an arcane proverb in French, which had been our first language. "I'd rather beat the stuffing out of you."

"Maybe you're in love." I trotted up the steps, though I well knew Arthur wasn't in love with Clarissa. Harry hadn't been either, and my own sentiments regarding Lady Clarissa's suitability as a wife made the vote unanimous.

I did not, in fact, even like her ladyship.

As I climbed the steps, I felt the toll taken by every dusty mile I'd traveled. I was not yet thirty years old, but war and captivity had aged me. My hair had turned white in France, though I had reason to hope some color was returning to the new growth. More to the point, I lacked the toughness I'd had as a reconnaissance officer.

My joints ached, my muscles burned, I was parched and exhausted. In short, I had overtaxed myself and had need of a hot bath followed by lengthy communion with a soft bed.

"God save me," Arthur muttered as a coach and four clattered up the drive. "She's posted spies, I tell you. Somebody doubtless recognized you riding through the village. I vow the damned woman will drive me to Bedlam."

"Waltham," I said, more than a little unnerved to see my brother, who never raised his voice much less his hand, muttering and cursing. "You sent for reinforcements, and I have come. Lady Ophelia will join me shortly if you ask her to—and even if you don't. Lady Clarissa can lay siege to the Hall all she pleases, but this citadel shall not crumble. Word of a Caldicott."

"Word of a blethering..." Arthur watched as the matched grays halted at the foot of the steps. Clarissa's auntie descended first on the arm of the liveried footman, and Enola Aimes was a fine-looking woman barely ten years Clarissa's senior.

I knew this little pantomime, having witnessed it many times. Mrs. Aimes was the advance party whose handsome figure drew appreciative glances, such that when Clarissa emerged, all eyes were already focused in the desired direction.

"Your Grace, my lord." Mrs. Aimes smiled up at us. "Clarissa, do come along. Our timing has been most fortunate, most fortunate indeed. Lord Julian is home, and you must greet him properly."

Lady Clarissa treated us to the expected performance. First, a dainty boot emerged from the coach, frothy skirts raised enough to provide just a peek at a slender ankle before the top of a fashionable bit of millinery, a slim gloved hand, and then the lady herself emerged from the coach.

She hesitated predictably on the steps—our moment to bask in her smile—then shaded her eyes because the pert little collection of silk and feathers on her head could not in any sense be called a bonnet. She next half turned, presenting us the near occasion of a *hip* to appreciate, gathered her skirts, and floated gracefully onto terra firma in a cloud of shimmery bronze silk.

The footman stepped back, and Clarissa remained beside the coach, beaming up at us. "Oh, Julian! How marvelous! I had no idea you were paying us a visit. We are simply delighted, aren't we, Enola?"

Her ladyship waited at the foot of the stairs, the most beautiful and least helpless woman I'd ever had the misfortune to know. Before guilt and manners got the better of Arthur, I moved down the steps and offered the lady a bow.

"Lady Clarissa. Good day. I have truly just this moment arrived, and thus I beg your pardon for greeting you in all my dirt. Let's go into the house, shall we, and you can tell me what you've been up to since last we met."

She simpered, I smiled, and I did not offer my dusty arm.

"I'd rather hear about what *you've* been up to, Julian." She gave me a look that suggested she'd worried about me, missed me, dreamed of me, and kept me in her nightly prayers.

Clarissa's features were on the dramatic side of perfection. Her hair was sable rather than the preferred blond. Her brows were a trifle heavy and swooping, her nose and chin a bit strong.

Her smile, though, was magical, full of warmth and mischief and suggesting all manner of quiet yearnings and unspoken wishes. What she said didn't matter half so much as what she *smiled*. Another man might have been enchanted by that smile.

"Do come along," Mrs. Aimes said, taking Arthur's arm. "I'm sure Lord Julian has all the latest *on dits*, and I vow I am absolutely parched for a cup of tea."

I waited for Lady Clarissa to gather up her skirts, gestured for one of her lapdogs to take her arm, and accompanied her into the house. Not for all the smiles in Sussex would I touch a woman I had trouble respecting, and certainly not when she was scheming to get her mitts on my only surviving brother.

~

As a prisoner of war, I'd been held in a cell that lacked windows. Candles had been denied me, and thus I had learned how time could expand or contract, bend back on itself, or stop. The thirty minutes of Lady Clarissa's visit reminded me of those dark, smothering times when I'd strain my ears to hear the scurry of a rat just to reassure myself that I was not dead.

Or deranged.

"We really must be going," Clarissa said, making no move to rise. "Julian, seeing you has been such a delight, not that Waltham isn't a delight, too, of course." She fired off a smile in Arthur's direction.

Arthur, enthroned in the wing chair closest to the parlor window, lazily stirred. "But you and Lord Julian haven't had a chance to catch up in any detail. We've been too busy hearing all about Lord Reardon's exhibition and Mrs. Aimes's missing puppy. Perhaps you two should share a hack tomorrow morning."

"Alas," I said, judging the distance between my brother's lap and the teapot, "I will need some time to recover from my travels, as will my poor horse. I will call at Valmond House when I am rested." Or when Prinny became a temperance advocate, whichever came last.

"You absolutely *must*," Clarissa said, as if her happiness depended on my visit. "We're much absorbed with preparing for Lord Reardon's exhibition, but we always have time for old and dear friends."

Who exactly was this *we* encompassed by Clarissa's regal pronoun?

"Lord Julian," Mrs. Aimes said, "before Lady Clarissa whisks me away, please tell us of the Makepeace house party. One heard of some lively goings-on."

"Just the usual bachelors and belles getting up to harmless mischief," I said, topping up my own tea cup. "A few little misunderstandings, a tiff and a spat, though all was well when I decamped." Not from me would she hear the juicy details, though I'd been in the thick of attempted kidnapping, slander, intrigue, and thievery.

"You men," Clarissa said. "You chatter amongst yourselves like schoolgirls at a quilting, but you never share the best bits outside your clubs."

And may God be thanked for that inviolable law. "Truly," I said, "the gathering was uneventful, though my reduced energies were taxed by even the tame entertainments typical of such functions."

Mrs. Aimes took the hint, getting to her feet. "We must leave you to recover from the journey, then," she said, offering Arthur a curtsey.

He was on his feet, too, of course, as was I. The last to rise—give the woman credit for dedication to her role at least—was Lady Clarissa.

"Waltham, we've taken up enough of your time," Clarissa said, presenting him her hand to bow over. "I'm sure Julian can see us out, can't you, my lord?"

She used my honorific strategically, sometimes flattering me with it—or so she doubtless believed—and sometimes brushing it aside to assume the familiarity of long acquaintance. Provided her coach was shortly tooling down the drive with her inside it, I did not care how she addressed me. Did she but know it, I was a legitimate bastard, in addition to my other shortcomings, and my title was more an irony than a courtesy.

"I'd be happy to see the ladies out." I headed for the door before Clarissa could take my arm. "Doesn't do to sit for too long following a long ride. Ladies, it has been a pleasure." I held the door for them, shot Arthur a glower, and left him to finish off the tea cakes in solitudinous splendor.

"You *are* looking well, Julian," Lady Clarissa said as we made our way toward the north portico. "One worried for you."

Her tone implied that *one* staggered forward under many burdens, but that anxiety over my wellbeing had figured most prominently among them. *One's* feminine fortitude was impeded by a gale-force headwind and blinding snow and probably a few brigands and witches too.

What tripe. "Thank you for your kind thoughts, my lady, but your concern would have been better spent on Harry." I preceded the ladies into the Hall's soaring marble foyer with a feeling of relief. Out damned spots, and all that.

"I *pray* for Harry's soul," Clarissa said, her tone reserved rather than wounded. "I *worry* for you. We hear things, Julian, even in the provinces."

Sussex was hardly the Outer Hebrides. Of course they'd heard the basics: I'd been a recluse in plain sight in London, I was not good *ton*, I still wore tinted spectacles, and my name was unflatteringly mentioned in the betting books.

Then too, when Arthur had needed my aid, I'd come hotfoot. Let's not forget that detail.

"Your prayers for Lord Harry are appreciated," I said, opening the front door before Cheadle could rouse himself to his station. "Though my brother died a hero's death and is doubtless enjoying eternity in the Anglican equivalent of Valhalla. Harry deserves to swill the best mead served by the comeliest Valkyries." I wished at least that for him.

"How fanciful you are. Lord Reardon shares your vivid imagination."

"Please give your brother my regards, and thank both of you ladies for making my homecoming more memorable." Not more pleasant, not more joyous. *Memorable* was as far as I would go.

The coach sat at the foot of the steps, the leaders stomping the gravel as if impatient to be away.

"The pleasure was ours." Mrs. Aimes gestured for a footman to escort her down the steps. "I am glad to see you looking recovered, my lord. Waltham seems to be feeling a bit more the thing too."

Oh ho? What had Arthur been up to while I'd been reading Etruscan poetry and battling nightmares in London?

"You must come see us tomorrow," Clarissa said, making no move to follow her aunt into the coach. "Reardon will want to show you his paintings. He's thinking of including a few battle scenes in the exhibition, and your opinion would mean much to him."

Viscount Reardon, Clarissa's younger brother, had not joined up, not even in the local militia, claiming weak lungs prohibited him from serving. Perhaps his lungs had been weakened in futile attempts to argue with his sister.

When Mrs. Aimes was unavailable, Lord Reardon was Clarissa's escort of choice, and Clarissa would guard his services jealously. As an unmarried female whose parents were frequently off taking the waters, she needed somebody's chaperonage if the proprieties were to be preserved.

"I am no sort of art critic, my lady, but I can tell you that your offside wheeler is favoring his outside hind leg. John Coachman should set the grooms to soaking that hoof as soon as you return to Valmond House."

I waved for the footman to get his handsome arse back up the steps. They were not the most noticing fellows ever to don summer livery.

"Don't be like this," Clarissa muttered. "I know we've had our differences, my lord, but that's all behind us. For Harry's sake, can't you let go of the past?"

"I have no inclination to hang on to the past, my lady, but I intend to keep a firm hold of my manners and what remains of my honor. I wish you good day."

Clarissa chose to cease fire, and I was supposed to think I'd won the war. I'd merely fought a skirmish to a stalemate.

I waited at the top of the steps until the coach disappeared into the shadows of the lime alley, and then waited a few more minutes, trying to parse what Clarissa had been up to this time.

"They'll be back," Arthur said, emerging from the house. "Lady Clarissa will want to look in on you as if you were still an invalid. You aren't, are you? That house party in Kent did you good."

"Leaving London, wielding some old reconnaissance skills, facing down talk, and making myself useful did me good. You are not to tell Lady Ophelia I said so. Does Clarissa seek to become your duchess?"

"One shudders to contemplate the possibility. I rather hoped she'd swivel her cannon in your direction."

Arthur had gone off to Eton when I'd still been in shortcoats. He'd been at university before I'd turned ten. Though we were only six years apart in age, he had been the heir, set apart from birth, and in truth, I did not know him all that well.

"She has you worried," I said. "Clarissa can't marry you without your consent, Your Grace."

Arthur took up a lean against a fluted Corinthian column. "Women wield weapons men know little about. Stealth, innuendo, opinion, guilt, appearances... One cannot blame them for using what's to hand, but I do not trust Lady Clarissa farther than I can throw Mama's pianoforte."

He made a lovely picture at his ease amid the Greek Revival splendor of the family seat, but his sentiments were less than gentlemanly.

"So you thought to distract her by parading me in her vicinity? Not well done of you."

"I thought to consult you regarding her schemes, but I also got word you might have been in difficulties at the Makepeace gathering. If you needed an excuse to decamp, I provided that and gave myself a chance to benefit from your insights regarding Lady Clarissa."

Like some old dowager arriving at the spa town, I needed a bath, some real sustenance, and a nap, particularly if Arthur expected me to revisit the past.

"I will happily join you for port after supper," I said, "but my wisdom regarding Lady Clarissa can be conveyed in summary: Avoid her like a plague ship full of sirens. Harry had a use for her, and she for him, but I want nothing to do with her, ever, on any terms, and that's final."

I tried for a grand exit, but Arthur merely followed me into the house.

"Does this have to do with Hyperia West crossing paths with you at that house party?"

Miss Hyperia West and I had had an understanding before I'd bought my commission. We had a different sort of understanding now. I wished her the best, we were friends, and not for the world would I tolerate Arthur casting any sort of aspersion in her direction.

"I esteem Miss West above all other women, save our mother and sisters," I said, "and you insult her at your peril. My regard for Hyperia has nothing to do with my enmity toward Lady Clarissa."

For a terrifying instant, I wondered if Arthur harbored designs on Hyperia. She was a treasure, having both common sense and compassion to an uncommon degree, as well as a fine sense of humor balanced by ladylike dignity. I had been fond of her before I went for a soldier. My feelings for her now were sadder, sweeter, and more complicated.

Hyperia deserved better than I could offer her, and in my estimation, even my ducal brother wasn't good enough for her.

"So you and Miss West did not embark on a courtship?" Arthur asked.

"We did not, but I refuse to solve your problem with Lady Clarissa by sacrificing myself on the matrimonial altar. Remain on your dignity—you do that exceedingly well—and she will eventually pursue a different quarry."

I started up the steps—why did this house have so many damned stairways?—and Arthur remained in the foyer.

"It won't be that simple," he called after me. "Foiling that woman won't be as simple as waiting her out."

"Of course it will. I'll see you at supper." I pulled our late father's trick and exited the conversation by the simple expedient of retreat.

Arthur, though, was correct. Foiling Clarissa, and the plots and schemes she embroiled us in, required much more than simple patience.

CHAPTER TWO

I had learned a few lessons at the Makepeace house party.

First, country air was good for me, provided I protected my eyes from bright sunshine.

Second, country air was good for Atlas, who tolerated Town well enough, but as an old campaigner, he preferred grass to hay and a good gallop across open country to a sedate hack in the park.

Third, I could endure a lot of annoyance provided I could periodically withdraw to privacy in even minimally commodious quarters. My old rooms at Caldicott Hall fit that definition, but I preferred a guest apartment to a bedroom in the family wing. The staff would report my comings and goings to His Rubbishing Grace, but I knew the Hall's every closet and coal chute.

I had eluded Napoleon's best spies and keenest lookouts. I could limit Arthur's surveillance of my activities, provided I kept myself as far as possible from the ducal quarters.

I'd had my effects taken to the Azure Suite. A parade of footmen filled a capacious bronze tub, and when they departed, I locked the door and sank gratefully into the water. No former soldier took cleanliness for granted, any more than he took warmth, a functional hat, or fresh water for granted. I scrubbed my hair clean—my no longer exclusively white hair—and lay back amid lavender-scented bubbles.

Above me, the ceiling fresco presented a blue sky, puffy white clouds, and soaring larks. The carpet and curtains repeated the blue-and-white theme with dashes of soothing forest green. I fell asleep pondering Arthur's real reason for summoning me.

When I awoke, the water was cool, my fingertips were wrinkled, and somebody was tapping on the door.

"Best get dressed, my lord," Cheadle said. "A coach is coming up the drive, and I suspect Lady Ophelia is soon to arrive."

"'Boots and Saddles.'" I cursed quietly in French as I rose, then switched to English as I toweled off. I'd left Ophelia in Kent less than a week before and had not expected her in Sussex for a fortnight at least.

By then, I might have been on my way back to London, doing my best impersonation of a ship in the night.

My godmother was a force of nature capable of decimating even Arthur's monumental self-possession. She could reduce me to blithering profanity without so much as raising her voice, then chide me for my loss of composure.

As a youth, I'd regarded her as something between an ally and an embarrassment, and as an adult, my affection for her was liberally laced with caution. Ophelia was devious and shrewd, for all she played the part of the scatterbrained, aging flirt.

"You come home," Arthur said when I presented myself, groomed and polished, in the family parlor, "and women tool up the drive."

"*I* tool up the drive at your invitation," I retorted, pouring myself a glass of lemonade from the offerings on the sideboard, "and mine host comports himself like a dowager who has misplaced her lorgnette and her ear trumpet. Why weren't you in Town this spring, Your Grace?"

"Why would I be? London during the Season is distasteful. Smithfield Market with the livestock in ballgowns and top hats."

Arthur would never be so gauche as to help himself to a drink before his guests had arrived. But then, he'd never known the pounding agony of dehydration, or the temptation to beg his captors for even a sip of water.

He was too well mannered to take a seat while he awaited his callers, but he'd also never been so exhausted he'd fallen off his horse and needed assistance to rise.

I settled on the sofa, lemonade in hand. "Is this why His Grace of Devonshire spends so much time traveling? He doesn't want to be auctioned off like a prize bull?"

Arthur winced. "When did you become so vulgar, Julian?"

"You're the fellow who brought up livestock."

Cheadle stepped through the open door. "Your Grace, my lord, Lady Ophelia Oliphant and Miss Hyperia West."

I was on my feet in an instant, both pleased and surprised that Hyperia had made the trek to Sussex with Ophelia.

"Lollygagging, Julian?" Ophelia said, swanning up to me and presenting her cheek for me to kiss. "Your Grace, don't look so dour. I'm here to help."

"Miss West." I bowed to Hyperia, who looked a bit fatigued, but as dear as ever. "You've come to help, too, I hope?"

"Help with what?" Arthur asked, bowing over Hyperia's hand, before she could answer.

"I've come to offer aid and wisdom regarding whatever situation required Julian to hare off hotfoot from a perfectly lovely house party." Ophelia and exaggeration were old and dear friends.

"Shall I order tea or something more substantial?" Arthur asked.

"No need." Ophelia beamed at him and settled into a wing chair. "I instructed Cheadle to rouse the kitchen. I'm famished, and this delightful creature"—she nodded at Hyperia—"is too polite to admit she's hungry as well. What seems to be the problem?"

Arthur muttered something about a surfeit of uninvited females, while I handed Hyperia onto the sofa and took the place a decorous foot from her. This was a ridiculous display of punctilio. We'd all but grown up together, been nearly engaged, and were honestly friends. Hyperia knew many of my secrets, and I hoped I was in her confidence as well.

"Waltham missed me," I said as a footman rolled in a trebuchet of a tea trolley. He fired off libation, biscuits, sandwiches, and cakes at the assemblage, all of which Arthur declined and Ophelia nearly inhaled.

"If His Grace missed you," she said around a mouthful of cheese tart, "he might have called on you in Town in recent months. He might have called on me, but no, of course not. They're starting to refer to our Arthur as His Grace of Wallflowers."

Nobody, with the exception of honored family or very close friends, ever referred to a duke by his first name. Nobody except Ophelia, who probably addressed Wellington as "Artie, my boy."

"Maybe I missed my brother," I said, rising to refill my glass of lemonade, "and being an obliging sort, His Grace invited me home for a repairing lease. House parties can be taxing." Particularly when an uninvited guest has been dragged to the gathering by his supposedly loving godmother.

"It's that Valmond woman, isn't it?" Lady Ophelia said, narrowing her gaze on Arthur. "She's plaguing you, so you summoned Julian to distract her. A ducal heir will do nicely when the duke himself can't be led to the altar. Clarissa is pragmatic, we must give her that."

Arthur shot me a look that was equal parts vexation and bewilderment: How did Ophelia know these things?

Ladies were great ones for keeping up their correspondence. When it came to social epistles, they were more conscientious than any senior clerk in the City or peer in Mayfair. My sisters doubtless traded dispatches with Ophelia, and her staff and the staff at Caldicott Hall were chummy.

"I'll thank you not to spy on me or my family," Arthur said mildly. "More tea?"

"I am family, you daft boy." Lady Ophelia passed over her cup.

"Your own dear mama asked me to have a look in on you two, and so I came posthaste. She's fine, by the way, but considering a remove from Lyme Regis to Bath."

Hyperia had been quietly demolishing a good portion of beef and brie sandwiches and was on her second cup of tea. I understood why Ophelia was on hand. The fireworks at the Makepeace house party were over, and Ophelia had come in search of fresh entertainment.

Why had Hyperia tagged along?

"I like Lady Clarissa," Hyperia said. "She doesn't put on airs, and she's all but raised her younger siblings."

"She puts on airs," Lady Ophelia said darkly.

"Not the sort of airs that stir unkind gossip in the ladies' retiring room," Hyperia countered. "Not the sort of airs that result in hurt feelings and ruined reputations. She's beautiful, her papa is an earl, and she hasn't settled for the first fop to fawn over her fortune. I commend her for that."

Before I'd gone to war, I'd regarded Hyperia as suitable wife material—pretty enough, though hardly gorgeous. Practical, unaffected, *nice*. We'd rub along when I eventually capitulated to fate and spoke my vows.

What an ass. What asses most wealthy, titled bachelors likely were.

My former intended had perfected the art of hiding her light under various bushel baskets. Hyperia dressed almost plainly. She danced adequately. She played the pianoforte competently and carried the alto line well in any duet.

Hyperia West was also blazingly intelligent, subtly stunning, and ferociously loyal. I was inordinately glad to see her. Missing a dear friend was a fine, normal emotion. One I'd not felt since returning from France.

I'd missed nobody and nothing for months, except a decent night's sleep, my appetite, and my manly humors.

"You must come with me," I said to Hyperia, "when I call on Lady Clarissa. Viscount Reardon is in the final throes of preparing for his first major London exhibition, and I have been invited to preview his offerings."

"He's quite good." Hyperia poured herself a third cup of tea. "A very talented artist. He aspires to study in Rome. Didn't he do a portrait of you, Your Grace?"

Arthur passed her the sugar bowl. "I seem to recall standing about looking ducal for a few afternoons last year. The result must be around here somewhere."

"Perhaps Lord Reardon should do a portrait of you, Lady Ophelia," Hyperia said. "He's quick, and a commission from you would lend him cachet."

If Ophelia sat to Reardon while he yet bided in the shires, that would keep Ophelia underfoot at Caldicott Hall.

Though it might also keep Hyperia underfoot, and I liked that notion quite well.

"You should consider it." I rose to take my glass to the sideboard, and because I needed to move.

"Have we any portraits of *you* since you were breeched, my lord?" Ophelia retorted.

"We do not," Arthur chimed in. "Julian was too eager to go up to university. He refused to sit for a coming-of-age portrait, and then he thought it bad luck to sit for a going-off-to-war portrait."

"And," I said, "I refuse to sit for a wearing-odd-spectacles and prematurely-going-gray portrait."

"Your spectacles are merely tinted." Ophelia had moved on to the jam tarts. "Your hair turned white, not gray. There is a difference, as you'd know if you weren't little better than a stripling."

I was approaching my thirtieth year. I did not know Ophelia's age. She was tallish, slender, and holding her ground in the battle against time. Hyperia, by contrast, was of medium height and had unremarkable brown hair and unfashionably abundant curves.

Ophelia dressed in pale silks and pastel muslins, accented with an assortment of jewelry, often even in the daylight. Hyperia had set aside the virginal palette for rich hues of burgundy, brown, and blue.

She wore the colors not of the schoolgirl, but of the lady who knew her own preferences.

"I must have a bath," Ophelia said, rising. "Hyperia will want one too. What time is supper?"

The interrogation was apparently over for the nonce.

"Country hours," Arthur said. "Supper is usually at six, though I've asked to have the meal moved back an hour in the event you ladies are inclined to nap. We do not dress for family supper except on Sundays."

"Splendid," Ophelia said. "Seven it is. I assume I'm in the Peacock Suite as usual? Where have you put Hyperia?"

Arthur rose and tugged the bell-pull. "Miss West will be in the Emerald Suite. Julian, perhaps you'd escort Miss West to the guest wing?"

"I'd be happy to."

Arthur deputed a footman to escort Ophelia from the family parlor, and thus I found myself arm in arm with Hyperia and standing in the doorway of the suite right next to my own.

～

Hyperia joined me in the rose garden, which was still making an effort, though past its peak. The gardeners were assiduous about removing any spent blooms, and that annoyed me. Blown roses had a beauty of their own and, in my opinion, ought to be left in peace to fade among friends and scatter their petals upon the good earth.

"Getting Miss Cleary situated was the work of a moment for Ophelia," Hyperia said, referring to a guest at the Makepeace house party who'd been in need of a change of scene. "Ophelia declared that she was bored. I suspect she's worried."

We ambled along a crushed-shell walkway between fragrant beds. My mother appreciated the scent of roses as much as their visual appeal, and thus the garden had a fair sampling of damasks. The requisite fountain several yards off—Cupid and Psyche reconciled—added the music of splashing water to the late afternoon warmth.

I wore my blue spectacles, but the closer the sun sank to the horizon, the less I'd need them. "What could Lady Ophelia possibly be worried about?" Besides me, of course.

"Your brother. Waltham has been least in sight during the Season for the past three years."

We ambled along side by side, while I examined my own anxiety where Arthur was concerned.

"For some of that time, he was mourning Harry." We knew not where Harry was buried, but Arthur had insisted on proper mourning rituals.

"And His Grace was mourning you, too, Julian, or preparing to. Let's look in on Atlas, shall we?"

Hyperia had guessed my intended destination. On reconnaissance and on the battlefield, my life had often depended on the courage, stamina, and gallantry of my mount. A gentleman did not neglect his cattle. A military scout took the welfare of his horses as a sacred trust.

"Waltham has become something of a recluse," Hyperia said. "You thought he was leaving you in peace in London, but that doesn't explain why he's all but dropped from sight socially. He'll take supper with the neighbors occasionally—he'll accept Osgood Banter's invitations without fail—but he doesn't entertain much himself."

"I haven't badgered my brother to share his calendar in recent years. What do you mean?" I'd been too busy badgering the French and then recovering from their kind hospitality.

"Waltham never goes north for the shooting," Hyperia said. "He refuses all house-party invitations."

"Wise man."

"He sits out the Season even if he votes his seat. The press of business and prior engagements prevent him from accepting any invitations. I'm told he doesn't even frequent his clubs much."

The stable sat on the other side of a copse of maples, just east of the garden. The whole was a two-story U-shaped structure that included grooms' quarters, carriage bays, a mares' wing, hay mows, harness and saddle rooms, and an assortment of loose boxes with adjoining runs.

A massive field maple held pride of place in the center of the stable yard. The tree was less than forty feet tall, but at nearly two hundred years old, it was full and sturdy. In autumn, the foliage turned to such a vibrant yellow that the whole yard seemed aglow, as if illuminated by a giant bouquet of daffodils.

I'd spent many a boyhood afternoon on the benches situated at the base of the tree, listening to the grooms gossip and swap stories while cleaning harness.

"What is it?" Hyperia came to a halt beside me. "We can call on Atlas another time."

"Ghosts." The ghosts of Harry and my father, the ghost of me before my memory had become problematic. They all haunted this peaceful, pretty stable yard. Pots of red salvia sat at regular intervals along the gray stone façade. A cat dozed in the shade cast by one of the water troughs. Horses lipped hay and regarded Hyperia and me over half doors as we approached one of the three entrances opening onto the yard.

"Happy ghosts?" Hyperia said. "Sad ghosts? Restless ghosts?"

"Dead ghosts, so a little sad, but they were happy in life, so let's not dwell on them. Tell me more about His Grace's situation."

"Not much to tell. Ophelia fears he's melancholic, but he never appears sad. Serious, reserved, preoccupied. Many weighty adjectives, but not sad."

Melancholia often marched alongside the common soldier and his superior officers. "The low spirits aren't always obvious. One of the most cheerful men I knew took his own life." An Irishman who'd seen his three brothers killed in battle on the same day. We'd buried him with full honors, and bedamned to what the churchmen thought of that. "My brother takes his ducal responsibilities seriously."

A vast understatement that I meant as a defense of Arthur's social deficits.

"Waltham takes everything seriously. Have you ever heard him laugh, Jules?"

I had not. Not even when we were children. "We can't all be like Lady Ophelia, flitting from one lark to the next." And yet, Ophelia had buried two husbands and two half-grown children. Was her determined good cheer simply melancholia stood on its head?

"She's worried, Jules. I suspect you are too. The Duke of Wall-flowers is not a kind nickname. For a time, there were bets placed about his matrimonial prospects, but even those have stopped. He will soon be regarded as an eccentric, and that's never a good thing."

We ambled into the barn, greeted by the predictable scents of horse and hay. I took off my glasses and looked about for Atlas.

"I am the family eccentric, thank you very much. Waltham is the family duke. We are quite clear on that. Where is my horse?"

"He's here somewhere," Hyperia said, stroking the velvety nose of Arthur's black gelding. "Greetings, Beowulf." She produced a carrot from a pocket and fed Bey half of it. "Shall we call on Lady Clarissa tomorrow?"

"I'm torn between 'best get it over with' and 'next year would suit.' Clarissa is up to something."

"Because she calls at Caldicott Hall where not one but two socially reticent titled bachelors can be found? Whatever could her motive be?" Hyperia held up a finger. "I have it—she's trying to be a decent neighbor! How devious of her. Surely, we must suspect her of nefarious motives."

"Cut line, Perry."

"I have a point, Jules. If Clarissa had been Vicar or Squire Huber come to swill tea and have a look at you, you would think nothing of it."

"Huber would be calling to gloat over my reduced state." He'd been the local justice of the peace for a time in my boyhood, and a more vindictive, pompous excuse for a magistrate had never befouled the English countryside. Harry had picked a few berries from a hedge, and Huber had tried to charge him with theft. The neighbor who owned the hedge had refused to testify against a hungry boy, and the matter had gone nowhere.

Of course, that boy had been the ducal spare and the neighbor nobody's fool.

"Huber's a twit," Hyperia said. "A lot of former officers become twits. Don't you be one. We will call on Lady Clarissa tomorrow and learn what the neighbors think of the local duke. Your father was generally well liked, but your brother hasn't earned such a warm reception."

"Arthur inherited at too young an age. He's been preoccupied seeing our sisters settled, and his brothers haven't exactly made his life easier. There's an end to it."

"Oh, right, by decree of Lord Julian, subject closed. Behold, your horse," Hyperia said, leaning on an open half door. "Jules, you rode him to flinders."

Atlas lay flat out in the straw of a roomy loose box, a posture a horse adopted only when sleeping deeply. He was covered in dust and breathing in a slow, deep rhythm.

"Somebody let him have a roll," I said, mildly disturbed to observe my noble steed so done in that he'd surrender all dignity within the confines of a stall. "He'll spend the night at grass and be fit for duty in the morning."

"Good. We'll ride over to Valmond House and then call at the vicarage. Stop for a pint and a pie at midday at the inn and have a nose around the village shops before returning to the Hall."

I was being managed by a commanding officer with a fine grasp of strategy. "You know I will oblige you because I'd rather not spend my morning dealing with Lady Ophelia." Then too, a call on the vicar and some excellent ale would be no imposition. "I will get even, Perry."

She patted my arm. "I'm counting on it. Until supper, my lord."

She swanned off, leaving me to regard her departing form with some puzzlement.

I was not keen on being touched. The French had handled me rather more than I preferred and in ways intended to convey pain and disrespect. Hyperia knew this, and yet, she also knew that with her I managed the usual courtesies comfortably.

A stroll arm in arm, a hand to hold when rising from a chair, a hug from my friend in parting or greeting.

That pat on my arm had been our sole contact for the day. Was she respecting my bodily privacy or being coy? If so, coy for what purpose?

I watched Atlas's slow breathing and pondered the possibilities while dust motes danced on the afternoon sunbeams slanting across his stall.

"You might as well show yourself," I said after a full minute of silence. "I know you're up there, and eavesdropping is an offense that should cost even a trusted retainer his post."

∼

"How'd ya know?" A slight boy of modest height dropped from the rafters as nimbly as a sparrow lit upon a breadcrumb. He was dusty, skinny, and grinning like a pirate newly arrived to his home port.

"Every time you move," I replied, "you disturb a raft of dust, and that dust wafts about, shouting of your presence. First rule of rural survival: If you seek refuge in a barn, keep still. The swallows, the cats, the horses, the dust, the hay and straw, the very dirt in the aisles... They all betray your presence should you so much as take a deep breath. What are you doing here, Atticus?"

The boy had no last name and little shame. I'd taken him into my employ at the Makepeace house party, with the understanding that he'd not change billets until the gathering disbanded. On Lady Longacre's staff, Atticus had been growing up illiterate, underfed, and without anything approaching a trade. My sensibilities had been offended by the waste of a bright young fellow eager to get on in the world.

My sensibilities were offended by the same fellow's unkempt appearance and complete lack of remorse for disobeying orders.

"Lady Ophelia said we shouldn't let you go off all on your own, what with you being dicked in the nob and all, and I was done at Makepeace, and everybody knew it. Canny sends greetings, and so does Miss Maybelle and Mr. Banter. I ain't never been to a duke's house before."

I used the handiest weapon of every governess, drill sergeant, and disaffected spouse in the realm and treated Atticus to a hard, silent stare.

"Wot?"

"You might well never see the inside of Caldicott Hall, young man. I gave you a direct order: Remain at Makepeace until Lady Longacre has wished her guests farewell. If you can't follow orders under calm conditions, how can I ever rely on you in battle?"

Atticus eyed me back steadily, offering a silent reproach of his own: I'd relied on him at Makepeace, and he'd not failed me.

"If Lady Ophelia was invitin' herself to trail you," Atticus said, chin coming up, "then I figgered you'd want me trailing her."

That defiant little chin yielded an insight. "You *figgered*," I said, exaggerating his informal diction, "if you showed up here at Caldicott Hall, then I'd have a harder time changing my mind about hiring you. I do not go back on my word, Atticus."

He scrubbed dirty hands over his dirty face. "Not sayin' you would, but you might forgetlike. You forget a lot. Said so yourself."

Atlas stirred, legs twitching. He lifted his head and assumed that "nestled in the straw" posture of all oxen assigned to nativity scenes.

"You woke the baby," Atticus said, peering over the half door. "Halloo, Atlas."

Atlas stood, shook like a wet dog, and came over to the door. Atticus, to my surprise, produced a lump of carrot.

"I do forget a lot," I said, yielding a fair point. "But not often.

When my bouts are upon me, Atticus, I won't know my own name, much less what employment arrangements I've made with various retainers. I forget what country I'm in, what day of the week it is, and where I live."

"You forget everything?"

I'd never considered that particular question. I took my turn feeding Atlas a treat. "Not everything. I know the difference between French and English when I'm *non compos memoria.* I know I am male. I can ride a horse easily enough, add figures, and mind my manners. But much else is temporarily lost."

"So you'd forget me?"

Touché. "I have forgotten who Miss West is, and I've known her for ages, though even in the throes of my befuddlement, I know instinctively that I can trust her."

"You should add something to the card in your pocket."

Clearly, while I was afflicted with a faulty memory, this boy had a mind that hoarded up every detail. A fine quality in a reconnaissance officer, but sad to see in a young child.

"I'm listening." All the card in my pocket said was that I was given to temporary bouts of forgetting, along with a few other and further particulars intended to get me safely home.

"Add a line about 'Atticus works for you, and you can trust him too.'"

This was why I'd taken the boy into my employ. He'd been going entirely to waste polishing boots and cadging meat pies belowstairs. He was not only smart, he was *canny.*

"I will consider your suggestion. You will consider my warning: You disobey direct orders at your peril, Atticus."

"Did you ever disobey direct orders?" He'd put an element of naïve curiosity into his question, which was clearly intended to distract me from my displeasure with him.

"Yes. I followed my brother Harry out of camp in the dead of night—that's about five standing orders violated right there—because

I thought I knew better than those silly old generals." I began to pace, rather than grab the boy by his worn shirt.

"Harry died in French hands," I went on, "I nearly died because I had the hubris to think I could free him. My stupidity has seen me labeled a traitor, because somebody let those nasty old Frenchmen know where to ambush an advance party of British infantry. A man who will disobey orders will likely betray his country, too, of course. But please, don't obey orders just on my say so. Consult your own vast stores of experience and make whatever decision suits your taste at the moment."

More than I usually admitted to anybody about my misadventures in France, and my diatribe was meant as a warning rather than a scold.

My horse, having exhausted the available supply of treats, ambled out of his stall into the adjoining run.

"Why is Lady Ophelia here?" I asked when Atticus merely regarded me with puzzlement.

"Don't know. She were twitchy as a skinny cat to get on the road, though. Your duke was invited to that house party."

"Many invitations are sent to ranking peers as a courtesy. In the same spirit of good manners, the peer declines the invitation."

"Waste of paper and ink. Lady Ophelia says the duke ought to marry."

God have mercy. If Ophelia's mission was matchmaking—again, some more—then there'd be no peace at Caldicott Hall until she was evicted, or until Arthur was ensnared in parson's mousetrap.

"You have an assignment," I said, heading for the nearest exit. "To the extent you can, you are to keep a discreet eye on His Grace, especially if eligible ladies are underfoot."

"The duke is frisky?" No judgment colored that question, nor did much curiosity.

"No, but my brother is a *duke*. Young ladies coveting the family tiaras might think to press their favors upon him just when a convenient sounder of gossips comes trundling along."

"A sounder is a group of swine."

"Right you are." I withdrew my tinted spectacles and emerged into the sunshine. I'd taken to testing myself, leaving the glasses off and trying to manage transitions from light to darkness without their aid.

The sunlight stabbed at my eyeballs, but not as it once had. The piercing daggers of pain were muted to mere darts, though at high noon, the story might be different.

"The duke is my only extant brother," I said, donning my spectacles. "I will defend his liberty as if it were my own."

Atticus hustled along at my side. "What's the difference between liberty and loneliness?"

Dratted boy. "To be imprisoned for life in marriage with the wrong person has to be the loneliest sentence known to man or woman. Arthur needs heirs, my humble self being a dodgy bet in terms of securing the succession. His marriage would have at least some intimate aspects."

"Ya mean he'd tup his missus. To hear the footmen tell it, that's the closest a feller gets to heaven, having his own missus to cook for him and cuddle with."

"And footmen are the wisest counsel to be had. Nearly as wise as grooms, undermaids, drunks, or courtesy lords. Before you show yourself belowstairs at the Hall, have a thorough wash at the pump. Comb your hair, take special care to get the dirt out from beneath your fingernails. Address Cook as ma'am and any male staff taller than you as sir."

"I know that part, and they're all taller than me."

Taller than I. I left the grammar lessons for another time. Rome wasn't sacked in a day. "Become equally well acquainted with the getting-clean part. Nobody likes to take his supper sitting next to a reeking urchin."

"Aye, guv." Atticus gave me a jaunty salute. "Any other orders?"

Yes, my lord. "None. Do you even have a comb?"

Now, he looked abashed. "Was going to borrow a comb the grooms use on the horses' manes."

Borrow being a delicate reference to larceny, no doubt. I passed over my pocket comb. "*Ask*, for the love of God. *Ask*. I am your employer. Your kit is my responsibility. Your turnout reflects upon me."

My comb, a pretty little affair inlaid with ivory and mother-of-pearl, disappeared into a pocket that likely held bits of string, linty lemon candies, a pair of dice, and an eye or two of newt.

"Maybe Lady Ophelia coming here wasn't such a bad idea," Atticus said as a trio of grooms came down the steps from the quarters over the mares' wing.

"Why do you say that?"

"When it comes to defending your liberty, you didn't manage so well in France, didja, guv? You might need some reinforcements, methinks."

I hoisted him over my shoulder, divested him of his boots, and deposited the naughty, disrespectful, clever, laughing whole of him into the nearest horse trough.

CHAPTER THREE

The Valmond family seat had likely begun life as a prosperous farmhouse. The owner, in the dim mists of time, had done some overlord a favor, or possibly lent money to a grateful monarch. Fortunate marriages had followed, aided by some plundering of the French countryside, and thus the Valmonds had been among the winners in the peerage sweepstakes.

Clarissa's father was an earl, though this realization had shocked me as a boy. Earls, in my juvenile opinion, were to be brave fellows mounted exclusively on white horses, broad of chest, noble of brow, never far from an assortment of gleaming, deadly weapons or some stirring martial poetry.

Clarissa's father was never very far from some crumbling bit of parchment that purported to explain how to create flying machines or perpetual clocks. His countess, likely in defense of her wits, had taken up a career as an invalid. She demanded her spouse's escort to various spa towns, which suited Lord Valloise quite well.

He disappeared to the nearest Druidic ruin or lending library—equally tantalizing to him—and left his wife to enjoy her afflictions among friends. The children had been raised by a succession of tutors and governesses, to the extent any adult had taken a hand in their upbringing at all.

My mother had occasionally intervened, and it had been she who'd first seen young Viscount Reardon's artistic talent. A proper drawing master had been dispatched, with promising results.

"Very good of you to come by," Reardon said, escorting Hyperia and me up the steps from the Valmond House guest parlor. Lady Clarissa had declared a pressing need to see to correspondence, which I took as a ploy to spare her yet another tour of Reardon's collection.

"His Grace sends regards," I said, though Arthur had done no such thing. "When does the London exhibition open?"

"In two weeks." Reardon fairly jogged up the steps. "One must wait a respectful time after the Royal Academy's annual show closes. My paintings are to be crated up and shipped to Town starting tomorrow. I will follow and oversee the uncrating. Clarissa will join me before opening day. I do wish the duchess could see the collection. She has always been a supporter."

Reardon was the fair-haired boy of English lore, grown up into a cheerful, blond young man full of energy and good humor. He'd been a pest in childhood, tagging after me and Harry, getting stuck in trees while spying on us, and dissolving into tears when we would not wait for him to catch up.

I had resented him then, and I resented him now. He bounced along with exuberant high hopes, while the feeble remains of my optimism had expired on some freezing mountainside in France.

My knee began to ache as we rounded the landing—and old injury—and I mentally chided myself for such petty sentiments.

"How many paintings will you send to London?" Hyperia asked.

Reardon went off into flights about how many was enough, and what if somebody made an offer on the best of the lot? How many reserves to bring up and of what kind? If the battle scenes sold first, did one hang another battle scene to replace it, or would an endless supply of one subject devalue the articles still on offer?

As he prattled on, I silently admitted that the pesky tag-along had become a budding artist with a frank—almost plebian—grasp of the financial realities of his calling. Clarissa's influence, no doubt. For all her fluff and smiles, she was shrewd.

Lord Reardon ushered us into a gallery that ran the length of the back of the house, perhaps eighty feet. Morning sunlight poured in through symmetrically spaced windows and a pair of central French doors. Fireplaces at either end of the room would have been inadequate to heat such a space, but comfort was irrelevant.

The gallery was a statement of elegant grandeur, a museum of family honor. The comparable room at Caldicott Hall wasn't much larger, though the ceilings were higher. Caldicott Hall had retained no less luminary than Antonio Verrio to paint the ceilings of its public rooms, while the Valmond House renderings had been done by James Thornhill.

The work above our heads was all very allegorical. Fortune smiling down on Prosperity and Bounty while tromping on the head of Fury, chubby putti flying through clouds conveniently arranged to shield any privy parts.

Against that backdrop, Reardon's work was starkly realistic. No gods or biblical figures filled his canvases.

"These are quite good," Hyperia said, moving closer to an image of an exhausted boy in regimental colors. He sat on the ground, head drooping at a dejected angle. His wrists, draped over his knees, conveyed the lanky strength of late adolescence. His pallor created a stark contrast with the blood stippling his face and arm.

Comrades lay in the lush grass around him, some given the gray pallor of death, one lifting a beseeching hand to the sunny heavens. Begging for water, no doubt. The fallen always begged for water—or a bullet.

A horse standing on three legs, the fourth cocked at an angle portending humane destruction, occupied a higher swell of the land. The horse's weary despair was the echo of the boy's.

"Accurate," I said, "right down to how the smoke drifts about.

When the smoke clears, the flies move in. Then the burial parties and the scavengers get to work. How shall you title it?"

Hyperia was looking at me oddly, while I moved on to another painting.

Reardon paced at my side. "Something somber. *Aftermath*, perhaps. *When Day Is Done. Battlefield Requiem.*"

"The expression on the lad's face," Hyperia murmured. "He has seen hell. You did that very well, Reardon."

He'd done it very well, and at least half a dozen times over. I tried to ignore the accuracy of his battlefield renderings and focused instead on the portraits and landscapes. Reardon didn't believe in prettying up his subjects, as the grand portraits of Sir Joshua Reynolds's era had done, but he also saw the beauty of the country-side and the people in it.

"Your cook?" The painting gave me a much-needed smile. The Valmond cook was the essence of jollity, an ageless bulwark of good cheer and generosity. I'd enjoyed many a slice of bread and glass of lemonade in her kitchen, and she'd patched up more than one skinned knee.

"Mrs. Felders," Reardon said. "The housekeepers come and go, the butlers retire, and the footmen run off with the dairymaids, but Mrs. Felders remains. Her eyesight's beginning to go, and I wanted to paint this while she could still see it."

"Such kindness in those eyes," Hyperia said. "You captured the humor and patience, and, of course, the skill."

Mrs. Felders had been painted in the company of her famous vanilla mousse, expertly garnished with orange slices and ripe red raspberries. To taste that mousse was to be transported to the realm of the gods.

"You can't place this wonderful rendering in the same room with all the..." Hyperia waved a hand. "Tragedy."

Lord Reardon preened, hands behind his back. "I thought I'd put the military subjects in a gallery of their own so the ladies and others of delicate sensibilities can spare themselves the more serious subjects."

"You did not serve," I said, moving on to a portrait of my own dear mama. "How is it your battle scenes are so accurate?"

"I kept in touch with every soldier I knew," Reardon said. "Lord Harry among them. I asked them for descriptions, sketches, impressions. You'd be surprised how poetical the average soldier can be when you ask him about his calling. How bitter, how insightful. I'd like to collect those letters into a book, but Clarissa says I'd need to ask permission of every correspondent and of the families of those who did not come home."

Hyperia pretended to study the duchess's portrait, but I could tell she disapproved of Reardon's scheme.

"Hang the battle scenes among the other paintings," I said. "Don't group them together, or they will lose their impact and be more easily ignored. Position that dejected, blood-spattered boy next to the duchess and title his painting *The Price of Victory*. That ruined lad is every bit as deserving of public appreciation as any duchess. Excuse me."

I had seen enough, or more than enough. Had I been in Spain, the stink of gunpowder in my nostrils, the screams of wounded horses all around me, and the French prisoners of war being marched off the battlefields in their weary scores, I might have borne up better under the onslaught of Reardon's artistry.

I had been swilling tea and cakes a quarter hour earlier, avoiding Clarissa's smiles and wishing myself back in Town. To see the destruction and tragedy of my past staring back at me from silk-hung walls was more of an assault to my composure than had I been attacked by footpads at high noon.

I tossed off a curt bow and strode for the door. I kept going until I was sitting on the Valmond House front terrace, fumbling to buckle on my spurs, and blinking madly against the bright morning sun.

～

I held a short, rounded silver spur in my hand, the type gentlemen donned more for show than for any equestrian purpose. The second spur adorned my right boot—and nice boots they were too—and I was sitting on the hard steps of some genteel country manor. Bright sunshine stung my eyes, and an ache in my throat left me with the uncomfortable suspicion that I'd been crying.

I realized that I did not know who *I* was. No name came to mind when I considered who I might be. I rose and regarded the gracious façade behind me. No sense of homecoming accompanied the sight of gleaming windows and a closed door of carved oak.

Lions rampant. Oak leaves. This might have been any one of hundreds of aging manor houses dotting the English countryside. Though, for that matter, was I in England? Was I English?

I was thinking in English, so I took it as writ that I was English.

"Your horse, milord." A groom led a big, sturdy, dark gelding to the foot of the steps. A second groom led a mare wearing a sidesaddle over to the ladies' mounting block.

The first fellow had spoken to me in English and referred to me as a lord—unless he was being cheeky, in which case his milording was an insult. Who the hell was I, and why couldn't I recall my own name? Was an excess of drink to blame? I did not feel as if I'd been taking spirits—no sour taste in my mouth, no vertigo, no roiling belly —but something had wiped my memory clean of all meaningful information.

"My thanks." I came down the steps, ignoring the urge to dust off my backside. "I must await the lady."

"Miss West is in good looks as always," the fellow said. "Will you be staying in the area long, milord?"

The man holding my horse was a groom, rather than a footman, and grooms were a generally less deferential lot than the indoor staff.

How did I know that? The fellow was also older than most footmen and addressing me with some familiarity.

"The duration of my visit is uncertain," I said. "You might as well walk him. Miss West could tarry a while inside." *Whoever Miss West is.*

I took in my surroundings, which were verdant and bucolic. Sheep grazed in a grassy park on either side of a slightly raised carriageway. Off to the east, the park gave way to a wood, while to the west, a lake mirrored the morning sun.

Summer, then, and the terrain had the look of the Home Counties. My mind apparently retained some sort of bedrock from which to reason, but few specific facts. I had the sense that surmising information through deductive processes was familiar to me.

But what did I know? Did I regularly misplace my wits? Why was I permitted in public if that was the case? I was attired as a gentleman. I had my own mount and silver spurs, and the scent of some sort of shaving soap wafted from my person.

The groom tugged on the reins, but the horse thwarted him and extended his nose in my direction. I held out a hand to the beast—he was a handsome fellow, though a bit on the inelegant side—and he ignored my gloved fingers, instead nuzzling the pocket of my riding jacket.

"Perhaps Atlas wants a tipple from your flask, my lord." The groom good-naturedly discouraged the horse's explorations.

I patted my pocket and felt a lump. "He smells this." I withdrew a piece of carrot and with it came a calling card of some sort. I passed the horse his treat—Atlas, a good name for such a substantial equine —and peered at the card.

You are Lord Julian Caldicott. You have written this card to remind yourself that your memory sometimes fails in its entirety. The lapses pass within a few hours. You have merely to be patient, and all will be well.

The card further informed me that my brother was no less than a duke, and my Town dwelling could be found on thus and such street. Town referred to London, and even in my diminished state, I knew I was nowhere near the Capital. The air was much too fresh, the sky too bright.

The card informed me that I had only to be patient, and my mind would right itself. I was not reassured in the slightest.

At that moment, a tidy, fashionably dressed young woman emerged from the manor house.

"At least you waited for me. Are you all right, Jules?"

Any lady presuming to refer to a ducal son by his given name was a familiar or some sort. *Miss* West, so not my wife. That conclusion left me oddly disappointed. The lady was only modestly attractive by fashionable standards—brown hair, a trifle curvaceous when Society favored blond sylphs—but her eyes were lit with keen intelligence, and her smile conveyed warmheartedness rather than frivolity.

"I was reading my card," I said, passing it over. "I assume you are familiar with my condition?"

A gamble on my part to entrust anybody with proof of what was apparently a chronic malady, but Miss West was the sort to inspire trust.

"Ah," she said, tucking the card in my pocket. "You were overdue for a forgetful spell, I'm thinking. The malady hasn't troubled you since you mustered out."

I was former military, then. Perhaps a war injury accounted for my lapse. "Might you get me away from this place? I know not who I am or where I dwell, but I'd rather not be parading about in public when I'm half-witted."

"We'll be off directly," she said, greeting her mare at the ladies' mounting block. "You are safe, Jules. You and I are old friends, we are barely a mile from your family seat, and by suppertime, you will be entirely yourself. I promise you that. You have blue spectacles in your breast pocket. You'd best put them on, because bright sunshine bothers your eyes."

Bright sunshine did not account for the lump I'd had in my throat, but I found the blue spectacles and donned them. They felt familiar, as did Atlas's gait when Miss West and I trotted down the drive.

"Don't fret," Miss West said. "The lapses of memory are as rare as they are complete." Her tone had the forced good cheer I associated with sickrooms and infirmary tents.

"And by supper, I will be myself." I circled Atlas and drew him to a halt, the better for me to behold the place we'd come from. "We were calling on the neighbors?"

Miss West turned her mare so we both regarded the manor house in the distance. No recollections stirred at the sight of it, no heart-strings vibrated. Perhaps I did not care for these neighbors.

"That is Valmond House," Miss West said. "Family seat of the Earls of Valloise. You and I are well acquainted with the earl's grown children, Lady Clarissa and her younger brother, Viscount Reardon. There's a younger daughter due to make her come out next year, Lady Susan. Reardon is preparing to exhibit a number of his paint-ings in London, and he's quite talented. We were admiring his work when you abruptly departed."

The house was pretty enough from a distance, but the potholes in the drive should have been filled in—summer storms would only make them worse—and the entire top floor of the house lacked curtains. Two lonely pots of some straggling greenery sat on either side of the front door, and the overall impression was one of creeping neglect.

"Was I angry when I decamped?"

"I'd say you were overwhelmed. Many of Reardon's works depict military scenes, and his style will be too realistic in the eyes of many."

"Gory," I said, instinctively concluding that I'd seen a fair amount of gore in real life. "We will wish Lord Reardon every artistic success, but somebody needs to take that house in hand."

Did I always notice details, or was my acumen a result of the near panic caused by the blank canvas of my recollection?

"I've always liked Valmond House, as Greek Revival structures go," Miss West replied. "Modest, but then, we can't all dwell in ducal palaces."

"That wood is overgrown," I said, gesturing to the east. "The park is overgrazed, and the place wants flowers. It's summer, for pity's sake, and if I'm not mistaken, that side terrace is beginning to subside."

Miss West looked from the sunny façade to me and back at the house. "For a man in the throes of a mental lapse, you see quite clearly. Shall we head to the village for a pint, or would you like to return to Caldicott Hall?"

What I wanted at that moment was to have my memories back. Then I realized that I'd been a soldier—infirmary tents were familiar only to soldiers—and realistic depictions of battle scenes had upset me, according to Miss West. Perhaps I did not want all of my memories back.

"Everybody will know me in the village. If you would please see me home, I will retire to someplace private and await the return of my powers of recollection."

Miss West turned her mare down a shaded farm lane, and I had little choice but to follow after. I had no idea in which direction my home lay, and if I lost sight of Miss West, I'd be as lost in reality as I was mentally.

She kept her mare to the walk, and after another hour of toddling along a placid stream, then through a wood, across a cow pasture, and up a hill, a large, stately edifice came into view below us.

"Caldicott Hall," I said. Not a guess. I beheld my boyhood home and the woman to whom I had once been almost engaged. "You were right, Hyperia. My memories are back. You wandered the estate with me in hopes they'd return sooner rather than later, didn't you?"

"And because I am not keen to answer Lady Ophelia's questions when she well knew we intended to be gone for half the day. Are you truly well?"

"Unaccountably tired, a tad disoriented, but well. Years ago, we tobogganed down this hill, and I had a spectacular crash into that oak over there. I was forbidden to toboggan for the rest of that winter, and Harry eschewed that pleasure out of loyalty to me."

"You remember Harry?"

"And I recall that he died and how. Let's have that pint, and then

I am to accompany you to the shops, where we shall spend enough to be appreciated, not enough to insult."

I urged Atlas onto the sheep track that doubled as a bridle path, and we were soon approaching the village in all its summer glory. A proper fuss was made over us by the innkeeper—the most recent in a long line of Mr. Foresters to hold that office—and the fare was as wonderful as ever.

As Hyperia complimented Mrs. Forester on the lemon cake, I was visited by another memory.

At the Makepeace house party, I had kissed Hyperia—with her permission—as a sort of experiment. Had my dormant manly humors stirred at all?

They had not, but neither had the encounter been distasteful. I'd taken encouragement from that much progress.

Sitting on our horses an hour past, assessing Valmond House as if I'd never seen it before, and my own name unfamiliar to me, I'd had the stray thought that this Miss West person taking such a kindly interest in my situation had a very pretty mouth.

Deranged as I had been, I'd noticed that, and I had been right.

CHAPTER FOUR

Spending the previous day in the village had been oddly pleasant. I'd toddled around at Hyperia's side while she'd pretended to dither over which length of ribbon best matched her eyes—none of them succeeded, in my opinion—and how sturdy a ladies' set of gardening gloves should be.

The shopkeepers all knew me, and the innkeeper's mother had even referred to me as Master Julian. The vicar had dropped a casual *my boy* into our chat. I might have temporarily forgotten these folk, but they would not forget me, and in that realization lay comfort.

The weather brought the opposite of comfort. A proper hot spell had got under way as Hyperia and I let the horses walk back to Caldicott Hall. No obliging thunderstorms had arrived at sunset to break the heat, and I'd passed the night dozing on the balcony and recalling many sweltering nights spent bivouacking in Spain.

I began my second full day at Caldicott Hall tending to the correspondence that had come down from my Town residence. A few polite notes acknowledged the pleasure of seeing me at the Makepeace gathering—one did not snub a ducal heir lightly, even if he was rumored to be a traitor—and others were invoices for goods and services.

I disliked the custom of paying the trades for a year's service in December. I lacked the optimism for such an approach and disapproved of living on credit in principle. For the average man, credit was a trap that could land him in jail. For the moneyed classes, credit amounted to an interest-free, unsecured loan, often carried from year to year by the humble tailor and tobacconist.

Arthur took the same view of credit that I did and that our father had: Bills were payable when received. Services were paid for when rendered. The Caldicotts endeared themselves to the mercantile and laboring folk with that philosophy, but came in for more than our share of sidelong glances and muttered asides in the clubs.

"Ye gods, it's hot." Lady Ophelia wafted into my sitting room through the open door. The windows were open as well, and through the blessed effects of a high ceiling and a slight breeze, the room was fairly comfortable.

"Godmama." I stood and bowed, though I did not put on my jacket. Ophelia had seen me as God made me, albeit not for at least a quarter century. "Good morning."

"You missed me at breakfast, I know." She subsided onto the divan, her morning gown drifting about her. "One prefers a tray to start the day. Social breakfasts are a waste of the best meal of the day. What news from Town?"

Ophelia likely knew all the news from Town, the shires, Paris, and north of the Tweed as well. "I owe my cobbler for new shoes for the indoor male staff. I am running low on claret, which is odd when I've become the next thing to a teetotaler. Ginny sends greetings and warns me against parenthood."

"Your sister is an *involved* mother," Ophelia said. "After another baby or two, she'll get over that nonsense. Why hasn't Arthur married?"

"That is none of our business." Though, as I'd tossed and turned on my balcony pallet, the same question had bothered me. Arthur was attractive, wealthy, titled, as loyal as an old dog to those he cared for, and utterly responsible.

Women would find that list vastly appealing. A romantic hero he was not—despite looking the part—but a dependable partner and father he would be.

"Don't be a noddycock," Ophelia snapped. "If His Grace doesn't marry, you will have to, and thus it becomes your business. Is he rolled up?"

"No. I reviewed the books with him when I mustered out. Besides, if he were rolled up, that would be all the more reason to make an advantageous match. You will please drop this subject, Ophelia. Waltham deserves your respect, and that means even you should accord him his privacy."

Ophelia's eyes narrowed, and I prepared for her sights to turn on me. Hyperia would say nothing to anybody about my lapse of memory yesterday, but Ophelia knew of my condition. She dismissed it—everybody's memory became dodgy if they lived long enough— and my mind always righted itself.

Hyperia rapped on my doorjamb. "Sorry to interrupt, but, Jules, Lady Clarissa is downstairs demanding to see His Grace. Something to do with the magistrate being off at the quarter sessions? The duke has gone to the home farm, so I said I'd fetch you. Her ladyship seems genuinely distressed."

Clarissa excelled at seeming genuinely distressed. Also genuinely charmed. Genuinely hurt. Genuinely enamored.

I rose and shrugged into my jacket, despite the heat, because I was genuinely a gentleman. "If her concern is of a legal nature, she'll want to convey it confidentially."

Ophelia waggled her fingers at me. "Go play gallant knight, but you never did answer my question."

"You ought not to be asking it." I ran a comb through my hair—I had a spare, of course—and left Ophelia to rifle my belongings or read my correspondence. She'd find nothing of any interest, but she'd enjoy the exercise, and it would keep her occupied for an hour or so.

"Clarissa is distraught," Hyperia said, striding along beside me. "She would not say what the problem is."

"The problem is she wants to marry Waltham." I jogged down the guest wing steps, Hyperia at my side.

"Unkind, Jules."

"But plausible. Arthur is Lord Lieutenant and thus has some say over the justices of the peace, who are all off drinking their way through the quarter sessions. A missing hatpin would be a pretext to intrude on his day." And to lure him into Clarissa's bedroom.

"Whatever has upset Clarissa, it's not a missing hatpin. She's in the family parlor. I'll see to a tray."

I put a hand on Hyperia's arm at the foot of the steps. "You will stay with me, please. I truly do not want to be alone with that woman."

Hyperia patted my knuckles. "As far as I know, Jules, you've never had memory lapses on successive days. You can go for months without having one."

We were alone in the corridor, and yet, I leaned closer. "Harry warned me against Clarissa, Perry. Said she is not to be trusted, and I'd best keep my distance, no matter what lures she cast. When Harry joined up, she did indeed cast lures in my direction, though she'd been swanning about with my brother a fortnight earlier. A gentleman isn't supposed to think poorly of a lady, but that was not ladylike behavior."

Hyperia stepped back. "Are you pouting because she chose Harry over you?"

"She unchose Harry the moment he bought his colors. I took longer to get together the money and find a commission in the same regiment as Harry. In those weeks... Very well, don't believe me. I'm making it all up, and she has no designs on Waltham. I hope you're right, and I'm wrong. I certainly have been before."

The truth was, Harry had conveyed an aspect of his relationship with Clarissa that baffled me. Money had been involved—money paid by him to her—and I was as bewildered by Harry's behavior as I was bewildered by Clarissa's. They were titled, wealthy, unattached... Clarissa was a *lady* and a Lady.

Why had Harry thought to offer her money for services? Why had she allowed it?

Did she think to somehow blackmail Arthur into marriage on the strength of that arrangement? Blackmail *me*?

I took a moment to calm my mind and mentally put aside my prejudices. Hyperia expected better of me, and thus I demanded it of myself.

"My lady." I bowed upon entering the family parlor. "Miss West tells me that you are most grievously upset and in need of the duke when His Grace is from home. Can I be of any assistance?"

"Julian!" She rose on a rustle of silk and lace and seized me by the arm. "Oh, Julian. You will think me ridiculous, but I'm his sister, and I know something is amiss. Lord Reardon did not come home last night."

Her distress certainly looked and felt sincere. She wore no earrings, her dress was as plain as any I'd seen on her, and her complexion was pale. Clarissa could produce tears or laughter with equal ease, but she could not make herself pale, could not manufacture unbecoming shadows beneath her eyes.

"The viscount has never stayed out all night before?"

"Not like this. Of course, he might tarry overnight after a dinner party if the weather turns foul. He stays the night with Squire Huber when their chess games run late, but he always sends a groom with a note. I know Reardon is an adult, and I'm not his nanny, but there's more."

Hyperia discreetly tugged the bell-pull twice—tray with all the trimmings—and wrestled a window open.

"Perhaps I should fetch paper and pencil?" she asked, moving to a second window. "If this is an abduction or foul play, somebody should take notes on what her ladyship has to say."

For God's sake, we were not dealing with an abduction or foul play, but neither did the situation have the ring of a stunt. Clarissa was genuinely beside herself.

I extracted the pencil and small notebook I kept in my breast pocket from long habit. "My lady, let us sit and review matters logically. When was the last time you saw Lord Reardon? What was he wearing? How were his spirits?"

Clarissa paused in her sniffling long enough to send me a bewildered look. "He would not take his own life, my lord. I'm insulted that you'd even imply that."

I handed Clarissa into a wing chair and took the seat facing her. Hyperia bustled about, pulling back drapes and generally impersonating a parlormaid. Chaperoning without being truly present.

"In the army," I said, "every officer became adept at locating missing persons. Desertion from both sides was a regular fact of life. The French deserted for the sake of British bread. The English deserted over rumors of good French brandy. Double deserting wasn't unheard of, and because both sides were short of seasoned soldiers, even that was often overlooked."

"What has this to do with my brother?"

"The penalty for desertion was death, but if a fellow voluntarily turned himself in, he could count on merely being sent to the West Indies or possibly India. Temporary banishment was considered preferable to a firing squad. If the deserter had any friends among his fellow soldiers, they'd make every effort to find him and bring him back. I was good at reconnaissance and a skilled tracker, so I was frequently called upon to locate the prodigal before the military police got wind of his wanderings."

And I'd often been successful, though my efforts hadn't always been appreciated by my quarry.

"My brother isn't an unhappy apprentice gone to join a traveling troupe of actors, my lord."

"Then perhaps he suffered a bump on the head and has temporarily lost his bearings. In which case, you need somebody who can track him down."

The tea tray arrived, and I asked Lady Clarissa to pour out in hopes the routine would soothe her. Hyperia took a seat on the end of the sofa and retired with her tea into silence.

"Was Reardon unhappy?" I asked when the footman had withdrawn. "The coming exhibition had to have put a lot of pressure on him."

"He was looking forward to it, Julian. I vow he was. That show was to be the culmination of a life's work and the means to fund a protracted stay in Rome. Nobody paints frescoes like the Italians, you know, and the Mediterranean light is marvelous. No dark, dreary winter where we go weeks without seeing the sun. Reardon longed for that joy, that freedom."

Did Clarissa long for it too?

"Very well," I said. "His lordship was in good spirits and had much to look forward to. What was he wearing?"

"Clothing." Clarissa took a sip of her tea. "How should I know? I take a tray in my room for breakfast, and when I came down, I was told he was out sketching. He is always out sketching. He has a little easel, and the legs are in a tube, and they screw into the easel-part. Very clever. He tosses that into a knapsack with his sketchbook and charcoal, collects a flask and some bread and butter. He whistles for his dog, and they are gone for hours."

"The dog came home without him?"

Clarissa stirred her tea. "I don't know. I assume so. I'm not sure."

I made a note to follow up. "Does his lordship have any favorite vistas, paths, or views?"

Clarissa shook her head. "Reardon's talent is so vast... He might be captivated by a cat sleeping in the sun outside the livery one day and fixate on a precise architectural elevation of the church bell tower the next. Last week, he did a sketch of Old Mrs. Forester, the granny, and before that, he was keen on memorializing the view above Caldicott Hall."

From the back of my mind came the usual litany of excuses: He fell asleep in the shade of some cow byre and decided to walk home in the morning. He's even now in his own bed, dreaming of Rome, but nobody saw him sneak in by moonlight. He indulged in a farewell tryst with some local widow...

The matter could not be dismissed so easily, however. Lord Reardon was Valloise's only son, the heir to an earldom. Kidnapping was a possibility. He was also a young man struggling for recognition in a field rarely frequented by peers-in-waiting, and he was on the verge of fame—or failure.

The artistic temperament had claimed more than one life and instigated tragedies aplenty.

Suicide was a possibility, as was—if I was to entertain even implausible theories—some jealous lesser talent pulling a prank in very bad taste.

More to the point, Waltham was not on hand to deal with the problem, and thus I would take Reardon's absence as seriously as I would a royal disappearance.

~

I questioned Lady Clarissa for more than an hour, trying to build a picture of Lord Reardon's usual movements and his most recent activities. For the whole of that hour, her ladyship did not so much as brush her fingers over my knuckles. She sipped two cups of tea and eschewed every other offering on the tray.

"Could Reardon's weak lungs have anything to do with him not coming home?" I asked as I escorted Clarissa to the north foyer. "Is he asthmatic? Might he have had some sort of rising of the lights?" Lord Reardon had not appeared consumptive to me. Not especially pale, no coughing, no hectic pink blush on his cheeks, but one did not mention fatal illness lightly to an upset woman.

"He does have weak lungs, but I've never known him to suffer any sort of seizure." Clarissa accepted her bonnet from me, while Cheadle hovered a discreet two yards away. "But you know how young men are. He could be expiring of an ague, and he'd claim he was right as a trivet."

Some young men were like that. I hadn't taken Reardon for a stoic. "I'm sure Waltham will want to interview your staff and have a look around Reardon's rooms. Until His Grace can make that inspection, please leave Reardon's effects absolutely undisturbed."

I certainly wanted to take those steps.

For the first time, Clarissa smiled. "What do a lot of wrinkled cravats or muddy boots have to say about an artist known to ramble the countryside by the hour?"

"The nature of the mud on those boots can tell me where he's wandered. Pond mud is different from bog mud, which is different from stable mud. Some plants are blooming now, while others have gone to seed. If I find spent blossoms of lady's-mantle on his coattails, for example, then I can look for tracks through the patch that's gone to seed nearest the house. We leave evidence of our passing on our surroundings, and our surroundings often do likewise with us."

Her smile faded. "You learned these skills in Spain?"

"I learned much about tracking right here at the Hall, rambling the home wood, playing along William's Creek, and pestering the gamekeepers." I'd also learned how to spot the signs of poaching. My father's tacit orders had been to ignore the occasional snare or patch of blood, unless evidence pointed to the presence of a poaching ring.

No Caldicott tenant family was to go hungry in a lean year while the woods teemed with game and the creek abounded with fish. The local folk reciprocated by stoutly repelling any overtures made by the professional poaching gangs.

Did Arthur still honor that approach, or might Lord Reardon have fallen afoul of the more violent game thieves plaguing half the realm?

I assisted Lady Clarissa into her cloak and escorted her down the steps to a waiting gig. No coach and four today and no chaperone or groom. The gelding in the traces was a venerable bay. He might not have the flashiest gaits, but a darting rabbit wouldn't unnerve him.

"I could escort you home," I said, assisting her ladyship onto the bench. "Have a look around Lord Reardon's apartment. He has a studio, too, doesn't he?"

Clarissa pulled on driving gloves and took up the reins. "I'd rather you informed His Grace of the morning's developments so I don't have to deal with the duke opening every cupboard you've just closed. Might I expect him this afternoon?"

"You can expect me, and His Grace if I can locate him. Try not to worry, my lady. Many a young fellow met with a batch of bad ale and needed a day or two to get back on his feet." Many a soldier had excused his absence without leave on those terms.

"I am worried," she said. "For Reardon to disappear a fortnight before he's due in London... that's not like him."

I stepped clear of the gig, and a final question occurred to me. "How did you know he was missing?"

Clarissa peered down at me. "I beg your pardon?"

"What made you realize that his lordship wasn't merely having a lie-in, or absorbed with a particularly challenging painting behind the door of his studio? It's not yet luncheon, and most ladies would take a tray in this heat rather than dress for breakfast. Something alerted you to the fact that Reardon disappeared into the undergrowth."

She stared hard at the horse's rump. "A feeling, mostly. Reardon does wander for hours at a time, but yesterday grew so warm, and he hadn't sent any notes, and... You will think me silly, but Valmond House feels different when Reardon isn't there. It feels different when Mama and Papa are on hand. The house has moods, and the mood now is, 'Where's Lord Reardon?' As if the very dwelling is concerned for him."

An interesting answer. What Lady Clarissa called a feeling might well be her eyes, ears, and nose noticing details that her mind had yet to build into a pattern.

I trusted feelings like that, for the most part. "Then you were right to bring the problem to His Grace, but I'd advise you against setting up a hue and cry, my lady. If Reardon does come home complaining of the effects of bad ale, or having slipped on some muddy bank and conked his noggin, you don't want to make a fool of him."

I expected an argument and got only a single nod. "So long as you find him, my lord. Tell the duke that. I don't care what it takes. I want my brother found."

She tooled off, and the gig created a plume of dust that hung in the sultry morning air. I did not like or trust Lady Clarissa, but I sympathized with her plight. Harry had gone missing from camp, and I had been compelled by fraternal loyalty, concern, curiosity, and instinct to follow him and bring him safely home.

If Clarissa's sentiments were a tenth as fierce as my own, then the hardest demands I could have made of her were for patience and inaction. I, however, had much to do. I sent word to the stable to have Atlas saddled and went up to my room, intent upon changing into riding attire.

Lady Ophelia had decamped, and Atticus was rifling the drawer at the foot of my wardrobe.

"Looking for something?"

"Who unpacked yer trunk?" He kept right on working his way down through rolls of stockings, neatly pressed handkerchiefs and sets of gloves.

I thought for a moment. "The first footman is Norse—that's his name, Norse. Big, blond fellow, looks like he could split you in two with his battle-ax, but he's actually quite merry."

"Did he do it right?" Atticus whipped dark hair from his eyes and sat back. "Is this how you like yer things stashed?"

Was Atticus covering for a bout of snooping, or genuinely trying to educate himself? "That arrangement will do, though in London, I have a whole dressing closet rather than just a wardrobe."

Atticus fished in a pocket and held my comb out to me. "Thanks for the loan."

The delicate comb looked incongruous in his calloused little mitt. "Not a loan. I cannot have a fellow in my employ going about unkempt. I have other combs. That one is yours. When we get to London, we'll see to your wardrobe."

Atticus rose, and his chin jutted disagreeably. "I ain't wearing no damned livery."

Ducal livery was nothing to be ashamed of. "Why not? You'll be taking my coin."

"Because you'll dock me wages for six months to pay for duds that aren't mine. Can't wear 'em anywhere but on the job, and if they get stained or wrecked because some fool spilled his tea on me, I have to pay for a new set, and there's another six months with no coin for honest work."

I shrugged out of my morning coat and retrieved my notebook and pencil from the breast pocket. "Get Helms to show you how to brush this jacket out and touch it up with an iron. Tell him I asked, and I will inquire of him before the day's out if you saw to the matter."

"He's the duke's man? Everybody calls him Your Grace and milord duke belowstairs. Everyone 'cept Cook."

"Helms is His Grace's valet. His uncle was my father's valet, and you can have no better tutor in the art of being a gentleman's gentleman." I took the time to wash off thoroughly, the morning having left me sticky as well as tired. "I'll need riding breeches—the oldest pair, please—and any shirt will do. The older the better."

"Why old?"

"Because my first stop is the home farm, and impressing the sows in their wallows is not on my schedule. In this heat, the less finery I'm wearing, the better. From the home farm, I will have a quiet word with the gamekeepers, some tenants, Granny Forester, Vicar, and if there's time, the grooms at Valmond House. No, you are not coming with me. I'll be on horseback, and time is of the essence."

"His Grace ain't on horseback."

I pulled on the worn breeches, which fit me like the old and dear friends they were. Not as loose as they had been a few months ago either.

"Why do you say that?"

"Because the duke left on foot at first light, and he weren't wearing no fin-er-y either. Did the same thing yesterday. I thought he was you, 'cept he took off his hat, and his hair was the wrong color."

"Was he alone?"

"Aye, and moving at a good clip. Right up the hill behind the house."

That was the opposite direction from the home farm and away from the village, but perhaps Arthur had meant to call on a tenant before the morning grew too warm.

Or perhaps he'd gone a-trysting?

I did up my falls and chose a shirt going a bit frayed around the cuffs. "I'll find him at the home farm, I'm told, and you will stay here, keeping your eyes and ears open."

Atticus perched on the sill of an open window. The drop behind him was a good twenty feet, and he could not have appeared more relaxed. Ah, youth.

"Somebody's pretty watch go missing again?" he asked, referring to an apparent theft at the Makepeace house party.

"Somebody's brother has gone missing. Viscount Reardon dwells on the estate just around the hill from us. He's an artist preparing for his first big exhibition, and he's the heir of a slightly eccentric earl. He did not come home last night."

Atticus began to bounce a heel against the wainscoting. "He's a grown feller, and he stayed out all night? Is he simple?"

"This is not London, where his lordship might have found a berth at his club, played cards all night with friends, or spent the hours with a ladybird. His sister is alarmed, and the duke is the closest thing to a justice of the peace in the neighborhood, so she sought His Grace's aid."

Atticus hopped off the windowsill. "You plan to find him?"

"Yes." When had I come to that conclusion and why? True, Clarissa was a damsel in distress, but she wasn't my damsel, and I wasn't any sort of legal official. Though I had been a tracker, and a damned good one.

"What if he don't want to be found? What if the bailiffs are on his tail, and you'll ruin him if you find him?"

"Don't be ridiculous. Lord Reardon would hardly plan a very public exhibition of his art if he was pockets to let and booked on a packet for Calais."

Atticus passed me a starched cravat from the selection hanging in the wardrobe. I whipped it into a loose mathematical, though any sort of cravat was rank stupidity in the growing heat. Not as stupid as putting the British infantry in wool uniforms and shipping them off to march across the Spanish plain in high summer. Very little could compete with foolishness on that order. Men had regularly died of heat exhaustion, and died wearing those wretched uniforms.

Atticus opened my jewelry box and passed over a plain gold pin. "Most important part of any cutpurse's rig is the distraction—the lady crying about her missing dog, the old man falling on the church steps."

The boy had a point. If Lord Reardon was in dun territory, then scheduling an exhibition could be a way to assure his creditors that he'd be back in Town for much of the summer. But could an earl's heir and only son *be* so deep into dun territory that he had to flee the family seat?

I jotted a few words on my notebook and shoved it into the pocket sewn into the tail of my riding jacket.

"Stay here, and stay alert." I arranged the pin among the folds of my cravat. "Reardon is apparently of sound mind, has no enemies, and has every reason to live. Kidnapping and suicide are unlikely, but he might well be at the bottom of some old mine shaft with a broken ankle or a broken head. Any detail—his childhood haunts, the quickest way home from his old nurse's cottage—could mean the difference between life and death, so keep a sharp ear in the servants' hall. Where the devil are my—?"

Atticus passed me the sleeve buttons that went with the plain cravat pin. I slipped them onto my cuffs and shrugged into my riding coat, but left the buttons undone.

"You taking a flask with you?" Atticus asked. "You'll miss your nooning, and it's hotter than holy damned hell already."

"Hotter than blazes," I said. "Hotter than perdition, the pit, the inferno. Hotter than a smoking coach brake. 'Hell' pushes the limits of gentlemanly decorum."

Atticus smiled and shook his head. "Hotter than fancy livery on a London summer day."

"The livery I had in mind for you was a tiger-striped yellow jacket—which your employer would provide at no cost to you, of course—but I suppose not, if you'd rather sport about in ragged trousers and a frayed shirt."

I had the satisfaction of seeing his mouth hang open, then snap shut. I made my exit before he could remonstrate with me—which the boy would do—and headed for the kitchen. The day *was* promising to be hotter than hell. I needed some sustenance and at least one flask full of lemonade, if not two.

I also had to uncover the answer to a question Atticus had pointed me to, but had not known to ask: Viscount Reardon was an only son and heir to the Valloise earldom. If Reardon's earthly sojourn had ended, who was next in line for the title, and had that person had any opportunity to advance his interests at Lord Reardon's expense?

I made another note to myself and took the footmen's stairs down to the pantries.

CHAPTER FIVE

"Reardon has done this before," Arthur said, his boot propped on the bottom rail of the fence overlooking a hog pen. Contrary to popular opinion, members of the porcine species were tidy creatures, dividing their quarters into dining room, sitting room, privy, and park. They wallowed in mud—not in their privies—to stay cool and were otherwise fastidious about their persons.

"Viscount Reardon has previous disappearances to his name?"

The sow sharing quarters with a dozen rambunctious piglets ambled over for a scratch about the ears. She would have done the horse artillery proud, if they'd had the sense not to eat her.

"Not exactly disappearances," Arthur said, obliging the sow. "Reardon falls asleep beneath a starry night, or wanders the country-side drunk on the vivid hues of wild flowers. Until a couple years ago, his absences meant we'd all turn out to literally beat the bushes, and then he'd trundle home that evening, his loyal hound panting at his side. I thought he'd outgrown his errant tendencies."

The sow nuzzled Arthur's hand. Another man—another duke—would have ceased petting the pig. Arthur switched to scratching her other ear.

"The dog worries me." I shrugged out of my jacket, lest the sun burn it from my shoulders. "If you are planning to elude creditors, for example, you don't take your dog."

"Maybe you do, if that dog is your most loyal companion."

How innocent Arthur was. "No, you do not, lest the dog be confiscated for resale to the bear pits to settle your debts. Then too, dogs require food and water. They require regular access to the out of doors. They mark you as different from all other travelers. People forget what sort of hat the man sitting next to them in the common wore, but they will recall his dog."

"That should make his lordship easier to track. Do you not recognize this sow? She's all grown up now, but you named her."

I took a closer look at big ears, white coat, and pink snout, and damned if the sow didn't appear to smile at me. "Guinevere?"

"The very same. She's a good mum and keeps the young sows in line. Pillar of the community and all that."

Pigs were smart, smarter than dogs in the opinion of some hog farmers. Pigs had a homing instinct to rival any pigeon, and they could remember a location where they'd found food years ago.

Guinevere appeared to remember me. She bumped at my hand, maybe the porcine equivalent of a greeting. I obliged by scratching both of her ears at once, and she tipped her snout up, just as she had when I'd offered her this same sort of attention when parting from her to go off to university.

"She has to be ten or twelve years old."

"Fourteen. Not our oldest breeding sow, but venerable. She has earned her pension, though Hopwood thinks me daft for pensioning a perfectly edible hog."

"Dukes are permitted their little foibles." Guinevere, having received her due, toddled off to slurp at the water trough. Each day, the trough was drained into the muddy wallow and fresh water provided for drinking. In this heat, a sizable creature like Gwenny would drink almost constantly.

On that thought, I took out my flask.

"I'm inclined to leave Lord Reardon to his foibles," Arthur said, watching the sow at the trough. "Getting the whole parish in an uproar when he's likely spent the night at some coaching inn... He would not appreciate being treated like a schoolboy."

The lemonade was tart, cool, and half gone by the time I offered Arthur my flask. "You must make some sort of effort."

"Why?" He took the flask and emptied it. "I'm a duke, as I've been reminded. I can give the fellow a day or two to canoodle with his light-skirts or capture the beauty of mating dragonflies."

Arthur was hot and troubled, and I knew not what bothered him. "If you take that attitude, then you allow any witnesses' memories to grow dim, and if we are to get any relief from this heat, thunderstorms are inevitable."

"I like a good, loud storm."

Innocent, innocent, innocent. "You would not like good, loud storms if you had any memory of French cannon booming out the doom of half your fellow soldiers. The more pressing problem is that rain will obliterate most signs of Lord Reardon's perambulations, and that considerably reduces the chances of finding him."

Arthur pushed away from the fence and handed me my empty flask. "Why are you drinking lemonade?"

"Because it's blazing hot."

"You avoid spirits?"

We stuck to the shade of the orchard, which in drought years could be shallowly flooded by virtue of proximity to William's Creek. Arthur was careful not to abuse that privilege. The creek turned the local mill wheel, fed the village pumps, and watered a good portion of the neighborhood's livestock.

"I had a bout of forgetting yesterday." I turned across the orchard toward the creek. "Hyperia was with me, and I had my little card in my pocket."

"I'm... sorry."

"I'm encouraged. An hour later, I was fine. Hyperia knew exactly what to do."

The shade was heavenly, and a number of spotted hogs were enjoying it with us. They lounged against the cool of the orchard's stone walls, panting gently.

"Encouraged?"

"A very short bout. At university, I went a whole day in a fog. I wasn't entirely over it until the next morning. I avoid overindulging in spirits because that, too, can cause forgetfulness. I can't see a connection between the two kinds of memory loss, but one doesn't tempt fate."

"Sometimes I envy you the forgetting." Arthur opened the gate on the stream side of the orchard, and we were greeted by the placid burbling of William's Creek. "Forgetting battles and captivity can't be an entirely bad thing."

"Forgetting one's name rather outweighs any benefits of forgetting wartime, and then there's the rush of recollection, when it all comes home to roost."

"Harry?"

"Harry most of all."

"That's why you will find Lord Reardon, because you could not find Harry."

I longed to take off my clothes and immerse myself in the cool, clear water, but time was of the essence.

"I did find Harry, trailed him right into the French garrison. I could not rescue him, though. Had he been a little less honorable, we might both have made it out of that fortress."

"He would not betray his country?"

"So the French commandant told me, but half of what that man said was lies, the other half untruths." I knew that French officer as Girard, but in my mind, he was Lucifer's handmaiden. I'd been warned that he was now sporting about among the English, having fallen heir to a barony. "Let us put old business aside. You are the closest thing to an acting magistrate, and Lord Reardon is missing. Ergo, you must do something."

"Or Lady Clarissa will be on our doorstep daily, wringing her hands and swooning into my arms?"

I took out my notebook and jotted another possible motive for sending Reardon into temporary hiding. Clarissa as a guest was an occasional penance. Clarissa as a woman seeking aid to find her brother was entitled to storm Caldicott Hall repeatedly.

"She's not awful, Arthur, and if you went missing, I would be distraught."

"I will not go missing." Arthur offered that not as a reassurance, but more of a lament. What on earth was wrong with my brother, and where had he got off to at first light?

"Will you come with me to Valmond House? I want to interview anybody who might have seen Reardon decamp, have a look around his apartment, and get a start on tracking him."

"Then I'm deputing you to take those very steps. I'll send Demming to nose around the old quarry. He'll be discreet and thorough."

The quarry, dating from at least Roman times, had been forbidden to every child in the shire. The best swimming was to be had there, of course, but the lip subsided from time to time, and thus on a tragic day in centuries past, some youth had lost his life in the dark depths of the small lake that half filled the old diggings.

His ghost was said to haunt the place, which only made it more attractive as forbidden territory. "You should drain that damned thing."

"No telling how deep it is, and draining a quarry is expensive. Besides, we need some sort of reservoir for the dry years, and the quarry serves. Go interrogate the Valmond grooms, and I will not expect you for supper."

I left Arthur perched on the orchard wall, gazing at the depths of the creek. I roused Atlas from his shady napping place, refilled my flask at the creek, and let Atlas have a good long drink too. I'd need to detour to the house for a few necessities, and given the building heat, I'd have to content myself with cursory questioning of the Valmond staff—enough to establish the general direction in which his lordship had taken off—and then I'd best get tracking.

Because rain was a constant threat, I'd likely be at that thankless task all night.

~

Reardon's studio had the predictable northern exposure, tall windows, and high ceiling. Artists used pigments that could be toxic if inhaled for too long or at close range, and light was as necessary to a painter as air was to a bird of prey.

"He works in here by the hour," Lady Clarissa said, coming into the room with me. "Reardon was very fast. He said a proper painter wasn't to be that quick, lest the public think him facile rather than talented. Why can't an artist be both?"

"Did the viscount paint through the night on occasion?"

"Often, which is why he has so much material for the exhibition. If it wasn't for Susan, I'd take most of my suppers alone."

Lady Susan was the youngest sibling, not yet out, according to Hyperia. "Is Lady Susan available for questioning?"

Clarissa picked up a sketchbook and opened it. "You make it sound as if she's a first former who knows how the frog got in the matron's bed."

"Clarissa, please don't touch anything. Reardon all but lived in this room, and details I find here can yield insights."

She set down the sketchbook. "Such as?"

I moved about, looking for what wasn't of a piece, for what didn't fit. "My father's desk, a beautiful old relic, had a succession of burns down the right side. He'd lay a cheroot on the edge, such that the ashes dropped onto the carpet, and forget he'd done so. The carpet and more especially the desk suffered repeatedly."

"And he could afford to abuse an antique, is that your point?"

Something about the whole room was off, but what? "When was Reardon most recently painting in here?"

"Night before last. He was up quite late, which is why I was surprised to learn he'd gone rambling on only a few hours' sleep. What is the significance of the late duke's marred desk?"

"In isolation, those burns might say merely what you conclude: He could afford to disrespect an antique. Those burns also tell us that His Grace would rather stay up until he was exhausted, poring over ledgers or correspondence, or simply swilling brandy, rather than join his duchess abovestairs. Perhaps those scars tell us he wasn't welcome to join the duchess. Maybe they suggest that the estate accounts vexed him to such a degree that he took his ire out on an otherwise lovely piece of furniture. No one fact is dispositive of the whole man, but a dozen facts can yield an insight."

The studio lacked the sense of industry I associated with an active workshop, and it also didn't... smell right.

"You've aired the room out?" The windows were cracked as I spoke.

"Of course."

Dratted woman. That was why even the scent of linseed oil was barely noticeable. "I asked you to leave the space untouched. You opened the windows, organized his brushes, tidied up the worktable, likely swept..." I continued my inspection and came upon a bouquet of dead yellow irises in the dustbin. "In fact, you meddled with the entire room."

Clarissa assayed her version of the timid, helpless smile. "Well, I didn't want you to see what a slob Reardon could be. He's very particular about his art, but not about his personal effects. Boots by the door, gloves tossed onto the mantel, pocket watch set on the end table. He focused on his paintings, and it's as if that exhausted his capacity for routine or organization."

I lifted the wilted flowers from the dustbin. "Had you left these in their vase, I might have known how recently they were picked. Because yellow irises love water, I know a few places to look for them, and thus I'd have some ideas where to find fresh sign. In the alternative, I'll find no fresh sign and have a list of areas I need not study further, because Reardon went there earlier in the week and had no interest in those locations yesterday."

"That bouquet was starting to wilt," Clarissa said. "Yellow irises are supposed to be cheerful—Reardon said they symbolized his passion for art—and they made me so sad. I can't just sit here, pretending all is well, working on blasted needlepoint, when my only brother might be *dead*."

She hurled the word at me as she flung herself into my arms. The last thing I wanted was to waste time comforting a woman I didn't much like, but Clarissa's distress was genuine. I patted her back and fumbled for my handkerchief, and at the first opportunity, I stepped back to hand it to her.

"How wilted were the irises, my lady?"

She gave me a look that said rumors of my mental deficiencies had not been exaggerated. "The flowers should have been tossed out the day before yesterday." She sniffed delicately and dabbed at her eyes. "They were well past their prime, Julian, and that is exactly the sort of thing Reardon would not notice."

I led her to a window bench, one of few places to sit in the whole studio. The breeze wafting in was warm, but at least it was moving air.

"What else did you tidy up?" Lady Clarissa would not trust staff to put Reardon's sanctum sanctorum to rights.

"His sketchbooks. He leaves them open to work from, and sometimes..." She began folding my handkerchief in quarters on her knee. "He does anatomical studies."

Nudes. "Of anybody in particular?"

"Mostly just parts. Hands, feet, ears. What can be so fascinating about an ear, for pity's sake?"

I left Clarissa to her prevarications and began sorting through the row of sketchbooks marching along a worktable. Reardon had devoted three whole books to anatomical studies, but in the next volume, the sketches took a decidedly erotic turn.

"Was he involved with Mrs. Probinger?"

Clarissa rose and gave me her back. "She modeled for him. I don't know if he felt sorry for her because she's widowed and needed the money, or whether there was more to it."

I finished inspecting the sketchbooks, finding everything from village portraits to a view from the lip of the quarry, to multiple renderings of a droopy-eared, brindle hound with enormous paws. I tucked one of those into my pocket.

"Could Reardon and Mrs. Probinger have eloped?"

Clarissa turned to face me. "Run off? I suppose so, but they can't marry. Mama would never stand for it. Reardon will be an earl, and he will marry according to his station."

Clarissa hadn't married according to her station, at least not yet. Was she that determined to snabble a duke? Was she wearing the willow for Harry, despite all appearances to the contrary?

Her unwed state was a puzzle, but not relevant to the instant inquiry.

"Your well-intended efforts to protect your brother's privacy might have made it impossible to find him, my lady. I'm off to the stable, and I hope somebody there saw which direction Reardon took when he left Valmond House yesterday morning. Unless you know?"

She shook her head. "You won't say anything to His Grace about Mrs. Probinger?"

"Waltham is essentially our acting justice of the peace. If it turns out Mrs. Probinger did Reardon an injury because he was preparing to throw her over for some wealthy Town heiress, then His Grace will have to know."

Clarissa took the wilted flowers I'd left on the worktable and dropped them back into the dustbin. "It won't come to that. It cannot come to that."

If she continued to interfere with my investigation, it well might come to that, or worse. "I'm away to the stable. I cannot insist that you work on your embroidery, but calm and logic will get you further than random poking about. If any detail occurs to you that might shed light on Reardon's situation, send for me.

Please do not go nosing into corners and obliterating evidence."
Again.

She looked on the verge of fresh tears, so I excused myself and had a footman direct me to his lordship's room.

"Don't go just yet," I said when the fellow would have withdrawn. "I assume the whole staff knows his lordship has taken French leave?"

"We're a bit worrit, milord." The footman was young, and his livery fit him loosely. "Himself does like to ramble, but it's been a while since he forgot to come home."

Quaint phrasing. "Does Lord Reardon use a valet?" Not every gentleman did when in the country. Formal attire was required far less frequently, and the estate laundresses and seamstresses could be trusted to handle masculine clothing competently.

"No valet, sir. The earl's man did for Lord Reardon when the family went up to Town. I look after his boots and such when he's down from Town."

My escort showed me into a comfortable two-room suite—sitting room and bedroom with dressing closet—that looked out over the shallow lake. This side of the house got the full brunt of the afternoon sun, but the windows had been opened here, too, and the ceilings were a good twelve feet.

Nowhere along the lake's banks did I see any obliging splashes of yellow flowers.

"Take a look at his lordship's dressing closet," I said. "Tell me if you see anything missing."

The footman made a job of it, counting items in the clothes press and peering into the jewelry box. "We're down a couple of shirts, milord, though those could be in the laundry, along with some under-linen and a cravat or two. I don't see his shooting jacket either."

A shooting jacket was cut loose to allow for handling a long gun, and while it kept off the damp, it wasn't a heavy item of apparel. More for autumn than winter.

"Nothing else is missing?"

"His lordship doesn't have much in the way of jewelry. He'd sooner spend his money on fancy paints and art books. Nothing missing that I can see."

The fancy art books were neatly shelved in the sitting room, which was an orderly, slightly worn space. I peered into the waste bin, finding it empty.

"Lady Clarissa told you to tidy up in here?"

"As soon as she came back from the Hall, though there wasn't much to tidy. The bed was slept in."

"No breakfast tray?"

"We set out the morning meal in the servants' hall by six o'clock, and his lordship would have helped himself to something on the way out the door. Not one for standing on ceremony."

"Who would know in which direction he tramped?"

The footman ran a finger around his loose collar. "Stable lads, most likely. Gardeners might. They like to get an early start when the heat's coming on."

"And Lord Reardon took the dog?"

"Aye, sir. That wretched hound goes into a decline when his lordship goes up to Town. We're hoping the dog goes to London with his lordship for that art show. The beast pines and mopes like a rejected runt."

Interesting. "What is your name, my good fellow?"

"Blaylock, sir. I'm cousin to Demming what works at the Hall."

"Thought I noticed a resemblance. You've been most helpful, though I cannot say the same for Lady Clarissa. In her efforts to keep busy, she's destroying valuable evidence and making it harder for me to locate our missing viscount. I realize you cannot be expected to order her ladyship about—"

"It's worth me life to remember me place, milord."

"—but if you and the staff would keep an eye on her, I'd appreciate it. She's going through a difficult time, and she and Lady Susan might benefit from a little more attentiveness."

Blaylock gave me a very unfootmanlike look. "I'll have a word with Mrs. Aimes, shall I? Suggest the young ladies could do with looking after?"

"As long as somebody is looking after Mrs. Aimes too. Is she at home?"

"Off to the village. The annual fete is next week, before the family goes up to Town. Mrs. Aimes and the vicar's wife are plotting over pies and sack races and so forth."

"Somebody's got to do it, I suppose. I'm off to the stable by way of the garden. Would it be possible for the kitchen to put together a few sandwiches for me?"

"Mrs. Felders will be pleased to oblige, my lord."

"Thank you, Blaylock. You've been most helpful."

I took a last look around Reardon's rooms, and again, my sense was that the space was too tidy, too organized, but then, the real man had likely been in evidence in the studio before Clarissa took to fussing for the sake of appearances.

"Demming speaks highly of the Hall," Blaylock said, his tone wistful. "Says the Caldicotts are fair and generous."

"We try to be." Though what point was Blaylock dancing around?

"Don't suppose there's lack of indoor help at the Hall, His Grace being a duke and all?"

For a footman to show any sort of discontent with his post was extraordinarily disloyal, though Blaylock was trying to be subtle.

"Lady Clarissa would take it amiss if we poached her best staff away."

"I do well with horses, sir, and I spent time in the garden with me uncle. I'm not much for the stepping and fetching, but a footman's job is inside work, and I thought..."

I waited, trying to look sympathetic rather than appalled. Surely, Blaylock was new to his ill-fitting livery to be offering me this confession under his employer's very roof?

"I thought I could make a go of it," Blaylock finished miserably.

"You're willing to return to outside work?" A social and financial demotion, but I was reminded of Atticus's disdain for livery he thought he'd have to pay for himself.

"Aye. I don't mind hard work, but the footman's job isn't what I took it for."

Perhaps the footman's wages weren't what he'd taken them for? A few pounds a year wasn't much—London wages were higher—but those pounds came with an allowance for beer, candles, and more, usually. Also very light duties on Sunday and a midweek half day.

"I'll have a word with His Grace. We tend to keep the staff we have, but younger fellows have been known to decamp for London or the New World without much notice."

"Thank you, sir."

"I'll see myself out."

"I'll send your tucker to the stable." Blaylock marched off smartly, and I tarried behind to have a look through Reardon's desk and night table.

I also examined Lord Reardon's second pair of field boots. His footprint would be a good inch shorter than my own, his right heel worn down slightly on the outside, and he probably tended to walk with his weight on the outside of the foot rather than on the inside.

Nothing of further interest came from my snooping, and the stable lads could tell me only that Reardon had disappeared into the woods at first light. He'd traveled along a web of game trails, farm lanes, and footpaths that connected Valmond House to Caldicott Hall, the village, and any number of neighboring properties.

The afternoon was half gone, and I had only a hundred miles or so of possible trails to inspect. *Jolly hell.*

My last stop before embarking on that task was the Valmond House gardener's cottage. After inquiring generally about the need for rain—"Aye, milord, we could use a mite,"—the misery caused by the heat—"the hydrangeas suffer so,"—and the possibility of an early autumn—"We live in hope, good sir. We live in hope,"—I got 'round to the reason for all the pleasantries.

"Where is the nearest patch of blooming yellow irises, Mr. Simpkins? A mature patch, plenty of blossoms, and at the height of their beauty."

Mr. Simpkins stroked a beard that would have been the envy of the King of the Elves. "Aye. A patch with plenty for picking, the best on offer, not a few bold specimens. When the trail from the park approaches the village, you take the left turning, away from the green. Another hundred yards, and you're along the creek, right at the foot of the Probinger property. Big patch there, and a right pretty sight they are too."

Well, well, well. I thanked him for his time and left him stroking his beard while I set out to familiarize myself with Lord Reardon's tracks. He and the loyal hound were easy to pick up—the path from the stable was dusty—but then I lost them on the grassy stretches approaching the village.

No worries, though. As I ate the last of my sandwiches and fed Atlas a few bites of carrot, I found clear signs of his lordship's recent travels right near the patch of irises on the Probinger property.

Quelle surprise, as my old nanny would have said.

CHAPTER SIX

"My lord, I am honored." Mrs. Probinger dipped a curtsey that said the honor was also a bit of a surprise and possibly a trifle inconvenient. She was a diminutive strawberry-blonde of perhaps thirty years, with pale green eyes and a sprinkling of freckles across the bridge of her nose. Her looks were too elfin to be considered beautiful —*nez retroussé*, point-ish chin—but she made an impact.

Those green eyes were bold, and that lush mouth looked to be on the verge of laughter or naughty asides. Reardon doubtless told himself he found her looks interesting.

I bowed, and she suggested we avail ourselves of her back terrace. I chose lemonade over tea and allowed as how my lunch had been late and lacking.

"One doesn't want to be rude," she said, taking a shady seat, "but when a Caldicott calls on a Probinger, tongues will wag."

Her house faced the church end of the village green, and I had doubtless been seen knocking on her door.

"Then the Caldicotts have been remiss." I took the chair across from her at a wrought-iron table. "I wish I could say I'm here to remedy the oversight, but I'm actually on something of an errand for His Grace."

"You're looking better," she observed, subjecting me to a dispassionate scrutiny. "Not as pale. Not as gaunt, and you are probably sleeping for more than forty-five minutes at a stretch."

I knew that assessing, measuring look. Had seen it from dozens of officers' wives. "Your husband served under Wellington."

"My husband served *and died* under Wellington. Made it all the way to Waterloo and was among the tens of thousands who never came home. He'd been injured before—I know the signs of a soldier waging a war against old ghosts—but I never thought... Bonaparte was exiled once for all, and then he was back again. The worst of bad pennies. I wish *l'empereur* every misery a man can suffer, and I make no apology for my lack of Christian charity."

"Moved, seconded, and passed," I said, feeling an odd kinship with a woman I barely knew. "But why settle here? We're an obscure corner of a rural shire." I had noticed Mrs. Probinger at services when I'd been recovering at the Hall, and we'd been introduced at some point, but I'd exchanged only pleasantries with her.

The tray arrived, and the abundance before me merited a silent and heartfelt grace. Sandwiches of pink, thinly sliced beef and cheddar. A bowl of glistening, sweet cherries. A small stack of shortbread.

"I have peace and quiet here," Mrs. Probinger said, looking out over a garden rioting with color. The flowers were the hardy sort—daisies, hollyhocks, and delphinium, with lush lavender borders running along crushed-shell walks. "I have no memories here to plague me, no regimental connections to pluck every nerve on the anniversary of every battle. I hope you don't intend to upend my hard-earned sense of tranquility, my lord."

Her tone, though light, promised that if I blundered in that regard, I'd be shown the door, ducal connections be damned.

"My errand is civil," I said. "Viscount Reardon has wandered off, and the duke has dispatched me to ask a few discreet questions. We suspect his lordship came this way recently and that you and he were well acquainted."

She chose a cherry. "I am unhappy with his lordship, sir. One might say I am furious with him. Have been for some time."

I asked the obvious question. "Did he trifle with you?"

She popped the cherry into her mouth. "I trifled with him, more like. Widows are permitted their comforts. The viscount was an enthusiastic caller in that regard, but then I awoke from a pleasant encounter a couple of months ago to find him sketching me, though I was in the altogether. He swore he was only trying to get my hair right, but he's a privileged young man who uses his art to avoid other responsibilities. He's truly talented, and he can also be unscrupulous. Has a bit of the rotten, sullen boy about him, for which I blame Lady Clarissa."

I started on a second sandwich. "You have given him his congé?"

"I sent him packing. I suspect he was trysting with me for the sake of his art, not immortalizing my beauty in his sketchbooks because our rendezvous were so delightful. Quite lowering. I might have forgiven him his artistic trespasses if he'd surrendered the sketches to me, but instead, he offered me money. I let him know what I thought of that overture, wished him every success in Town, and haven't spent time with him since."

She munched another cherry, and it struck me that her conscience was clear. Of course, many a soldier committed murder by the hour and concluded his battlefield labors with a clear conscience and even pride in his work.

"When did you last see his lordship?"

"Earlier this week. He was mooning about by the river, stealing irises from the patch at the foot of the garden. That was three... four mornings ago. I caught a glimpse of him striding by yesterday at dawn, knapsack and hound at the ready. He was walking in the direction of Squire Huber's parcel, though why anybody would call on Huber so early in the day defies explanation."

I debated whether a third sandwich would be ill-mannered and decided to refrain. "You don't get on well with Huber?"

"Other than the Valmonds, few in the area do, as you should know. The squire is arrogant, wallowing in the past, and chronically disappointed by a life most would call well blessed. He is my bad example. Have some cherries. They enjoy such a short season, I devour them on sight."

She held the bowl out to me, and I took a single ripe fruit. The cherry was perfectly sweet, a small delight. I took another.

"What do you mean, Huber is your bad example? He was supposed to marry my great-aunt or something. I shudder to think he might have been family."

"John Huber is family to the Valmonds. Second cousin or some sort of cousin to the present earl, though they aren't far apart in age. Huber took his wife's name along with her fortune, and the fortune is still going strong. What I mean by my bad example is that Huber is the thing I must not become. Yes, he lost his wife, but he has three grown sons and two daughters, along with grandchildren, and they all toady to him. I will not let my husband's death turn me into the bitter, demanding, bumptious creature Huber has become."

I took one more cherry. "The squire was a veritable demon as magistrate, but I'd forgotten he's connected to the Valmonds by birth. Lord Reardon played the occasional game of chess with him."

"Reardon felt compelled to call. Said those evenings were more about cheap brandy and a repetition of regrets—if only Mrs. Huber hadn't gone to her reward, if only the Americans hadn't proven so ungrateful, if only young people today were not so frivolous."

I set the bowl of cherries before my hostess. "Is art frivolous?"

"For a peer's heir, it's supposed to be. Reardon will put aside his paintbrushes when he inherits the title. His sister will see to that, and Reardon knows it."

Mrs. Probinger offered me the shortbread next, and the buttery scent alone decreed that I take a sample.

"You don't care for Lady Clarissa?"

"I don't *know* her, but I suspect another motivation for Reardon's visits here was masculine rebellion. He has more the nature of a sixteen-year-old than a man who has attained his majority. Lady Clarissa has discouraged him from the usual pursuits that help a fellow leave boyhood behind. An earl's heir and only son was unlikely to have served in the military, but the viscount's role has been limited in recent years to that of Clarissa's escort, her confidant, her project..."

"And is his art also a rebellion?" Was his lordship staging a bit of an uprising by going missing as his exhibition loomed?

Mrs. Probinger went back to demolishing the cherries one by one. "Reardon's art is a genuine calling, but Clarissa pushed him to do the exhibition. Most aspiring artists would have applied to join the Royal Academy's summer show and taken their lumps if none of their work was included. The usual recourse is to try again, year after year. Lady Clarissa convinced her brother to make his own splash, though Reardon would rather have gone the traditional route."

"You are saying Reardon is henpecked?"

"By a prime biddy. Clarissa alternatively spoils him and manipulates him. She's his greatest supporter and the first to whine if he steps out of line. I was a step out of line for him, but one she could ignore. I certainly ignore her to the greatest extent possible, though one does pity the woman."

Clarissa couldn't ignore Reardon's protracted absence. "Why pity her?"

Mrs. Probinger considered the empty bowl. "You came across enlisted men who would never rise beyond sergeant, didn't you? Shrewd fellows, tough, charismatic, dead shots, endlessly brave, but their rough speech alone meant they'd never command more than a night patrol. At the same time, prancing buffoons by the score strutted around wearing a lieutenant's uniform simply because their papas could buy them a commission."

"And those enlisted men," I said slowly, "had to watch in silence, eyes front, while the prancing buffoons ruined good soldiers and even got them killed. You suspect Clarissa is that enlisted man?"

"She is mortally unhappy, my lord. If you can't see that, you need to stop wearing your tinted spectacles. Reardon swore all Clarissa's worldly aspirations were focused on him because her own dreams had come to nothing. Lord Harry might have figured prominently in her disappointments."

Oh, him. He figured in my disappointments as well. "Harry has been gone for some time. I suspect Clarissa has set her sights on the duke."

Another laugh, this one genuinely amused. "More disappointment in the offing. Mind you don't come into her ladyship's crosshairs, my lord. For Reardon's sake, I hope he's taken ship for Rome. Clarissa can have her exhibition, but Reardon won't be one of the items on offer."

"And for my sake, I hope the viscount is doing an impromptu portrait of Huber's younger daughter." I rose, though a nap wouldn't have gone amiss. A nap in some obliging hammock rather than in Mrs. Probinger's bed. "Thank you for your hospitality and assistance."

Mrs. Probinger popped to her feet. "Huber would like that—he's hinted at a match between Reardon and Eunice, though he pretends to disapprove of the notion. Reardon was fond of Eunice, or so he claimed. I do not envy Eunice his lordship's variety of esteem, and my conscience is easier for having removed myself from his orbit. To hear Huber tell it, Eunice and Reardon were all but courting."

"Huber has also spoken of taking the Americans to task and giving the Regent a piece of his mind. Shall I give him your regards?"

"Best not. He already refers to me as 'that jezebel' and worse—when he isn't ogling my bosom, of course. When I first set up housekeeping here, he sought permission to court me, and I... gently declined the honor."

"You see before you a former officer bent on tactical retreat before he says something truly stupid. Miss Hyperia West and Lady Ophelia Oliphant are visiting at the Hall. May I send them to call on you?"

"You may. But why?"

Mrs. Probinger called for my hat and spurs to be brought out to the terrace. I'd left Atlas munching grass at the foot of the garden, and a whistle brought him trotting to the terrace steps.

"We are neighbors," I said, taking up the girth. "I realize my brother is somewhat retiring, but His Grace is a good sort, and he truly does prefer country life to doing the fancy in Town." I realized I might have just made a mortally stupid comment. "I don't suppose His Grace calls here?"

She stroked Atlas's muscular neck with cherry-stained fingers, and he turned a limpid horsey eye on her.

"The duke has never called on me in the sense you mean, and not in any other sense either. Reardon was an indulgence, but ultimately not worth the bother. He's an unhappy, frustrated fellow. Sometimes I felt a sense of hopelessness from him that reminded me all too much of life on campaign. I'll look for more mature fruit the next time I go a-maying."

There would be a next time, apparently. This woman knew what she wanted and how to obtain it. I bid her farewell, swung into the saddle, and refrained from offering her a salute.

I aimed Atlas back toward the creek and tracked Reardon and his hound onto Huber's property. Only as I was rapping on the squire's door did it occur to me that I might already have broken bread with the cause of Reardon's disappearance.

Mrs. Probinger was an army widow and thus no stranger to violence, gore, and death. She was discontent, for all her talk of seeking peace, and Lord Reardon had betrayed her trust and insulted her.

Was she angry enough to have sought retribution for the wrongs he'd done her? Mortal retribution?

I would have jotted those questions in my notebook, except that a graying housekeeper had opened the door and was giving me a most unwelcoming inspection.

∼

"It's been ruddy Smithfield Market here lately," the housekeeper said, hands on ample hips. "Coming and going, going and coming, and now the Quality must show up again, uninvited. I'll have that hat, my lord, though I'll likely be handing it right back to ye. Himself is in a towering pet, but when ain't he?"

In her pristine apron and mobcap, Mrs. Wingate had the indomitable substance of the old Spanish fortified towns. High on their precipices, they'd kept watch over the plains and pastures by the century. Wellington's sieges had toppled a few, but not without tremendous effort and loss of life.

My guess was nobody had besieged Mrs. Wingate in living memory, and even Squire Huber would quail at the thought.

"I do apologize for my intrusion," I said, handing over my hat, "but I come on a matter of some urgency. Is Squire Huber in?"

"Of course he's in," she said, her gaze pitying. "He's always in, unless it's market day or the Sabbath. Miss Eunice is keeping a close eye on him in this heat, for which God be thanked. If ye have a flask, I'll cheerfully fill it for ye, but Squire will begrudge ye a tea tray. Too hot for tea anyway."

I passed over my flask. "Cold tea, water, lemonade, cider... Anything to quench thirst would be appreciated, but no spirits, please."

"Cold meadow tea with a spot of honey, best thing for summer. Come along." Mrs. Wingate led me down a dim corridor to a combination library and parlor. In Mrs. Huber's day, the room had likely had matching carpet, curtains, and upholstery, but time and the squire's bulldog sensibilities had turned the parlor stuffy, cluttered, and masculine.

A long gun hung over the mantel beneath a portrait of Huber in his youth, a brace of pheasants in hand, a pair of adoring hounds at his feet. No fire burned in the hearth, and the andirons—lions couchant—added another pugnacious touch to the décor.

The rest of the art on the walls was the predictable assemblage of hunt scenes and one landscape of Huber Manor. The style appeared to be Reardon's, but the signature, I was astonished to note, was J.V. Huber.

"Did that in my misspent youth," Huber said, entering the room at a brisk march. "Nicely done, if I do say so. Mrs. Huber liked it. What do you want?"

A long swim in the quarry pond, a longer nap in a shady hammock, a pleasant evening strolling in the gloaming with Hyperia...

"I seek a moment of your time," I said, nodding rather than bowing. Might as well give Huber more grist for his endless sense of injured pride. "Lord Reardon has gone missing, and Lady Clarissa is concerned. I'd like to know whether his lordship passed this way and, if so, when."

Huber scrubbed a hand across his jowls. "You aren't the magistrate. You have no authority to make these inquiries."

He had avoided addressing me by name or title, avoided offering me any greeting whatsoever, and was ignoring the dictates of rural hospitality. His determination to cause offense was nearly as pathetic as it was predictable.

I'd had senior officers like him. They needled, pushed, and insulted their inferiors until some fool stepped out of line and got himself a flogging or a demotion. Reconnaissance had been dangerous, but not as dangerous as some of Britain's own officers.

"You are correct, sir," I said. "I have no authority to ask questions, but I am concerned. A gentleman and good neighbor does not ignore a lady's distress." I wasn't about to tell him I'd left the Lord Lieutenant himself idling along the creek several hot, dusty hours past.

"Clarissa thrives on distress." Huber was aging, or perhaps the heat took a toll on him. His mane of white hair was thinning at the top. His face was more lined than I recalled from my previous visits. "Her mother is the same way. If it's not a misplaced earbob, it's a sneeze portending a fatal lung fever. Reardon wanders off in defense of his wits."

Huber crossed to the sideboard, poured himself a brandy, downed the lot, then poured another. "Care for a tot?"

"Thank you, no. In Spain, I learned to go easy on the spirits during hot weather."

"In New York, I learned to live on spirits. You never saw such a hellish winter, young man. The horses could barely stand it, the cold was so bitter. But I was a third son, so off I did march."

Was that the wellspring of Huber's misanthropy? Enforced service in the colonies?

"Papa, do we have guests?" Miss Eunice Huber joined us and offered me a pretty curtsey. That this lovely lady of nineteen summers could have bloomed on Huber's branch of the family tree proved nature's talent for surprises.

"Miss Eunice." I bowed properly. "A pleasure to see you."

She opened both windows and aimed a glower at her sire. "You are being naughty, Papa. Making his lordship endure this airless cave. Come to the formal parlor, my lord. I'll have a tray brought around, and you can tell us all the news from Kent. You were at the Makepeace house party, weren't you?"

I could feel Huber marshaling his patience, and Eunice's arrival had inspired other transformations. The paternal chin was no longer jutting in general indignation. The faded blue eyes had gone soft with affection.

"Might we chat on the terrace?" I asked. "I really can't stay long, and I wouldn't want the kitchen to go to any trouble when supper preparations are under way."

"We'll have a cold collation this evening, given the weather,"

Eunice said. "Very well. Papa, show our guest to the terrace, will you? And tippling is not good for your gout, sir. I will tattle to Dr. Heller if you persist in your wayward behaviors."

She offered me a smile and another curtsey and decamped, the very air in the room more pleasant for her brief appearance.

"Blighter will break her heart," Huber said. "Young ladies take that sort of thing hard, while you pawing stags never give it a thought."

Miss Eunice had not seemed in the least heartbroken to me, but then, I was not her devoted papa. "You refer to Lord Reardon?"

"Lord Randy." Huber stomped from the room, and I followed. He ceased marching when we'd reached a flagstone expanse at the back of the house. All was surgically trimmed privet, latticed roses, and potted mint here, a stark contrast to Mrs. Probinger's exuberant flowers.

"I know how it is with young men," Huber said, casting a skeptical eye over me. "You don't think. You disport with this one, waltz with that one, drive out with the other. Constant rut, that's your natural state, but a gentleman doesn't yield to his base nature every time the sap rises."

"Does your disappointment in Lord Reardon have anything to do with his friendship with Mrs. Probinger?"

"*Friendship*. Do you typically cavort as God made you with your *friends*? Perhaps you do. Ducal families are a law unto themselves, as is known to all who have the misfortune to encounter them, and the Caldicott men disdain marriage in the general case."

He was in fine form today, while I was hot, tired, and increasingly worried. "If it's any comfort, Lord Reardon is no longer welcome to call on Mrs. Probinger. Hasn't been for some time. Did his lordship come by here yesterday or earlier today?"

"So what if he did? As far as I'm concerned, the viscount can sketch himself right into the sea. Eunice adores him, and all he can think of is his perishing exhibition. He'd take ship for darkest Peru to escape from Clarissa if he had the blunt."

The more scorn I heard heaped on Clarissa's head, the more sympathy I felt for her. "Is Lady Clarissa the impediment to your marital ambitions for Eunice, or is Reardon's devotion to his art the real problem?"

Huber left off studying his formal parterres to glower at me. "Art. Bah. Reardon has talent. I had talent. A gentleman is supposed to be competent at rendering an image, just as he's expected to have a passable singing voice and know his way around a dance floor. He's also supposed to have a few pretensions to honor, about which I'm told you know precious little."

Of course Huber would get around to accusing me of treason. As an old soldier, he'd feel particularly entitled to strike at that wound.

"I was held captive by the French and tortured before I escaped. My brother was similarly tormented—to death, if I can believe what I was told. The military cleared me of any suspicion of wrongdoing, and while I respect that you have served our country loyally and well, you have no right to insinuate that my honor is lacking."

A few months ago, I would not have taken issue with Huber's insult. I myself could not be entirely certain what had happened in that French garrison. My captors had denied me food and water, kept me in cold and darkness, and likely drugged me as well. I know not what horrors Harry endured, but my French guards informed me that he'd died honorably.

In recent weeks, I'd entertained the possibility that they'd lied to me. The French were nothing if not shrewd, and their purposes might well have been served by contending that Harry had died without yielding any sensitive information. A ducal spare might have been allowed a hero's death, when Harry's lapse could instead be conveniently attributed to me.

To break under torture was human. To lie under torture was all but predictable. Every fiber of my soul and a thorough military investigation concluded that I'd done neither, but I could not as confidently speak for Harry.

Which was none of Huber's bloody business.

"You don ducal dignity most convincingly," Huber said, offering me a mocking bow. "Why isn't your older brother chasing about after Reardon?"

"Because His Grace is of the opinion that if a young man is determined to make an ass of himself, discretion promises to better thwart the tantrum than does setting up a hue and cry."

"Still not your job," Huber said. "Reardon was here yesterday morning. I was at breakfast, but I saw him with Eunice in the garden. Down there, by the bowling green. Taking liberties in broad daylight, like the damned fool he is. The lad's no better than his dimwitted father, but then, his mother is no prize, and his sister has been left to manage as best she can. One fears for young Lady Susan."

Genuine worry colored that last observation.

"You have confirmed my suspicion that the viscount passed this way. I'll not trouble you further."

"See that you don't, and tell your brother if he's the Lord Lieutenant, then he ought to be on his horse, riding after Reardon in hot pursuit. In my day..."

In the slanting afternoon shadows, the squire looked old and bitter, and also sad. He took out a flask and tipped it up.

"In your day, sir?"

"Never mind, and don't tattle to Eunice. She thinks she's confiscated my flask, but a soldier learns to carry a spare. Reardon might well have left for Rome early, you know. Clarissa was driving him mad."

"He told you that?"

Huber pocketed his flask and wiped his mouth with the back of his hand. "I endured the occasional night of bad chess listening to Reardon sing his laments. We played for pennies, and the boy never did pay up. He'd always get back his own next time, he said. I took that as a bid for another invitation, so I humored him.

"He had nobody else to lament to," Huber went on, "and one feels a duty to the less fortunate. He was a man beset, to hear him tell it. Unable to serve his country because of a faulty constitution, forbidden to study under proper masters abroad lest his sister feel abandoned. His parents are a rackety, self-indulgent pair... Even I had to admit his grounds for complaint were legitimate."

And yet, somehow, my compassion for Reardon was ebbing by the hot, dusty hour. "Was his lordship despairing, sir?"

Huber's glower faded. "All young men get to despairing at some point. I'd say yes, the viscount was gloomy about his prospects and rather dreading the whole remove to Town."

"Thank you, sir. That could be a helpful insight."

"Tell it to your brother. The viscount might well have taken a fatal leap into the quarry pond, and His Grace can't be bothered to have a look."

Huber apparently wasn't about to make that effort either. "The duke has already sent trustworthy, *discreet* eyes to inspect the quarry, sir, but as cold and deep as the water is, a dead body wouldn't surface there for several days at least."

That factual recitation sent bushy brows upward. "Suppose not."

"What direction did Reardon take when he left?"

"Toward Semple's patch," Huber said, gesturing to the north. "Plenty of places to cross the creek there, and the boy could have picked up the track in the woods that turns back toward the village. I have no idea where he went, and even less do I care. He's treated Eunice far too cavalierly."

"While I do care, and I suspect Miss Eunice does as well." I turned to go and was halfway back to the house when Huber's voice caught me.

"I don't have the bloody gout," he said. "I lost four toes in the colonies. Leather boots are no protection from cold such as that. I can drink as much as I please, but you will not tell Eunice I said so."

He likely had gout in addition to missing toes. "Your secret is safe with me, sir."

I all but dashed for the house and found my flask tucked into the crown of my hat. I took a fortifying sip of cold, sweet meadow tea—mint, bless Mrs. Wingate for all eternity—and headed for the stable.

I was already in the saddle when Eunice came hurrying down the path. "My lord, please wait. You are trying to find Lord Reardon, aren't you? Might you spare me a moment before you ride off?"

I swung down and prepared to become the repository for more secrets, as thankless as that office would prove to be.

CHAPTER SEVEN

"Let's walk the lane, shall we?" I asked, looping Atlas's reins around a hitching rack in the shade of a towering maple.

"Not the lane." Eunice sent a grimace in the direction of the manor house. "Papa can see much of it from his study. That's partly why he lurks in there so much. On the alert for callers—he is so lonely—not that we have many. Come."

She led me around the side of the barn to what was likely the groom's favorite loafing bench, out of sight of the house, facing east and thus in shade during the warmest hours of the day.

"Lord Reardon has gone missing, hasn't he?" she asked, collapsing onto the bench with a decided lack of grace. "I knew he was planning something stupid."

"His lordship did not come home last night." I perched about a foot away from her. "Lady Clarissa is worried."

"For herself, of course. Without the viscount to toady to her, Lady Clarissa will have to rely exclusively on Mrs. Aimes, won't she?"

Another member of the Committee to Consign Lady Clarissa to

Perdition. I hadn't exactly been a founding member, but my own shabby opinion of Clarissa bothered me increasingly.

"If you know something, Miss Eunice, something that would help me find his lordship or give up the search as unnecessary, please don't keep me in suspense."

"I know Reardon loathed the notion of this grand exhibition. That was all Clarissa's idea."

For a man reluctant to show off his work, Reardon had certainly waxed enthusiastic to Hyperia and me. "The proceeds will finance a journey to Rome, I'm told. One admires a young man attempting to support himself with his abilities."

Eunice gave me a scowl very like her father's. "Do you support yourself with your abilities, my lord?"

"Fair point." Though in the military I had subsisted on my officer's pay, and I now lived on investments initiated with an inheritance from my grandmama's side of the family. "You are saying Reardon resented this exhibition?"

Eunice scuffed her slipper against the bare dirt. "Real acclaim comes from recognition by the Royal Academy. Everybody knows that. Reardon submitted a few works to them last year, and they passed on every one. The Hundred Days were ongoing when the committee made its selections, and smiling portraits were all the crack."

The Hundred Days being the months following Napoleon's escape from Elba, when all the world had been dreading the battles necessary to send the demon back into exile—and rightly so. One out of four soldiers at Waterloo had not come home, or had not come home whole and healthy. Tens of thousands had been maimed or killed in a day, and the entire Continent had lost sons, husbands, and fathers overnight.

"Did the viscount take you into his confidence, miss?" Or had his lordship sketched for Eunice the portrait of his situation most likely to gain her sympathy? Oppressed by his sister, determined to make his own way in the world (until he inherited the title, of course), suffering for his art...?

She stared at her hands, a lady's graceful, pale appendages. Clean nails, a thin gold bracelet winking at her wrist.

"Lord Reardon and I are close," she said. "I esteem his lordship greatly and believe my sentiments are reciprocated. I know he has his diversions—we are not engaged, and he's a vigorous young man—but..."

I wanted to be anywhere rather than on that bench, listening to a young woman make excuses for the bounder who'd treated her trust lightly and then disappeared.

"But you hoped," I said. "Hoped that, in time, those sentiments might blossom into a commitment and a shared future."

She curled her hands into fists. "Lord Reardon hoped too. He told me as much, and that is why you must find him."

I would locate his lordship so that I, perhaps aided by Huber and Mrs. Probinger, could administer a sound thrashing to him.

"Miss Eunice, please do not take offense at my next question: Were you intimate with the viscount?"

She sat up straight. "That can have no bearing on where he might be at the present moment. None whatsoever. He's taken a fall, run afoul of brigands, crossed paths with highwaymen, or worse."

Highwaymen on the farm lanes of Sussex. Making off with his lordship's rickety easel and dented flask. Oh, of course. "Are you carrying his child?"

She popped off the bench and marched a dozen paces away, keeping her back to me. I followed, though I remained out of slapping range.

"I am not suggesting his lordship would evade his responsibilities, miss, but if somebody disapproved of a match between his lordship and you, then spiriting Reardon off to Paris might give him time to reconsider his options."

"Reardon will not reconsider," Eunice said, rounding on me, "but he doesn't know... That is, I didn't have a chance to inform him... and it's too soon to tell anyway." Her shoulders slumped, and she took to blinking hard at something over my left shoulder. "It was only a couple of times. Well, three, or four. Reardon said we mustn't indulge again until he gets his situation sorted out."

Oh, ye gods and stupid young men. "Nothing I know of his lordship or the Valmonds suggests that he'd willingly shirk his duty to you. But he's gone absent without leave, and that is cause for concern."

Or had he removed to Rome early, as Huber had put it, the better to avoid fatherhood? Eunice might not be sure of her condition, but Reardon, an artist with an acute eye for detail, might have noted changes in his lover's body.

His current lover's body, the rutting clodpate.

Or had Clarissa press-ganged him onto a packet bound for Calais, then sounded the alarm in the fashion of skilled pickpockets everywhere, crying, "Thief," at the top of her lungs while her own pockets were full of guilt? Reardon was supposed to marry money, and Eunice Huber, lovely as she was, did not qualify as an heiress.

Clarissa had at least one motive for seeing Reardon whisked into the figurative wings.

Eunice sent her next glower in the general direction of Valmond House. "Reardon said just yesterday morning that I wasn't to worry. He said the whole situation would come right if I could be patient."

Were those the general platitudes a young fool offered the woman he'd put at risk of ruin, or had Reardon been speaking of a specific scheme? What if he'd meant that his will provided for Eunice, and his mortal remains were at that moment floating about in the Stygian depths of the quarry pond?

What if Huber, disgusted with Reardon's faithless rutting, had given him a push into the Great Beyond?

"Did Reardon mention how long you'd have to be patient, miss?"

She shook her head. "A little while longer, something like that, but I might not have a little while, my lord. Papa is all bluster and noise, though when it comes to his family, nothing escapes his notice.

Mrs. Wingate has mentioned herbs, but I'd never want to do anything to harm my baby."

Her baby might someday be Earl of Valloise—if he wasn't the cause of his mother's permanent exile among Welsh cousins.

"Did Reardon have any enemies that you know of? Anybody who'd delight to see his life made difficult? A jealous fellow artist? Somebody with a grudge against aristocratic heirs? A supposed friend with a glint of avarice in his eye?"

"You think Reardon might have been *kidnapped*?" She seized on this possibility with far too much enthusiasm. "He is an only son. His parents dote on him, and they would pay any sum to see him safely returned to Valmond House."

"Kidnapping is unlikely. I ask for the sake of thoroughness."

"Lord Reardon isn't lost," Miss Eunice said with far more conviction than she'd mentioned roving highwaymen. "He knows this neighborhood better than anybody does. Knows every lane, bridle path, game trail, and ford. Knows where the foxes dig their dens and where the bluebells first bloom."

"My hope," I said, "is that he's turned an ankle or dislocated a knee. That can happen to the most sure-footed among us. He'll come limping up the carriageway, or bouncing home in some farmer's cart before nightfall, his hound and his knapsack beside him."

Eunice was back to scowling at me. "I've remembered something."

Not the scent of Mrs. Probinger's perfume lingering about his lordship's person, please. "And?"

"It's about his knapsack. Lord Reardon has a system. His sketchbook slides into this pocket, pencil case into that one. Canteen here, sandwiches there. An old saddle blanket rolled up atop the lot, for sitting on boulders and such. He has an ingenious portable easel, too, and the legs fit into a cylinder that he straps to the bottom of the knapsack."

Get to the point. "Something was different about his knapsack?"

"The whole thing looked fuller to me than usual—more bulges and whatnot—and the easel cylinder was missing."

"Perhaps he hadn't planned to use his easel."

"He always took it with him, my lord. That contraption was as much a part of his rambles as Touchstone panting at his side."

"Touchstone is the hound?" Also a Shakespearean fool.

"Lord Reardon loves that smelly old dog." Mis Eunice punctuated her sentiment with a sniff. "Clarissa can't stand the beast, which I'm sure only endears Touchstone to his owner all the more."

The more people I spoke with, the more my picture of life at Valmond House shifted. Something was seriously amiss between brother and sister, and I hadn't picked up a whiff of it when I'd taken tea with them.

Perhaps Hyperia had some insights to offer.

"I will find his lordship if he wants to be found," I said, risking a pat to Miss Eunice's shoulder. "And believe this if you believe nothing else: Your father loves you. He would never blame you for the ill-timed enthusiasm of a smitten young man."

"Thank you, my lord."

"When Viscount Reardon left you, which direction did he go?"

"Into the woods. He loved the woods, loved the birdsong and wild flowers and all the varieties of light."

The Semple farm lay adjacent to those woods. Huber probably hadn't misdirected me.

"Then I shall follow him into the woods, though I'd ask you to send a groom to Caldicott Hall. Please let my brother know that I'll likely be out quite late and might camp in the countryside tonight, the better to get an early start tomorrow."

"Of course, my lord, and thank you for your efforts."

I bowed my farewell and collected my horse. As Atlas ambled in the direction of the trees, I thought back to all the sketchbooks I'd perused. For a man who professed to love the woods, Lord Reardon had not immortalized any sylvan scenes in his notebooks.

But then, many a wayward fellow delighted in the woods because they were an excellent place to hide.

~

I lost the light, but I did not lose Viscount Reardon. To my surprise, the crushed undergrowth and bent bracken suggested he'd bedded down for a nap within earshot of the creek. His hound had reposed beside him, and based on the depressions in the soil, they'd whiled away much of the day in slumber.

That puzzled me. Clarissa had said that Reardon had gone short of sleep the night previous to his wanderings. Why not remain at home, lounging about in robe and slippers, swilling chilled hock on a shady balcony?

I considered that question while I watered Atlas at the millpond. Reardon's perambulations had traveled a wide circle, and he'd probably stopped beside the pond to allow the hound a drink. The spot was peaceful, save for the occasional burst of cheering from the posting inn a quarter mile up the road on the village green.

Other than the darts-night revelers, the evening was quiet. The plop of a frog hopping into the water, an owl hooting a warning to any who'd encroach on her territory, the inevitable chorus of crickets. To any former soldier, those sounds were the music of safety and a good night's sleep.

Had Lord Reardon heard them as such?

Atlas lifted his head, chin dripping, just before a quavery voice called, "Who goes there?"

"Lord Julian," I called back. "Good evening, Mr. Sawyer." I put the hour at nigh ten o'clock. Past Old Man Sawyer's bedtime, surely.

"Ah, the young master come home from the wars. Out for a moonlit ride, are ye?" Mr. Sawyer shuffled forward on the path that circled the pond. "Too hot to stay indoors on such a night."

"I'm trying to locate Lord Reardon," I said. "He left Valmond

House yesterday morning and hasn't come home." I stopped myself before asking if Mr. Sawyer had *seen* his lordship.

Sawyer was blind, or as good as, though he navigated familiar surrounds with ease. The loss of sight had been gradual, and I'd never heard him grumble or complain about it. He carried a walking stick to Sunday services, but made no other concession to his disability.

"That one..." Sawyer took off a battered cap and slapped it against his skinny thigh. "He was here last evening, standing right in the very spot you occupy. You can hear that dog o' his panting a mile off."

Sawyer had heard the dog, while I would likely not have noticed that panting at all. "How do you know it was Lord Reardon and not, say, Squire Huber on the lookout for poachers?"

"Firstly, your exalted brother don't mind an occasional hare ending up in a local goodwife's stewpot, so nobody need venture onto Huber's land in a lean week. Secondly, Huber don't wear that prissy Hung-a-ree water. Thirdly, his lordship talks to that dog like it was his drinking companion, which it prob'ly is, given that most canines will accept a bowl of ale, though it does 'em no good."

"Is there a fourthly?"

"Aye." Sawyer beamed at me. "The young viscount swims like an otter and had hisself a dip in the pond before moonrise. He's been swimming about this pond since he were a tadpole, and I know the commotion he makes. Took hisself a bath, using good lavender soap to get clean."

Sawyer owned the water mill, there being some sort of kinship between sawmill families and grain mill families. His sons and grandsons ran the facility now, but the old man was still the authority of last resort. He could tell by the feel and scent of a handful of grain if it was ready for milling. The sound of the beaters working the threshing floor revealed more secrets to him, and he could divine exactly how long milled flour would last before turning.

I'd forgotten about Old Man Sawyer's blindness, and he might have forgotten about it too.

"Did Viscount Reardon know you observed him?"

"Nah. Nobody sees the blind man, Master Julian. I know where the shadows fall, and I keep to 'em. The viscount waited in the trees until a good hour after the birds stopped singing, and that would be as dark as it gets this time of year before moonrise."

How did Sawyer know where shadows fell? What phase the moon was in? Memory, perhaps, or some instinct honed in absolute darkness. That same degree of darkness, part of my captivity by the French, had driven me half mad.

"Finding him has become urgent." For Eunice's sake, if not for Clarissa's.

"Then look ye to London, sir."

"He went north when he left here?"

"He went no farther than the gates of this fine establishment, whereupon he did flag down the king's mail. Ye cannot get a sizable dog onto the roof of a public coach without somebody resorting to profanity, and the hound was none too pleased either. Lord Reardon has gone up to Town, or at least traveled in that direction."

Good news—Reardon's mortal remains weren't floating about in the quarry pond—and bad news. The British coaching system was the envy of all of Europe. From our corner of Sussex, Lord Reardon could be halfway to Scotland by now.

"Do you think anybody saw him board the stage?"

"He tarried here, before and after he used this pond as his personal bathing tub. Then he waited at the gate, had hisself a piss and a tot of brandy while he loitered, and yes, I can smell the difference. He didn't want nobody to see him sneaking off after dark, that's for sure, and it's a safe bet he got what he wanted. Darkness sends most folk indoors, but it's all the same to me."

What an expansive view Sawyer took of his situation. "Your keen attention has saved me a lot of pointless bother, sir, though if you don't mind, I'd like to bide here for a while and consider these developments."

"That's a new mill wheel your brother had built for us, and it turns so sweetly because your grandpa took a hand in fashioning a proper millrace. Thanks to him, we could switch from an undershot to an overshot wheel. The old duke said that would more than double the power, and he were right. You bide as long as you like, Master Julian."

"Thank you." I turned to my horse and loosened the girth.

"Heard you had a hard time of it with them Frenchies," Sawyer said.

"Lord Harry had a worse time yet."

"Lord Harry was allus tryin' to charm his way outta corners when he shouldn't oughta been in them corners in the first place. Not sayin' he got what he deserved, but way I heard it, you went after him when he was bent on some foolishness."

"Who told you that?"

"Never you mind who told me that or where I happened to over-hear it when somebody thought I was napping. I known you and your brother, man and boy. Lord Harry were bullheaded. He were a lord, so we're supposed to say he had determination. He were stubborn, and he'd fib his way out o' a birching if he could, while you..."

What an extraordinary—and not entirely inaccurate—exegesis on my brother's character. "While I?"

"We're glad you're home, and the duke is the gladdest of all. Don't let him make you think otherwise. Sweet dreams."

"Same to you."

He shuffled away into the darkness, not so much as a fern bobbing in his wake.

I made a dry camp, using my saddle as a pillow and the saddle blanket for my pallet. The necessities I'd collected from Caldicott Hall hours ago included a few toiletries, clean socks, and underlinen. I tended to my ablutions as best I could and settled down to the lullaby of Atlas munching grass nearby.

The day had been a complete and exhausting waste in one sense. Lord Reardon had led me a dance, past women he'd treated ill, a potential father-in-law whose compassion for a peer's heir was exhausted, through secluded woods, and thence to a deliberately furtive leave-taking.

Had I questioned Mr. Sawyer first, I'd have learned what I needed to know without exhausting myself in the miserable heat. I would not, though, have learned that Mrs. Probinger was furious with Lord Reardon. He'd turned a discreet romp into a means of ruining the lady's good name. Eunice Huber might well be furious with his lordship as well—he'd done a few anatomical studies of her too—or she might simply fear her own reputation if he'd done a bunk.

Squire Huber, by contrast, had posited the notion that Reardon had decamped for his own good reasons—sibling pique, artistic pride, fear of matrimonial limitations. All plausible, and avoiding confrontation was consistent with what I knew of Reardon's personality.

As these thoughts circled in my mind, lightning flickered overhead, though rain posed little threat now. The stage coaches followed predictable routes, and in the morning, my tracking would take on a different and less interesting nature.

I'd need to stop by Caldicott Hall and Valmond House before trailing Lord Reardon in the direction of London, and that brought another thought into my weary mind: I was hardly in fighting shape, but I was regaining some of the fitness I'd had on campaign. The day had left me exhausted, nonetheless.

Lord Reardon had walked a distance that I'd covered mostly on horseback, and he'd finished his day with a hearty swim.

That was not the behavior of a man with weak lungs. Clarissa was propagating a falsehood about her brother's health, and that begged the question: What else was she lying about?

CHAPTER EIGHT

"You haven't found him?" Arthur went on piling eggs and ham onto his plate and hadn't so much as looked at me when he'd posed his question.

I'd returned to Caldicott Hall at first light, handed Atlas over to the grooms, and bathed in the laundry. I was famished, which pleased me inordinately. For months, I'd had no appetite, but a day spent rambling my home shire, and I was ready to fill my plate twice over.

"I don't know where his lordship is, but the trail hasn't gone cold yet. He hopped the northbound night stage in a clandestine manner and is now thirty-six hours away."

Arthur took the place at the head of the table. No footman stood watch over the sideboard, by decree of the duchess. She preferred for the family to start the day in relative privacy, though the staff knew everything anyway.

"He went up to London early and forgot to leave word?" Arthur mused, appropriating the nearest rack of toast. "Perhaps he has a mistress in Town, and she summoned him for some romping."

"He had a mistress in the village, of sorts. Save some of that toast for me." I took the place to the left of Arthur—Harry's place had been to the right—and spent the next quarter hour summarizing yesterday's findings.

"Huber might have the right of it." Arthur stared at his empty plate. "His lordship might be running away from home, either to avoid holy matrimony to Eunice, or because Mrs. Probinger has threatened to stir up trouble between Reardon and Eunice and demanded that his lordship absent himself. Why not call off the search and let him come home, wagging his tail behind him?"

"Because the Lord Lieutenant himself has tasked me with ensuring that Reardon hasn't come to any harm."

Arthur poured himself a third cup of tea. "Reardon is not Harry. I tasked you, now I'm un-tasking you."

"Not so fast, Your Grace." I debated whether to go back for seconds and decided to let my meal settle first. "Does Huber resent that you've passed over him for the magistrate's job?"

Arthur topped up my tea cup and set the honey and cream beside my plate. "'Resent' is too tame a word for Huber's sentiments. He feels personally insulted that the Americans gained their independence. They weren't paying their taxes, and yet, they wanted their vast frontier secured from French incursion for free—the same frontier the Americans themselves sought to plunder at will, despite British treaties with the native inhabitants. Loyal subjects the Americans were not, and Huber will snub an American on sight to this day."

I fixed my tea precisely as I liked it and took a delicious sip. "So Huber bears a grudge against life. What has that to do with Lord Reardon's disappearance and you putting forward some other fellows for the magistrates' posts."

"Huber was supposed to marry one of our great-aunts or cousins-at-a-remove. I forget the details, and I wasn't born yet. He's a younger son of a younger son, and he wasn't good enough for a Caldicott when it came time to work out settlements."

"Hell hath no fury like an ambitious young man thwarted by a lack of coin."

Arthur sipped his tea. "Easy for us to say."

I was never sure of Arthur's politics, but he was something of a reformer on a few carefully chosen topics. Rotten boroughs drove him nigh barmy, the Bloody Code drove him past barmy. Centuries of hanging children for stealing spoons hadn't stopped children from stealing spoons, according to Arthur's research on the topic, or from picking the pockets of those attending the hangings.

I had heard Arthur refer to the Corn Laws as the Starvation of the Poor Laws, but only the once, late at night, after a few brandies.

"I gather your political views don't march with Huber's?"

"I didn't march at all—left that to you and Harry—and Huber regards my lack of military experience as a character flaw. One among many. I coddle the tenants, overpay the staff, ignore poachers, and am a disgrace to the masculine gender."

"Everything that's wrong with the peerage?" I mused. "Huber sounds perilously American."

Arthur rose and took his tea to the French windows, which were open to the morning breeze. "Huber is right, in the eyes of many. Ignore poaching, and the woods will soon have no game. Pay generous wages, and those who cannot afford to do likewise soon have no employees. Coddle the tenants, and they become lazy."

I had never heard Arthur confess to this degree of self-doubt. "Having spent hours in the local woods as recently as yesterday, I can assure they are still teeming with game, forest fruits, and deadfall. The wages you pay are still less than what's expected in Town, and your coddled tenants out-produce Huber's by a wide margin. I still ought to find Lord Reardon."

"Because Huber won't let me forget it if Lord Reardon disappears onto the Continent, leaving Miss Eunice to pine away, another Huber who wasn't good enough for the local nobs."

"She might well be pining away for her reputation, Your Grace. Lord Reardon took liberties."

Arthur finished his tea and returned to the table. "He took liberties with Mrs. Probinger," His Grace observed, "and not in the carnal sense, but rather, the artistic sense. He took unpardonable risks with Eunice, and he's leaving his sister to manage the upcoming exhibition or explain why it's being called off. I'd say Reardon bears women the same sort of enmity Huber bears me and the Americans."

"Irrational loathing? For a man who loathes women..." But then, I'd met many an officer who lived to go romping at the local brothel on Saturday night, and yet, he regularly vilified women as a gender. Women, these fellows loudly proclaimed, were weak-willed, selfish, hard-hearted creatures who thought only of their own pleasures and ambitions.

"It might be the sort of loathing he doesn't recognize in himself," Arthur said, biting off the corner of a piece of cold, buttered toast. "The best hypocrites are sincere in their contradictions."

Of whom was he speaking? "Waltham, where did you go on the morning Lord Reardon disappeared? You were seen out walking up the hill behind the Hall early in the day."

He set down his piece of toast. "I went for a walk before the heat started to build. Sometimes I hack out, sometimes I walk. The first hours of the day are for me to spend how I please, and the rest is for... business."

My brother was lying to me. About where he'd gone and why, and also about Huber's grudges. Those grudges were real, at least to Huber, and I was convinced something personal lay between Arthur and Huber.

"Huber loved being a justice of the peace," Arthur said, peering into his empty tea cup. "I don't love the Lord Lieutenant's job, and yet, I'm much better at it than the other candidates would be. Huber had been justice of the peace for years, despite many complaints, and then he took a fall in the hunt field. I was prevailed upon to step in, because even Huber could not protest giving the magistrate's duties to another at that point."

"Has Valloise ever been the magistrate?"

"Don't be ridiculous. The countess could manage the job, but the earl would forget to dress for his own parlor sessions. Besides, gentry keep a jealous hold on the magistrate's bench in the usual course, and well they should."

True enough. I hadn't realized Arthur had become Lord Lieutenant only on sufferance. He'd never complained about being the duke—the lord lieutenancy was generally held by a peer—but I had the increasing sense that his station in life brought him no joy.

I wanted to ask him what made him happy. Was it those first hours of the day? Or had he been off trysting during that hour with an unsuitable parti? I believed Mrs. Probinger when she said Arthur kept a distance from her, and I also believed that Arthur was entitled to some privacy.

"I intend to pursue Lord Reardon," I said. "He has either caused trouble, or he's in trouble, and Clarissa has asked us to intervene."

"And what Clarissa wants, she usually gets," Arthur said, rising. "Be careful, Julian. You've been away for years, and then you were recuperating. The old neighborhood isn't quite what it once was, and I'd hate to see Huber taking out his grudges on you."

"I have no intention of provoking Huber, but I do want to call on Clarissa. Who was it that insisted loudest of all that Reardon had weak lungs?"

"The same sister who forbade him to buy his colors?"

"Precisely." I rose as well. "And his lungs are no more weak than Lady Ophelia's nature is shy and retiring. Clarissa also tried to hide evidence that might have aided me to locate Reardon, and she hasn't been entirely forthcoming about this exhibition."

"Neither have I." Arthur plucked a strip of bacon from the offerings on the sideboard. "Reardon did a portrait of me a year or so ago."

Somebody—Hyperia?—had mentioned this portrait. "I have yet to see it." I wanted to know how Reardon had portrayed a peer who was much that Reardon was not.

"I didn't care for it, truth be told. Reardon wanted to include it in his exhibition, and I..."

"You were noncommittal, which anybody with a modicum of sense knows is a polite refusal."

"He took it poorly, begged leave to discuss the matter. I put him off again. The last thing I want is a lot of London snobs using my likeness for target practice."

Arthur was a good-looking devil, everything a duke should be, save for having dark hair when the preferred shade was blond.

I helped myself to the bacon as well. "Your secret is safe with me, Your Grace."

That jest only made Arthur withdraw into frosty dignity. "What secret?"

"That you truly *are* shy and retiring. I won't tell a soul, but I suspect the neighbors are on to you."

He shoved me on the shoulder. "I'll show you shy and retiring. If you weren't my heir..."

I wasn't supposed to be his heir. Harry was, at least until some little dukeling showed up in Arthur's nursery.

"Who is Valloise's spare?" I asked, demolishing more bacon. "If Reardon should meet with misfortune, who is the next Earl of Valloise?"

Arthur wiped his fingers on a table napkin. "I don't know. Lady Ophelia might, and Clarissa certainly would."

"I will ask Clarissa." She'd dither and protest and sigh, but I'd get it out of her.

"Take Miss West with you to Valmond House, Julian. That is not a request."

I elbowed him in the ribs. "It's a humble plea, if you know what's good for you. Go tend to your business while I continue my search for the runaway."

"If that's what he is." Arthur padded toward the door, but paused before leaving the room. "I'm glad you're home, Julian. I realize the shires hold little appeal compared to the hum and bustle of London, but it's good to have you here."

I wanted to dash him with a cup of tea, but the only weapon to hand was the greasy table napkin, so I balled it up and flung it at his chest. He caught it and set it on the table, his expression guarded.

"I slept wonderfully last night, Arthur, *outside*, on the hard ground by the millpond where we used to camp as boys. Rest like that is impossible for me in London. Old Man Sawyer spoke to me like I was eight years old. Biddy Wingate filled my flask without my having to ask her. London isn't home, and it never will be."

Arthur was silent for a moment, then his lips quirked. "Then welcome home." He marched off, and I did not know whether to laugh or cry. Whatever had just passed between us, it mattered, and I apparently mattered to Arthur.

As he did to me. Very much.

Clarissa wore a morning gown several years out of fashion when she received Hyperia and me. Her hair was in a simple chignon, and her slippers were worn. This was, I supposed, the costume of the wretchedly anxious sister, forced to remain at home with no comforts save prayer and worry beads while her brother lay beaten and bleeding in a ditch.

"Shall I ring for a tray?" she asked, leading us to the family parlor. "I haven't much appetite myself, and it's so perishing hot...." She cast her gaze to the open window, as if she'd lean out and cry to the heavens to send her brother home to her.

"You need not bother with a tray on my account," Hyperia said. "My lord?"

"No, thank you, though I would like to have another look around Lord Reardon's studio."

Clarissa's weary languor faltered. "Why? You've already poked about there at length."

"Indulge me," I said, heading for the door. "Miss West will keep you company, and when I've finished with my inspection, I will deliver a full and reassuring report regarding my efforts to find your brother."

"You've found him?" Clarissa clasped her hands together. "Please tell me you've found him."

"He was last seen heading for London, very much alive and well. Details to follow." I slipped out the door and left Hyperia to deal with Clarissa's consternation, because that had been consternation I'd seen in her ladyship's eyes, not relief.

My errand abovestairs took me first to Lord Reardon's studio. I conferred briefly with a footman thereafter and then had a look around Clarissa's bedroom, two doors down from his lordship's. A brief inspection of her ladyship's dressing closet revealed a surprising paucity of gowns—the better selections were doubtless kept in Town —and the item I'd sought.

Naughty Clarissa.

I rejoined the ladies in the parlor and brandished the cylinder that held the legs to Lord Reardon's field easel. "Guess where I found this?"

"What is it?" Hyperia asked.

I'd briefed her generally on my findings yesterday, but had kept my suspicions regarding the portable easel to myself.

I unbuckled the leather cap on the cylinder. "This is proof that Lord Reardon has left the shire of his own volition." I upended six lengths of wood into my hand. "These screw together to form the legs of an easel, which his lordship was known to use when sketching *en plein air*. He never left on a sketching sortie without it, according to one source."

"What source?" Clarissa asked, staring at the pieces in my hand.

I returned them to their case and put the cap back on. "You, for one, mentioned this device to me, as did others. Reardon didn't take it with him when he left on his dawn march. You realized this and realized the implications."

Clarissa put a hand to her throat. "What *implications*? Reardon has his debut London exhibition in less than *two weeks*, I've invited everybody we know, and now you're... *What are you saying*?"

Had I been a betting man, I might have wagered that a swoon

would follow. Thinking up clever excuses was not the work of a moment for most of us, but Clarissa remained very much on her feet.

"I'm saying you know that Reardon has not been kidnapped and has not come to harm. You know he left the house without any intent to sketch, much less return by nightfall."

She looked me up and down and apparently decided on a tactical retreat. "I know nothing of the sort. That case was in my wardrobe, but I found it only this morning, and I have no idea why Reardon left it there. For safekeeping, I suppose? Perhaps as a memento? That little easel was such a clever device, and he spent many happy hours... Oh, Lord help me, what has that foolish boy *done?*"

Hyperia wasn't buying this performance, and neither was I. "I'll tell you what he's done," I said. "He's sneaked onto the northbound night coach with a knapsack full of necessities. More than enough to get him as far as Town, or to a friend's summer residence in the Borders. My guess is he'll choose the friend. Easier to lie low in one rural household than to avoid running into a familiar face in London."

"You are saying he's deserted me?" Clarissa's fading-blossom act evaporated in an instant. "He's taken ship? Vanished of his own accord?"

"Not vanished. Hopped the stage under cover of darkness, after planning to decamp by those very means. He took leave of Miss Eunice Huber, told her not to fret over his actions in the near term, prepared for his travels, waited patiently for the stage, and arranged fare as an outside passenger, where, again, he was far less likely to risk recognition."

Clarissa's cheeks acquired two becoming spots of pink. "You are saying that Viscount Reardon, heir to the Valloise earldom, rode away from the village on the roof of the public coach like a... common laborer?"

"Precisely." I did not mention the dog, but that beast worried me. A man intent on leaving for good was more likely to take his loyal hound with him than was a fellow just nipping over to Kent for a few days.

The path I'd traveled in Lord Reardon's wake the previous day had kept near sources of water, suggesting he was a conscientious enough owner to ensure his pet was regularly offered something to drink on a hot day.

His lordship might carry a grudge against females, but he doted on that dog.

"I cannot explain this," Clarissa said, sinking onto a sofa. "I cannot... Surely you are mistaken, my lord? In the darkness, your eyes might have deceived you."

The darkness had not deceived Old Man Sawyer's ears or nose. "I am not mistaken, but like you, I cannot explain Reardon's actions. I do have another question for you."

"I am all befuddlement," Clarissa said, "but you will ask anyway."

She appeared angry rather than befuddled. Had Reardon bungled his assigned role? Thwarted his sister's plans for him? What did Clarissa know that she wasn't admitting?

"Are you your brother's heir?" I asked.

Clarissa's brows twitched down. She glanced at Hyperia then at me. "How would I know? The estate is entailed, but if Reardon even has a will regarding his personal assets... I have no idea."

A dodge. Clarissa was the brains in the Valmond family, a role passed down from the countess before that lady had become a professional invalid. The Valmond womenfolk would know to the letter and the penny what provisions had been made for them by the earl or the viscount.

"I can ask your solicitor, then," I said. "An express to Town over the ducal signature should result in a swift reply. His lordship's finances are increasingly of interest to the whole inquiry."

Clarissa's scowl was thunderous. "If you must involve the duke, then get him out looking for Reardon instead of sending pointless letters. He should be interrogating the tenants and offering a reward or something, not poking into Reardon's private affairs."

Hyperia stated the obvious. "If we know why Reardon has gone missing, then we'll have an easier time finding him. A look at Reardon's finances can help us rule out blackmail, for example."

"Blackmail?" Clarissa nearly wailed the word. "Why would anybody blackmail my brother? He's as dull as day-old bread. All he does is paint, and escort me about, and talk about painting."

Hyperia once again stepped into the breach. "He walked Eunice Huber home from services a time or two, didn't he?"

"*Her.* That one is no better than she should be, and she would love to get her hooks into a future earl. Eunice is as bitter and self-centered as her father, and I've told Reardon as much to his face."

"If Reardon has caught Miss Huber's fancy," Hyperia began gently, "then he might be removing himself from temptation by quitting the surrounds. Taking a repairing lease in Rome."

Clarissa rose and began to pace, and my imagination started the introduction to Mozart's "Queen of the Night" aria. *Hell's vengeance boils in my heart. Death and despair blaze about me...*

Clarissa stalked from the cold hearth to the window and back again. "Reardon might well have left the shire to get away from Eunice. She could not compromise herself with him, so she might instead threaten to spread lies about him. She's like that, and I would put nothing past her."

Eunice was not like that. She was kind to her curmudgeon father, worried for Reardon, and entirely too trusting.

And I was growing alarmed. "Clarissa, who is the Valloise spare? If Lord Reardon dies, who inherits after your father?"

"Squire Huber, I suppose, and he has three sons and a troop of grandsons. Papa reminds Mama that the succession is secure every time she tries to find a bride for Reardon."

How had I not seen this? "Huber inherits the earldom, Valmond House, and the lesser estates?"

She nodded. "How does that bear on Reardon's situation?"

Huber's motives for removing Reardon from home and hearth—and the reach of a protective older sister—just became sinister. That's how.

"If Huber becomes the heir presumptive," I said, "he benefits enormously, even if Reardon emerges from exile ten years hence. Huber's access to credit, his social standing, his ability to make a match for Eunice and his granddaughters... On every hand, he has reasons to wish Reardon to perdition." Huber couldn't bring any legal petition to be declared the heir for years, but he'd benefit from improved expectations the moment Reardon was feared dead.

"But Huber wouldn't..." Clarissa resumed her seat. "Eunice's papa would move heaven and earth to protect her good name and to keep her with him. He was a soldier. He can be ruthless and rigid. He's a very unhappy and lonely man."

"Would he threaten Reardon?"

Clarissa put a hand to her belly, and the gesture seemed genuine. "You're saying Huber might have chased Reardon from the shire? Are footpads awaiting my brother in London even now?"

Would I go that far? Could I afford for Reardon's sake *not* to go that far? "I don't know what Huber is capable of, but His Grace gives the man a wide berth. Then too, Huber is not the only party who might wish the viscount ill. Mrs. Probinger is none too fond of him, he might well have artistic enemies, or he might be leaving England for reasons of his own."

Though if I were intent on quitting England, I'd head for the coast rather than the capital.

"Then you simply have to find my brother before any harm can befall him." Clarissa was back on her feet and striding toward the door. "I'll show you out, and you can be on your way to London in the next hour."

We made our farewells, mounted up, and turned the horses for Caldicott Hall.

"You're off to London," Hyperia asked.

"I'm off to pick up whatever trail I can find."

Hyperia was quiet until we'd gained the hill above the Hall. "Jules, Clarissa was clearly distressed, and some mischief is afoot, but she pronounced herself all befuddlement."

"And?"

"And I've never met a less befuddled woman in my life. She either knows or can make a good guess at where Lord Reardon is."

Hyperia's judgment was reassuring and traveled in tandem with my own. "If she leaves Valmond House, she'll be followed—I had a word with the staff—and if she sends any suspicious correspondence, the direction will be noted. Without Reardon to escort her, her ambit is limited. I'm counting on finding Reardon before Clarissa warns him that I'm closing in."

"Good," Hyperia said, giving the mare a loose rein. "And then maybe we can get some answers."

"From your lips to God's ears."

Alas for me, the riddle would prove more complicated than simply locating his lordship's last known whereabouts.

CHAPTER NINE

"You shouldn't go alone." Atticus, exuding the indignation of an offended rooster, glowered up at me, his hands fisted on his skinny hips. "What if you have one o' them spells?"

The boy voiced my own chronic fear, did he but know it. "Then I have a spell, but they never seem to come in close succession." I spread a laundered saddle blanket on my bed. "Watch what I'm packing, because you might well be expected to do likewise for me in future."

"In future." He made those two words into a curse and perched on the nearest windowsill.

I tossed clean linen, spare socks and cravat, an extra knife, and two spare shirts onto the saddle blanket.

"What's the knife for?"

"In case I need it. You put the clothing and whatnot in the middle half, fold the sides over, and roll it all as tightly as you can. The horse's saddle blanket serves as the pallet, and this one will be my blanket, should I need it."

I demonstrated while Atticus impersonated a gargoyle.

"What about a spare flask?" he asked. "Weather has turned hotter than perdition."

"I'll take a proper canteen in addition to my pocket flask. I'll also bring a spare pair of tinted spectacles and keep them on my person. Toiletries go in the saddlebags, along with another knife."

Atticus drew up his legs to sit tailor-fashion on the windowsill. "Why all the knives? You only have two hands."

"Because one knife—good, sharp, and serviceable—saved my life when I was wandering the slopes of the Pyrenees during a cold and miserable spring. I speared fish with it, fashioned snares, dressed game, and defended myself, all with that one blade."

More significantly, that knife had given me hope. If I could eat, I could survive. If I could defend myself, I could survive. If I could mark the passage of days on a stout walking stick, I might even survive with some of my wits intact.

"You ain't going to no Pyrenees, whatever they are."

"They are nasty big mountains straddling the border between Spain and France. A small army could never prevail in that terrain, and a large army could not survive there for long. Wellington had his hands full."

"Bad business."

"Bloody bad business." Seventy different passes through those mountains, and the French had been ready to defend them all. "Hand me a couple more cravats."

Atticus hopped off the windowsill and opened the wardrobe. "You'll bind that thing up with cravats?"

"Plain ones, no starch. A cravat makes a passable bandage, or it can be pressed into service as a sling."

Atticus produced the required articles and another scowl. "The duke oughta be goin' after this fella. You ain't the magistrate."

I secured the left side of my bedroll. "The duke *ain't* much of a tracker, and he's asked me to do what I can." I held out my hand for the second cravat.

Atticus tossed it to me. "*Isn't*. You should say, 'The duke isn't much of a tracker.'"

"Then you do know proper speech, but you simply can't be bothered to use it?"

"I'm not a toff. Why should I talk like one?"

"Because you deserve more from life than an endless procession of muddy boots that the toffs expect you to clean late at night, when a growing boy ought to be abed, and speaking of which, don't wait up for me."

He would, the little blighter.

"You're not coming back here?" Atticus tried for a casual tone, but the studied diffidence with which he pushed his hair from his eyes told another different story.

I gathered up an old jacket and collected my saddlebags, which I'd packed before my pint-sized governess had arrived.

"I will be in pursuit of Lord Reardon, possibly for the next few days, but I'll send reports back to the duke each day."

"And I'm supposed to beat any news outta the duke?"

He probably could, or he'd die trying. "The duke will inform Miss West of pertinent developments, and she will inform you."

Some of Atticus's ire seemed to deflate. "You still shouldn't go alone."

I sat on the cedar chest at the foot of the bed. "I have instructed my brother that if anything happens to me, you are to be raised as his ward. You will be given a trade, at least. You might enjoy being a gamekeeper." Rambling around outside, his own dwelling, his own man for much of each day.

"Nah. I don't like killin' things. Birds especially."

"We have that in common. Made military life something of a challenge."

"Is that why you were a scout? No killing?"

"Less killing. While I'm on patrol for the duke, you think about what interests you, what you'd like to learn more about. You've watched kitchen work at close range and might make a good cook.

Maybe the stable appeals, though it's hard work in all weather. Think about it, and for God's sake, don't pike off while I'm gone."

Ah, a smile. The devilish smile of a boy pleased to contemplate mischief. "I might do that. I might go have a look at them Pyrenees."

I rose. Time was of the essence, though Atticus's fears were justified, and Atticus's wellbeing was of the essence too.

"Very well, off to the Pyrenees with you, my lad. You'll need to speak French or Spanish, if not Basque, and seeing as you disdain to use proper English, you'll find the journey challenging."

"Can you speak French and Spanish and that other?"

"I have only a few words of Basque, but French was my first language, Spanish not a long leap from there, and I can get by in Italian. My German is serviceable as long as we're talking about military subjects, horses, or women, and now I really must be going."

Atticus nodded, but I could see him struggling with the impulse to keep me from walking out the door.

I gave him my best impersonation of Arthur in all his ducal froideur. "I shall return. Get Miss West to start you on your letters. A fellow must be able to write his signature."

Atticus closed the wardrobe doors and mumbled something.

I had good hearing—the French hadn't stolen that from me. "You have two names, you little ass."

"Just Atticus ain't—isn't—two names."

This poor child. This poor brave, stubborn, wonderful child. "Atticus Caldicott has a nice ring to it, but I leave the challenge of choosing middle names up to you. One or two good ones should suffice."

I'd stumped him, an inordinately gratifying victory. I tousled his hair—as much affection as I dared impose on him—and made my escape.

∼

Luck was with me for a change, and I had Touchstone the Hound to thank for much of it. A large dog traveling on the roof had made Reardon's progress easy to follow. That I'd taken a sketch of Touchstone with me made the task even simpler.

The journey to London was a good fifty or sixty miles, depending on the route, and for public coaches, that meant four or five changes of horses.

The coach Lord Reardon had taken had apparently hit a rut and broken a wheel at the midpoint between our village and the first change—more good luck for me. His lordship and the other passengers had chosen to walk those five miles in darkness rather than wait for good fortune to tool along in the middle of the night.

Reardon had thus arrived at the first change shortly after two a.m. He was apparently reluctant to travel by day, because he'd taken a room at the Belle and Boar and not decamped until last night's northbound coach had come through.

Fortunately for me, my brother kept teams at all the coaching inns between Caldicott Hall and Town, and thus I made good time in the duke's curricle. A packed hamper sat at my feet and were it not for the heat, the wretched dust, and the traffic, the outing might have been pleasant.

For Lord Reardon, traveling with a sizable hound in the short hours of a summer night, progress had not been as impressive. I had to stop and ask questions at each possible change, but Touchstone's likeness kept my conversations short. Nightfall saw me at The King's Man, still twenty miles shy of London. The inn occupied a crossroads and was joined by a cluster of modest houses. The location barely deserved the appellation *village*.

"With a hound, you say?" the proprietress asked, running a thick finger down her guest ledger. "Big hound, too, and bred for sport, not some mongrel. I recall the dog because he did not fit with his master."

"How so?"

"That is a nice dog. Good manners, good breeding. The fellow, though, he ain't so fine. Dusty, like he'd been riding up top since May.

Short-tempered, took the best rooms despite having only a battered knapsack. Expected us to allow the dog upstairs. Wouldn't eat in the common, but must have a tray when half the world has taken a notion to travel and my cooks are nigh run off their feet. Uppish and twitchy, though he were in want of a bath and dressed like a shepherd."

"Might I see the room he took?" With luck, the waste bin hadn't been emptied, and Reardon might have sketched me a clue or two.

"Can't allow that." She swiped a graying wisp of hair back from her temple and tucked it under a dust-streaked mobcap.

"What if I hired the room myself?"

Her smile was tired. "Can't allow that neither, sir. He still has it booked."

Yet still more wonderful luck—Reardon was either lounging about in his quarters, or he'd return to there eventually—and yet so much good fortune made me cautious about confronting him.

"Is the hound up there?" In a hand-to-hand scuffle, a loyal hound tipped the odds in favor of his owner. More than one Spanish farmer had defended his land by setting his dogs on any intruder—French, English, or Spanish. That hounds did not climb trees had preserved me from several bad maulings.

"Hound is in the stable. Mr. Reynolds left him there when he went out at midday. Poor thing looked so bereft I had Cook give him a hambone."

This development was not on the list of possibilities I'd antici-pated. "Mrs. Clark, I realize you cannot allow me to have a look around *Mr. Reynolds's* rooms, but might you take a peek? I'm concerned that Reynolds has abandoned his dog, and if ever a canine was beloved by his owner, Touchstone is that lucky pet."

Had Reardon gone off to meet somebody in the humble environs of The King's Man? Was he off sketching of all the outlandish notions? Squire Huber's observation, that all young men get to despairing from time to time, also rang in my ears. What the hell was Reardon about now?

"Aye," Mrs. Clark said. "I can have a look. What am I looking for?"

"The general state of affairs. Did Reardon—Reynolds, I mean— eat his breakfast? Did he use his shaving water? Was the bed slept in? I'm sure you have a keen eye for the difference between a room that's ready for the next guest and a room that's occupied. Focus on those differences."

"Avoiding his creditors, was he? We get a lot of those, though they're usually heading on down to Portsmouth because the beadles keep a watch for 'em in Dover. Such doings..."

She bustled up the steps and left me fretting by the front door. The King's Man was busy, but not as the London coaching inns were busy. An air of good cheer prevailed. The maids were well fed and sturdy, the hostlers quick with a change, but relaxed about it.

If Reardon had been intent on abandoning his dog, this inn was a good choice. Not so close to London that Touchstone could end up in the bear pits, not so busy that he'd be forgotten altogether.

Mrs. Clark lumbered down the steps, a piece of paper in her hand. "I don't like this, sir. I don't like this one bit."

She passed over a single page of good-quality paper bearing a sketch of Touchstone.

Please see the noble hound conveyed into the keeping of Lady Clarissa Valmond. Valmond House, West Waltham, Sussex. My thanks for your assistance. R.

"He left a sovereign on the pillow." Mrs. Clark shook her head. "A sovereign."

Until that moment, I'd considered the possibility of Reardon committing a rash act of self-harm minuscule. One scintilla away from impossible. But the sovereign, the touching concern for the dog, the soul-deep sorrow of that young soldier in Reardon's battlefield painting...

Perhaps weak lungs had been the family's polite label applied to a propensity for melancholia. "What else did he leave?"

Mrs. Clark glanced up the steps. "His dusty old knapsack. Should I send that to the lady too?"

Rubbishing hell. "I can get the knapsack and the hound to her ladyship. Might I have a look at the room now? He's apparently left the premises on foot and paid his shot."

"He'd paid a sight more than he should have." In Mrs. Clark's weary eyes, that generosity was clearly suspect rather than cause for rejoicing. "Who does that? Mayhap he were famous, like them kings that disguised theirselves as paupers. Or maybe he was dicked in the nob."

She turned a speculative gaze on me. "Suppose there's no harm in you having a look. Keep the door open. If anybody asks, you mistook his room for yours. Happens all the time when the guests linger at the bar. His room is all the way back, has a view of the river."

I left her muttering about sovereigns and, "What is the world coming to?" and "How was I to get a dog to some almighty ladyship in blooming Sussex?" I jogged up the steps, dreading what I'd find in Reardon's abandoned room and cursing my luck.

~

The image I beheld in Reardon's sketchbook disturbed me: Lady Clarissa, looking winsome and sweet, was embraced by her loving brother. Both siblings were smiling. Their expressions suggested a string quartet gamboling through a Vivaldi allegro in the background, genteel laughter, and good company just beyond the borders of the sketch.

I had never seen Clarissa look that genuinely happy. As for Reardon... His gaze was affectionate, and sad. The remaining pages were blank.

"A farewell," I murmured, putting the sketchbook back into the knapsack and pulling the drawstring closed. "A beautifully executed farewell." Would Clarissa smile or cry at that image?

I sat on the bed in the middle of an airy, tidy room. A balcony gave on to a pleasant view of paddocks, the stable proper being on the other side of the inn. Between lush green hills, a distant silvery ribbon of water gleamed in the fading sunset.

From that direction, a low rumble of thunder sent further foreboding rippling down my spine.

Storms were all too reminiscent of Waterloo.

Wellington had known that Napoleon was intent on attacking Brussels, but he hadn't known the exact route, so he'd waited and watched until the damned *empereur* had marched right across the border from France. The allied forces had been left to take up their positions in the middle of the night in a pounding downpour, which had made maneuvering artillery a bloody awful job indeed.

Not nearly as bloody awful as what had followed.

Though now was not the time to wallow in nightmares. I removed the pillowcase from the topmost pillow and collected Reardon's knapsack. When I returned to the common, Mrs. Clark was nowhere to be seen, so I stopped a passing maid and explained my situation.

She summoned another maid, the one responsible for the better rooms, and that good woman had noticed Reardon's direction when he'd left the premises.

"That is very helpful," I said, "and now I need to find the hound in the stable, the one who arrived with Mr. Reynolds."

"Follow your ears," the chambermaid replied. "Through the yard, around the back, and you can hear him whimpering and wailing. Not used to being tied is my guess."

"Thank you. I'm off to find him." I turned to go, but the maid's voice called me back.

"Your man was carrying something. Not a satchel, but something dark like an old satchel. He was too far away for me to make out what he had with him. Could have been a sack of food, could have been an extra hat."

"All I need is the direction he went, and you've given me that." I sprinted for the stable, taking the pillowcase and the knapsack with me.

The dog was in a miserable heap by the barn door, gazing woefully across the paddocks and occasionally baying at nothing.

"Touchstone."

His floppy ears twitched, and he stopped howling long enough to look at me. I wasn't his beloved owner, but I had his attention.

No water bowl lay within sight, so I purloined a bucket from down the aisle, filled it at a trough, and set it before the dog. He slurped greedily, coughed, and sat back on his haunches. I produced the pillowcase.

"He's out there," I said, holding the pillowcase up to the dog's nose. "The chambermaid saw your viscount ambling off between those paddocks shortly before noon. Your job is to track him down faster than I ever could."

Lord Reardon had not asked for some sandwiches to take with him. He'd not told anybody his destination, if he'd even had one. Nobody knew if he'd brought a pistol with him, or a rope, or poison...

I untied the rope securing Touchstone and led him to the path where Reardon had last been seen. The dog began sniffing and whuffling, his tail low. Compared to a sight hound, who had to keep game in view, scent hounds tended to work more slowly.

Not Touchstone. He caught the trail of his errant owner and nigh hauled me off my feet as we followed the track. Down past the paddocks, out into the grassy fields newly shorn at haying. We wended our way closer to the river, then veered off and began to climb one of the rolling hills that would eventually join up with the South Downs.

The dog, having been tied all day and eager to find his master, had far more energy than I. I let him half tow me up the path, the inn in the distance below us a dark shape against the gathering night. Another rumble of thunder sounded, closer and louder, and I was tempted to turn back.

I was on a steep path of increasing elevation as night descended, far from any dwelling, and in unknown terrain. A bad fall here could end in disaster for me and for the hapless dog. When the weather reached us, the downpour would be tremendous and might keep up for hours.

And yet, a hound could track on damp soil as easily as dry, even more easily, according to some foxhunting enthusiasts. How well Touchstone could find his master's scent after a drenching rain was another question.

"Let me rest," I panted, giving the makeshift leash a stout tug. "Sit, damn you."

The dog's expression turned reproachful, but he sat, sides working, tail thumping restlessly against the earth.

I breathed deeply, resenting my lack of condition. In Spain, I'd become tireless.

"We're not in Spain, old boy," I muttered, "and God be thanked for that." I trudged onward, the dog snuffling the ground and straining at the leash.

The ground rose and rose, and had the clouds not been obscuring the moon, I would have had a better sense of how steep the drop was to the left of our path. The river below gleamed dully, and a raindrop smacked me on the cheek.

The track led to the summit of a sizable hill. From the inn, the landscape had looked to roll alongside the river, but the hill was, in fact, sliced flat by the river. The inn side sloped down to the little cluster of buildings, while the river side was a long and precipitous drop.

"Keep walking," I said to an absent and possibly no longer extant Lord Reardon. "Keep walking right down the other side of this hill."

Touchstone paused at the highest elevation and snuffled back the way we'd come, then forward a few yards. He looked to be casting for Reardon's trail and repeated his efforts three times without success. He then took to sniffing the edge of the drop, then hunkered onto his haunches and howled into the abyss.

God, no. The rain was picking up, and a flash of lightning illuminated the scene for an instant.

I stood on the very lip of the precipice, and the river roiled along some fifty feet below. A pretty view on a fine day—also a fatal drop onto a rocky rapids washed by a strong current. I waited, growing increasingly cold while the hound whimpered and paced, until another flash of lightning obliged.

I could not be sure—the rain was coming down hard—but as I peered into the depths swirling far below, I thought I saw the shape of a boot being carried away by the storm waters.

"You bloody fool."

Touchstone looked at me anxiously.

"Not you. Well, perhaps you too. Why did he bring you all this way only to abandon life while you were tied in a barn a mile away?"

The dog whined, then settled on all fours, and put his chin on the toe of my boot.

"We can't wait for him," I said. "He won't be back this way."

I tugged on the leash, and Touchstone, good soul that he was, padded along at my side. I hadn't the heart to tie him in the stable again when we reached the inn, so I piled straw in an empty stall, made myself a makeshift bed, and spent the night in the barn with the malodorous, grieving dog.

～

The day dawned with the bright, refreshing quality that so often follows a hard summer storm. The air was cooler and less humid, the dust had been put to rout, the sky arched above in a dazzling blue rather than leaden white.

I'd donned my tinted spectacles while yet indoors, so piercing was the sunshine—and so piercing was my sense of failure.

I gathered up Lord Reardon's knapsack—a pitifully light testament to his life—collected the dog, and prepared to journey back to Sussex. My last task before departing was to prevail on Mrs. Clark to contact me if anybody came by inquiring for Lord Reardon or Mr. Reynolds, or offered to take in the orphaned hound.

"He's a good beast," Mrs. Clark said as Touchstone panted gently at my feet. "A dog that ought not to have been left behind like that. You say Mr. Reynolds was a lord?"

"A courtesy lord, but yes. He had a title, and now I am off to inform his family that he's... gone missing."

"Been years since anybody jumped off yonder leap. Sad business. Very sad business indeed."

I didn't *know* that his lordship had leaped to his death, but his hound had been unable to track him past the clifftop.

The trip back to Sussex went quickly. No need to stop at each coaching inn, no need to ask questions of the hostlers or have a look around the commons. I debated whether to travel straight to Valmond House or stop at Caldicott Hall. The Hall won in the end—call me a coward—in part because I wanted to report to Arthur in his informal capacity as acting justice of the peace and in part because I needed a damned bath.

Then too, Atticus—and Hyperia—would worry. Not so much for Lord Reardon, but for me.

I climbed the steps of the north portico at the Hall, feeling about eighty years old. A night in the straw with five stone of bereaved hound at my side had yielded little in the way of slumber. I stank of the stable and of a bungled mission.

"Lord Reardon apparently jumped," I said when Arthur and Hyperia were assembled in the family parlor. I did not dare risk befouling the furniture in my untidy condition, so I stood near the open windows. "He made arrangements for Touchstone to be returned to Lady Clarissa, amply paid for all services rendered, and on a fine summer day... seems to have put period to his own existence."

"You're sure?" Arthur asked, pouring two glasses of lemonade and passing one to Hyperia and one to me. "No other explanation?"

"He could have climbed down the cliff face," Hyperia said. "He arrived there in full daylight. He apparently knew the area, and he could take his time with the descent."

"Reardon was fit," Arthur observed. "Rambled the countryside by the hour. He might have been able to negotiate such a feat."

I wished now that I'd tarried at The King's Man and assessed the terrain more carefully, but a torrential downpour would have obliterated much of the relevant evidence supporting Hyperia's theory.

"If he did negotiate a safe descent," I said, "then somebody else lost a boot attempting to do likewise and did not retrieve that item upon reaching the riverbank."

"You saw a boot?" Arthur asked.

"A man's boot, as best I could make out. Probably landed in the shallows, and as the rain moved in upstream, the rising current caught it."

"Clarissa will be devastated." Hyperia said softly. "But she won't be any more or less devasted if you take an hour to eat and put yourself to rights, Jules."

I agreed, but I still appreciated that Hyperia would tell me so. "Somebody needs to see to the dog. I left him in the stable..." Looking heartbroken and confused. "Maybe Huber can add him to his kennel."

"Huber is more likely to shoot that beast," Arthur said. "Touchstone was a babbler, giving tongue when he couldn't stay on the line of scent, running riot, ignoring commands when the huntsman lifted the pack, backtracking to the confusion of his fellows. As a foxhound, he was a complete disaster one day and then brilliant the next."

Arthur did not ride to hounds. He claimed he hadn't time to indulge in all-day meets, but the reality, I suspected, was that he felt for the fox.

"How do you know Touchstone's dubious past?" The dog had been eager to work when I had asked him to trail his owner.

"I've crossed paths with Lord Reardon on many a hack and hike about the property. I asked why such a handsome animal was relegated to pet status."

"Touchstone is more than a pet," Hyperia observed. "That dog was in the nature of a familiar for Lord Reardon. A creature with whom he could communicate without speaking. Poor wretch. Clarissa won't want to deal with a bereft hound, so let's sort him out another day. Jules, I've ordered a bath for you, and if we're making a call, I must change as well."

She could think rationally, while I was too preoccupied with what had happened on the hill behind The King's Man. I nonetheless sought my bath and was nearly startled out of my skin when Arthur let himself into my sitting room.

"No need to get up on my account," he drawled as I reposed in a tub full of tepid bliss. "I've brought the knapsack, because it might be considered evidence in the event of an inquest." He helped himself to a sandwich from the tray on the stool beside the tub.

"You'll hold an inquest?"

"If there's been a death, it's certainly suspicious. The question is not whether to hold an inquest, but when." He settled into a wing chair. "This whole business doesn't feel right."

Arthur must be very troubled indeed to seek me out at my ablutions.

I swirled a hand through the water. "I agree. The exhibition looming in London, the day spent pretending to sketch in the neighborhood, that vague warning to Eunice Huber... I can't make sense of it. Reardon was on the verge of launching an artistic career, he's heir to a title and means, he's reasonably likable... Suicide is scandalous, a sin, a tragedy..."

"The coroner won't rule suicide," Arthur said, finishing his sandwich and reaching for another. "He'll rule death by misadventure."

"Because you will tell him to?"

"Because it serves no purpose to rule otherwise, and for all we know, Reardon slipped."

"Reardon spent eternities navigating outdoors, Your Grace. You noted as much yourself. I found no evidence at the inn that he'd been imbibing. He was well rested and fit. He did not slip."

"Was he pushed?"

"No sign at any point on the trail of a companion. No sign he met somebody at the summit. And who had cause to push him?"

"Huber, Mrs. Probinger, some other artist who resents Reardon's talent—he is very talented—or roving brigands. Plenty of those about in recent years. Or maybe he did slip." Arthur tipped his head back and closed his eyes. "Reardon might have had weak lungs after all, and you describe a steep climb in excessive heat. He grew light-headed, lost his balance, and a tragic mishap ensued."

This conversation ought to have been awkward, but Harry and I had enjoyed exactly the same informality. I had the sense Arthur had sought me out precisely because he wanted a discussion he could never have had with me in any public drawing room or salon.

"Is that what I'm to tell Clarissa even though we know Reardon's lungs were in excellent working order? A tragic mishap? She'll be in mourning for at least a year now, possibly two."

"Six months for a sibling," Arthur said. "She'll be back in good form by next Season. She might even go ahead with the exhibition."

"She'd call it a tribute to his memory, the least she owed him, devoted sister that she is." I submerged myself and got my hair thoroughly wet, then availed myself of the tinned lavender-scented soap made by the Hall's laundresses. "I always associate this fragrance with home."

"I associate it with the old man," Arthur said, referring to the late duke. "Brisk, unfussy, hard to ignore. Close your eyes, and I'll rinse you off."

I obliged, the cooler water a lavish pleasure when sluiced over my head. Arthur handed me a towel and took the last sandwich save one.

"I won't ask for an inquest just yet," he said. "No rush when we don't have a body."

In the usual case, the remains would be on display at the inquest, which was often held at the largest local inn. The proprietor would do a grand business in drink and gossip, and the whole town would witness the proceedings.

"Can you have an inquest without a body?" I asked, scrubbing at my hair with the towel.

"It's done, particularly in cases of drowning if the deceased isn't recovered, or when the deceased has been burned beyond recognition. Lord Valloise and his countess deserve time to receive the sad news and make the journey home, if they so desire."

I rose, and Arthur tossed the bath sheet to me.

"One feels reluctant pity for Clarissa," I said. "She'll have to manage this—this too. She might not want her parents to come home."

"She will want them to make the effort, though I suspect Valloise forgets half the time that he has progeny of any kind."

I wrapped the towel around my waist and stepped from the tub. "Inbreeding," I said, quoting the late duke. "The aristocracy is too damned inbred."

"Not as inbred as the monarchy," Arthur replied, which surprised me. "I'll have the coach brought around. Your errand to Valmond House requires all the dignities."

"Not the coach, please. An open conveyance if I'm to take Hyperia. If we use a closed carriage, Lady Ophelia will have to chaperone, and I'm not up to that."

"She's still off haranguing the vicar. Divine justice, to subject him to sermons for a change." Arthur held out the sandwich tray. "You're still too damned skinny, and good food shouldn't go to waste."

I took the sandwich and wondered how often Arthur had been teasing me with humor so subtle I'd missed it entirely.

"Where were you really going the morning Reardon disappeared, Your Grace? The grooms say you do hack out regularly, but that day you were on foot."

"Would you like to be the justice of the peace, Julian? I can have that arranged, you know. You can snoop about as Huber did, lurking between lines of laundry, listening at keyholes, wreaking ill humor on all you survey."

"Get out, or I will have to report a crime. A thief has stolen my sandwiches. Takes the very bread from my tray. Bold fellow, and he must be stopped before I toss him in yonder tub."

Arthur looked about with all the hauteur he was capable of. "I see no thief. You are imagining things."

"Away with you. I have sad news to break to my neighbor." Though, as Arthur had said, the whole business didn't feel right, didn't follow any logical pattern. Reardon wasn't Young Werther, thwarted in love and wallowing in sentimental excesses.

Arthur paused by the door, his back half to me. "When the kitchen sends me a tray of sandwiches, they are the size of tea cakes. A dab of butter, a few leaves of watercress. If Cook is feeling generous, I get a slice of cheese or ham so thin you can see through it. The parsley is arranged into some damned Christmas wreath, and a vase of flowers always accompanies the tray. I ask for food and get kitchen art."

"And you want to dash that tray against the wall, because you will be hungrier after you eat what's on it than when you rang for it."

"Cook is trying to be respectful of my station, serving food to suit my supposedly refined palate. Such respect can leave a man starving." He slipped out the door, and I dressed in solitude.

Not until I was tying my cravat did I realize the duke still had not answered my question about the true purpose for his early morning ramble.

CHAPTER TEN

"My lord, Miss West." Lady Clarissa curtseyed to us as we were shown into the gallery. She looked a bit more the thing today, less wan and weary. The gallery, situated at the back of the house and well ventilated, was relatively cool, though half the paintings I'd seen here previously had been taken down.

The missing artwork imparted a sort of silence to the room, a sense of lost purpose. A few landscapes yet remained, though those did not look to be Reardon's work. An underfootman was trimming ivy on the balcony and sweeping the clippings into a dustbin.

"My lady." I bowed, because as Arthur had said, the occasion called for dignity. "We come bearing upsetting news."

Clarissa sighed gustily. "Reardon refuses to come home? I suppose he might as well stay in London. The exhibition looms at hand, and we'd soon be going up to Town anyway. Enola has claimed all along that Reardon is simply having a fit of the artistic vapors."

"What makes you think he went to London?" Hyperia asked. From her, the question was mere polite curiosity. From me, it would have been the start of an interrogation.

Clarissa walked off toward the furniture grouped at the far end of the room. "Where else would he go but the Valloise town house? Mama and Papa are to meet us there next week, and I have had nearly all the paintings shipped. I just wish Reardon hadn't indulged in these pointless dramatics about a simple change of plans."

Was she too calm? When I'd last parted from Clarissa, she'd been beside herself with worry, and willing to let all and sundry know of her concerns. Now, she posited that Reardon had merely nipped up to Town—a journey he'd normally have made on horseback or in his own conveyance—and her attitude approached blasé.

"I have reason to believe that your brother has met with ill fortune on the way to London," I said. "Might we sit?"

Clarissa looked from me to Hyperia and back again. "Ill fortune?"

Hyperia settled onto the sofa, Clarissa took a wing chair, and I took the place beside Hyperia. A footman wheeled a tea trolley in at the far end of the room, but Lady Clarissa gestured for him to wait.

I did not particularly want an audience for this discussion, but somebody might be needed to fetch smelling salts, so I forged ahead.

"I followed Lord Reardon along the coach road as far as The King's Man in Surrey. He spent the night there, then went walking yesterday rather than travel on to Town." If Town had ever been his destination.

"He broke his journey in Surrey? That doesn't make sense."

For once, Clarissa and I were in agreement. "The King's Man lies near a sizable waterway, and I gather walking the riverbank is a local pastime. The trail rises along a headland at one point near the inn, and the drop to the river is precipitous."

"Why are you telling me this?"

"It appears that his lordship slipped from the heights into the river. The fall could well have been fatal."

I had delivered news of a man's death to enough war widows to know that some took the whole business calmly, almost resignedly, some went to pieces, and others appeared to bear up while saving for another, more private hour, a complete loss of composure.

Clarissa merely stared at me as if I'd switched into some arcane French dialect. "Slipped? Reardon was part mountain goat."

Did mountain goats have weak lungs? "He might have underestimated the impact of the heat on his stamina and balance."

Clarissa rose. "Reardon racketed about the countryside in all sorts of weather. Up to Scotland, over to Wales, because the scenery God saw fit to give us in our little corner of Sussex wasn't dramatic enough. He knew how to deal with heat. He knew how to protect himself from the cold. He detested Mama's medical preoccupations and was determined not to emulate them."

Still no mention of weak lungs. Interesting. "My lady, Reardon left generous payment at the inn and asked that Touchstone be conveyed to you here at Valmond House."

"What would I want with that smelly old...?" Clarissa sank back into her chair. "You think Reardon did himself a mortal injury." She stared hard at me, blinked twice, then shook her head. "No. That is not possible. That makes no sense at all. I have moved heaven and earth to get this exhibition organized, *spent money on it*, and Reardon would not... I need to think."

Never in all the times I'd had to inform a lady of her bereavement had her response been, *I need to think.*

"I have Reardon's knapsack," I said, going to the door and retrieving the article from the corridor. "I'll need it back, in the event there's an inquest, but I wanted you to have a look at the contents. A sister might see what everybody else will miss."

Clarissa left off staring distractedly at nothing. "Give it here."

She systematically emptied the bag, putting a flat wooden panel on the floor—the drawing surface of the portable easel perhaps—some clean linen, a wrinkled and none-too-fresh shirt, soiled neckcloth and stockings... dirty laundry, the sketchbook I'd examined in the inn, and a balled-up handkerchief.

The pile on the floor was pathetic, but how many soldiers had left behind even less when they departed life on some fly-infested battlefield?

I went to the window, intent on giving Clarissa what little privacy the situation afforded. The view below gave on to the same overgrazed park, the same half-crumbling terrace I'd seen previously, but the whole seemed so much sadder given recent events. Behind me, I heard Hyperia murmuring to the footman, then the sound of cutlery and porcelain tinkling.

Reardon could have taken Valmond House in hand. Could have stepped into the shoes his father had never filled very well. Eunice Huber had been willing to marry him and seemed to value his esteem, and even Clarissa, in her way, had doted on him.

The footman, a more venerable specimen than Blaylock, wheeled the tea cart across the room, then paused and gestured vaguely to the detritus on the carpet. "Shall I... tidy up?"

"No need for that," I said, lest our man totter off with what Arthur considered evidence. "That will be all, thank you."

He sent a worried look in Lady Clarissa's direction, then decamped with his empty tea cart.

Hyperia poured us each a glass of some pink, lemony-smelling libation garnished with mint leaves, while I knelt on the floor and repacked the knapsack.

"You were supposed to find him," Clarissa said in low, flat tones. "I relied on you to find him."

"I failed." The words should have been followed by abject apologies, but something about the wrinkled shirt and balled-up socks caught my attention.

Clarissa was clutching the sketchbook to her chest, knuckles white. "I asked you to find him, Julian. You dithered about here..." She bowed her head. "This doesn't make sense."

No, it did not. Lord Reardon had been many things, but most of all, he'd been an artist.

No pencil case lay among the orts and leavings of his life. No set of pastels, no erasers, no pen case or ink bottle. *None* of the accoutrements of his art. True, he could have fallen to his death with pockets full of art supplies, but Eunice Huber had said the knapsack had been *bulging* when she'd seen it.

The knapsack he'd left at The King's Man had been far from bulging, and the articles that would have been most dear to him were nowhere in evidence.

"Lady Clarissa," Hyperia said, holding out a glass. "Drink something, please. Have some shortbread. You need your strength."

Clarissa ignored the proffered glass. "I cannot abide lemonade that's too tart, but Cook refuses to sweeten the punch. Not even with honey, though Reardon puts honey on everything and thus we always manage to have some on hand. Julian, why are you staring at me?"

Puzzle pieces were shifting about in my mind, trying to form a coherent image. The aging staff, half-empty wardrobes, the kitchen hoarding sugar and honey, the overgrazed park...

On instinct, I rose and examined one of the landscapes hanging by the nearest fireplace. No signature, but the style was unmistakably a Reynolds. A constable look-alike hung across from it. As I surveyed the remaining paintings, they all shouted a very close resemblance to some dead master's work. A circuit of the room confirmed that not a one of them was signed.

"Clarissa Valmond," I said, marching back to the ladies' end of the room, "what in the hell have you done with your brother?"

~

Clarissa tried to maintain the role of bewildered, outraged sister. "What I have done?" she retorted. "I've supported Lord Reardon's every ambition, worked tirelessly for his success, and introduced him to every fashionable family I know. What have *you* done to find him?"

Hyperia sipped her drink, made a face, and set the glass down.

"I have trailed him all around hell's nether acres, tooled halfway to London and back, and spent the night condoling his grieving, reeking dog, though the viscount is still extant, isn't he? Did you think up that bit about an old boot on the riverbank, or was that a flourish he added?" The chamber maid had seen something in Lord Reardon's hand, something dark.

A man's tall boot was dark.

Clarissa dragged the knapsack closer to her feet and yanked the drawstring closed. "What are you going on about?"

"I'm going on about an earl who is never home so his creditors can't find him here. Is Valloise truly taking the waters, or did he and the countess repair to the Continent and lay a false trail? I'm going on about valuable paintings quietly sent off for sale because Reardon had the talent to create replicas with nobody the wiser. I'm talking about your horses—some of whom probably trotted off the Ark—and your jewels, which I'm guessing have also been pawned."

"My lord," Hyperia murmured, "we take your point."

"Sugar and honey are both dear," I went on, "and art supplies are expensive. Lord Reardon salvaged those from his luggage and nothing else. They meant more to him than the clothes on his back. Mrs. Felders has been your cook since Methuselah dandled Noah on his knee, and she toils on because you cannot afford to pension her."

There was more—the land tiring, the side porch subsiding. I'd seen that clearly enough when I'd not had memories of finer days to cloud my perspective. I nonetheless desisted, because Clarissa's expression had turned from ire to patience.

"Are you quite finished, my lord?"

"I will not be finished until I uncover whatever scheme you concocted *to put your brother's name on everybody's lips.*"

"What an interesting idea," Hyperia said. "However did you come up with it?"

Whereas I wanted to shake Clarissa to within an inch of her smelling salts, Hyperia's question inspired a wan smile.

"Am I incapable of interesting ideas?" Clarissa asked.

Oh, for pity's perishing sake. "You are incapable of honest answers, Clarissa, so I will remind you that I am acting on behalf of the Lord Lieutenant in the absence of an available magistrate. Your prevarication amounts to interfering with a lawful investigation."

I had no time for bullies in the usual course, but I was plagued by the sense that Clarissa's scheme, whatever its particulars, had gone awry, and time was yet of the essence.

Clarissa sighed, she presented me with her pretty profile, she nudged the knapsack with the toe of a worn slipper.

"When Gainsborough died," she said, "his work tripled in value virtually overnight. Sir Joshua's works also appreciated enormously when he went to his reward. Reardon once commented that we ought to be investing in Sir Thomas Lawrence's art because Sir Thomas is getting on a bit. I thought the remark ghoulish at the time."

"But then," Hyperia said, "you began to see the possibilities."

Clarissa rose and went to the sideboard. She opened a drawer and extracted a honeypot and a sugar bowl, then used the spoon to drop two lumps into her lemonade. She passed the bowl to Hyperia, who did likewise. The honeypot she left on the sideboard.

Stashed in the drawer for Reardon's sweet tooth, no doubt. Our hostess was resourceful. If I focused on that, rather than on my frustrations, the conversation would be more productive.

"What I saw," Clarissa said, putting the sugar and honey back in their hiding place, "was the physician's bills mounting. Mama is truly ill this time. Dr. Heller made that plain to me, and even Papa seems to grasp the truth. She's seeing specialists who prescribe bleeding her, or who forbid her to be bled. They recommend the juice of oranges heated with cloves and cinnamon, or they lecture her to avoid spices of any sort. Regardless of the prescriptions, they all want to be paid, immediately and exorbitantly, while Mama continues to fade. I sometimes think the worry is killing her, or perhaps the shame."

"I'm sorry." And what moved me to genuine sympathy was the weary dispassion with which Clarissa reported her mother's poor health. "Sorry that the countess is ill, and sorry that she cannot have the comfort of your presence."

"As am I. Mama prefers home, but Papa cannot be in residence, for reasons stated. He cannot be jailed for debt, but he can be dunned without mercy."

Hyperia passed me her drink, of which I took a cautious sip. Clarissa observed this familiarity without comment, but then, I had not been offered the sugar or the honey, had I?

"Reardon's art is needed to save the family from ruin?" Hyperia asked.

Clarissa picked up the knapsack and tossed it at my feet. "Reardon's art was supposed to at least staunch the bleeding. I was to have married the late Lord Harry, but Harry wasn't having that. Off to war he did go."

With a ducal connection by marriage, the Valmonds could have lived longer on credit, but not indefinitely. They might also, though, have been privy to more lucrative investment schemes, better prospects for Reardon, and a cooperative approach to estate management.

Clarissa's ambitions had been rational, however desperate. "Harry failed you?" I asked.

"Harry *employed* me," she retorted. "Paid me well to swan about on his arm as a means of foiling the matchmakers. That meant, of course, that everybody assumed I was spoken for. Harry made it plain I could be his hired escort or his nothing in particular. Those were my options. I took his money, though he knew his devoted company cost me other prospects."

And worse than that ungentlemanly behavior, which was bad enough, Harry had warned me off Clarissa lest I get wise to his scheme. He'd never come out and said she was taking money in exchange for sexual favors, but he'd certainly implied as much.

What a rotten, selfish thing for a brother of mine to do. No wonder he'd slunk off to Spain. "Harry behaved badly. I apologize on his behalf."

Clarissa shrugged. "He behaved generously and kept his mouth shut about the money. It helped, but bad harvests, falling rents, the usual litany of woes among the landed class, and the problem is now beyond what I can manage."

That she'd even tried to salvage her family's finances spoke of determination, courage, ingenuity, and loyalty.

Virtues all, and yet, she'd played the part of the self-absorbed flirt so convincingly. I well knew the toll donning a role took. I'd been a drover, a shepherd, a French deserter, an English deserter, a Spanish monarchist, and more, all the while knowing an unconvincing performance could see me killed.

"My lady, you must be exhausted."

"I am so tired," Clarissa said, "I cannot think straight. I cannot think at all, and now this..."

"Reardon has forgotten his lines?" Or Reardon, like Harry, had used Clarissa for what benefit she could do him and then scarpered.

"We had a plan." She stirred her lemonade and took another sip. "I admit that much. I could not tell the world Reardon was dead— bad luck, that—and Huber would get ideas. Reardon was to go missing immediately before his exhibition. Talk would spread, half worried, half mean. The betting would start, the talk would pick up momentum, and a nine days' wonder could turn the exhibition and subsequent auction into something truly lucrative."

"And what of Lord Reardon?" Hyperia asked. "Is he supposedly delirious with a summer fever and relying on the care of a beautiful widowed stranger? Did he smack his head on the way down that cliff-side and lose all recall of his former life? What will the story of his miraculous resurrection be?"

"He was to be kidnapped and ransomed in time to appear a few days after the auction, much the worse for his ordeal."

I, and the whole world, had underestimated Clarissa badly. "Kidnapped by whom?"

"That part's a bit vague." Clarissa had the grace to look sheepish. "We'd hint at jealous rivals or disaffected former soldiers desperate for coin and resentful of a peer's heir who did not serve. I would imply that the villains had warned us to exercise utmost discretion. Only our closest friends would hear any details at all."

"As stunts go," Hyperia said, "this one was certainly ambitious."

"Would have been ambitious," I said. "But it's all gone to blazes, hasn't it, Clarissa?"

Clarissa glowered at the knapsack resting at my feet. "Dear Reardon has apparently deserted the cast. This business of leaping off a hillside, sending me his wretched dog... That wasn't remotely what we'd discussed. If Reardon hasn't done himself a serious injury, I might see fit to deal him a few blows myself."

A fine speech, full of frustration and bravado, but Clarissa was clearly terrified for her brother, and well she should be.

～

The storms that had drenched me in Surrey had yet to grace my corner of Sussex, and thus breakfast was served in the shade of the back terrace. Arthur had already been out for a hack, while I had dropped off to sleep only as the birds had begun their matutinal hymnody.

Hyperia and I had explained the latest developments to His Grace and Lady Ophelia over supper the previous evening, also served on the terrace at Godmama's insistence. Too late, I'd realized her tactic.

"You were informing the staff last night," I said, passing her the teapot. We occupied a square table in the cool shade, Arthur and Hyperia making up our foursome. "Apprising any maid or footman with sense enough to linger by an open window of Reardon's odd behavior."

"Nonsense. I was ensuring I did not expire of heat exhaustion before the fruit and cheese arrived. I vow Scotland begins to appeal quite strongly."

Then you should go... I kept that riposte to myself for selfish reasons. If Lady Ophelia decamped, Hyperia would have to leave with her, and Hyperia had been invaluable at winkling the truth from Clarissa.

Hyperia had also handled my most recent memory lapse with sense and kindness, and she brooked no nonsense from Arthur.

Lady Ophelia had also contributed much to last night's discussion, pointing out that Reardon had doubtless been resented in artistic circles for hosting his own exhibition rather than participating in the Royal Academy's annual do. Clarissa's rumor about jealous rivals would be credible, particularly if Ophelia gave it a nudge in that direction.

"You do look to be on the point of expiring from the heat," I said, "if one ignores how becoming that shade of rose silk is on you."

"Flattery is always appreciated, provided it's skillful." Ophelia handed the pot on to Arthur, and I realized that dining al fresco served another purpose: We could not be as formal, and in particular Arthur could not be as frosty, when the table was barely six feet square, and pigeons paced along the balustrade, exuding birdy self-importance.

"The question is," Arthur said, spreading jam on his toast, "do we continue to pursue Reardon's disappearance or let him have his sulk on his own terms?"

Hyperia took the jampot out of range of Arthur's knife. "Lady Clarissa wants and needs to have her brother found. Her mother is failing, the Valmond family finances are failing, and Reardon is her only ally. He's also a peer's heir, and the notion that somebody could be blackmailing him or truly holding him for ransom bears consideration."

"I was not through with the jam, Miss West."

Hyperia put some preserves on her plate. "You have lost the knack of sharing, Your Grace, and there are three other people at the table." She handed the little pot back, and Arthur set it in the middle of the table.

Lady Ophelia looked vastly amused, while I waited for Arthur to retreat from the affray with some excuse about the press of business calling him to his study.

He munched his toast instead, and Lady Ophelia and Hyperia exchanged a smile. Clarissa was apparently not the only female with plots afoot.

"I agree with Hyperia," I said. "Whatever Reardon is up to, he's a man with few allies and fewer resources. He has, as far as I know, some clothing, some coin, and some art supplies. How far will that get him in rural England?"

"It will get him farther in France," Ophelia observed. "Suppose we should set a watch at the ports?"

Arthur had a vast army of homing pigeons stationed around the country and even a few on the Continent. He kept an equally large loft at Caldicott Hall to deploy as needed. He could get word to the ports before noon, if necessary.

"I am not inclined to spend much more effort on the business," Arthur said. "The viscount is an adult. We have no real indications of foul play, and if his father has creditors, then his lordship must as well. A hue and cry would serve only to set the wrong sorts of people on his trail."

The old duke had had one maxim for business that eclipsed all other concerns: The trades must be paid.

"You'd shield Lord Reardon from creditors?" Lady Ophelia asked. "Is that now part of a Lord Lieutenant's duties?"

"I'd shield him from blacklegs and tipstaffs until his creditors apply to the authorities through proper channels. Let him sell his paintings. He's very talented, and Clarissa is right that if the artist has mysteriously disappeared, his work will attract more interest."

"The artist," Hyperia said repressively, "might have been *made* to disappear by the very people you seek to *protect* him from by ignoring his situation entirely."

"The dog bothers me," I said, tucking into my eggs. "If Reardon was merely lying low for a couple weeks, why send the dog back to Valmond House?"

"Because Reardon is off to the Continent," Ophelia replied, "abandoning his family when they most need him, eluding creditors, and pursuing his art, or pursuing opera dancers in Paris, which might amount to the same thing in the mind of a young male aristocrat."

"Or," I countered, "Reardon feared for the dog's wellbeing."

Arthur retrieved the jampot and resumed troweling preserves onto a piece of buttered toast. "You assume that creditors, rivals, or potential kidnappers picked up the viscount's trail?"

"If I wanted to squeeze money out of the Earl of Valloise," Hyperia said, "and I knew that peers cannot be jailed for debt, I'd take his only son and spirit Lord Reardon off until after the sale."

"Because..." Lady Ophelia murmured, "then the family would have at least some coin, a sum more or less public by virtue of the nature of an auction. My dear, I'm impressed. You think like a criminal."

"Where's the ransom note?" Arthur retorted. "Where's the lock of his hair, or a sketch of his proving that he was seized from the clifftop in Surrey, though Julian reports no signs of an altercation?"

Our debate was cut short by the arrival of Squire Huber, escorted by a sniffing Cheadle.

"Your Grace, my lord, my lady, Miss West. Squire Huber has come to call, and he insists his business is urgent. Apologies for the intrusion."

The heat truly did not agree with Huber. His cheeks were scarlet, sweat sheened his forehead, and his thinning hair, when he snatched off his hat, was matted to his pink scalp.

"Good morning, all," he said, offering a terse nod to the ladies. "I have urgent business with His Grace, and that business is best discussed *in private*." His chin jutted in bulldog fashion, while Cheadle, joined by two muscular footmen, tarried by the terrace doors.

"Oh dear," Ophelia said. "Whatever this private business is, I'm sure it's better discussed on a full stomach, but we haven't room for a fifth at the table. I'll excuse myself, shall I?"

I'd half risen to hold her chair when Arthur spoke. "No need to excuse yourself, my lady. Whatever Squire Huber has to say can be discussed here and now."

Some battle of wills ensued, with Huber silently fuming and Arthur refusing to yield an inch.

"Very well." Huber sent a fulminating glance at the footmen, who ignored him in eyes-front, parade-rest fashion. "So be it. His Grace, as Lord Lieutenant, has failed to see sufficient numbers of justices of the peace appointed. Witness the present circumstances, when all serving on the magistrate's bench are off carousing at the quarter sessions. Lord Reardon has been kidnapped by person or persons unknown, and His Grace has done nothing—not one thing— to bring the criminals to justice or see his lordship safely returned to his family. I shall formalize my complaint in writing not later than tomorrow."

He gave Arthur a look of scathing contempt. "I can see myself out."

"No," I said, "you cannot." I rose, rather than give Huber the satisfaction of snorting and pawing while we sat before him as a captive audience. "As you well know, I was deputed by His Grace to make quiet inquiries regarding Lord Reardon's situation. Your posturing is so clearly self-motivated that it rises to the level of interfering with a lawful investigation. As we attempt to sort out next steps, to balance discretion for a family already beset by difficulties with the vagaries of a young man's artistic temperament and the demands of justice, you bumble in here with no purpose other than to make a grab for the duties you prosecuted with unseemly zeal in years past."

"Julian." Arthur spoke quietly. "You need not insult the man. His concern is for his daughter."

"My daughter is above reproach in every particular," Huber thundered. "My concern is for a neighborhood that once enjoyed some order and dignity, some respect for the law. With your hand guiding the choice of magistrates, sir, the poachers run rampant, drunkenness characterizes every market day, and hanging felonies are committed with impunity. Valloise is not about to stir you to action, but I am here, by God, and you will face consequences for your inefficacy."

What in the hell was Huber going on about? He well knew that I —better suited to the job of nosing about—had acted without ceasing and with some results. Perhaps the facts had been garbled in translation between one servants' hall and the other, or perhaps I'd got it right the first time: Huber wanted the magistrate's post back and would stop at nothing to get it.

But as to that, the justices of the peace were not Bow Street Runners, haring off to poke their noses wherever they pleased to. Huber, of all people, knew that.

"You expect His Grace to find Lord Reardon by tomorrow?" Hyperia asked. "The man only went missing four days ago. If finding him is so simple, why haven't you done it yourself?"

Huber stared at Hyperia as if a potted palm had spoken. "These matters are no concerns of yours, Miss West."

Hyperia rose, and her chair scraping back against the flagstones should have warned Huber to flee hotfoot over the balustrade.

"You malign my friends," she said, balling up her napkin and tossing it onto the table. "You discount Lord Julian's tireless and productive efforts, while you barely deigned to yield him the few pertinent facts you had to offer. Perhaps the proper authorities ought to be made aware of how little the former magistrate has done to assist in this matter? Perhaps Miss Eunice should be told that her papa is more concerned with finagling his old job back than finding Lord Reardon?"

Huber tried the same silent battle of wills—he was determined, let it be said—but again went down to defeat.

"By the first of the week, then," he said. "I want that man found, or there will be consequences. His Grace has appointed a lot of drunken bumblers to the bench, and this is the result. And, Waltham, you'd best explain to your brother that you might well have been the last person to see Lord Reardon alive."

He stalked out, and with a nod from Cheadle, the footmen followed him.

"How unpleasant," Lady Ophelia said. "The tea's gone cold, I fear. Why is it, even in the heat, I want hot tea to start my day?"

"Because," Arthur said quietly, "we are English, and human, and prone to a certain inflexibility in our expectations. If you will excuse me."

He rose, bowed to the ladies, and walked off across the terrace and down the steps—the opposite direction of his study.

"Go after him, Jules," Hyperia said. "I've never seen His Grace more upset. Huber deserves to be whipped at the cart's tail, and, I guarantee you, the squire has little notion how perilous Eunice's situation is."

I had never seen Arthur looking more composed, but an instant's reflection told me Hyperia had the right of it. I grabbed a piece of buttered toast slathered in jam from his plate and went after my brother.

CHAPTER ELEVEN

"I never appreciated," I said, "how vexing being a duke must be." I tore the piece of toast in two and passed half to Arthur. "Mind if I have a seat?"

He gestured languidly to the opposite bench in the duchess's gazebo. Papa had built it for her to celebrate their tenth anniversary, or to placate her for ten years of his nonsense. The view was lovely—the Hall on its stately rise, the hill behind it, dense woods flanking the vista, and summer verdure adorning the land.

How many times had I prayed for just one more glimpse of my home? And my prayers had been answered, a steadying thought.

We ate our toast in silence. I did not know how to pose the questions I needed to ask, and Arthur probably wanted time to fashion his answers. I'd found him in the first place I'd looked for him, to all appearances merely taking his ease on the padded benches and enjoying the relative cool of the morning air.

He dusted his hands together, crossed his legs, and rested his arm along the railing while he munched his toast. A relaxed posture, though I wasn't deceived. Arthur was braced for battle, and that broke my heart.

"Why does Huber hate you?"

Arthur's lips quirked. "As obvious as all that?"

"He is choleric by nature and hates easily—the Americans, inebriates, beggars, women who know how to enjoy themselves, and radicals for starts. His antipathy toward you is personal."

"Huber... has his reasons."

"Did you trifle with Eunice?" I could not imagine Arthur trifling with anybody, for any reason. He wasn't a trifling sort, but Huber was as angry as a man who'd failed to protect his daughter.

Arthur closed his eyes and tipped his head back. "My dear Julian, I would not know how to trifle with Eunice."

Whatever did that mean? I thought back to my conversation with Huber earlier in the week. What had he said? *The Caldicott men disdain marriage in the general case.*

At the time, I'd thought he was digging at me for breaking off an understanding with Hyperia.

That comment could also have been aimed at Harry, who'd—to appearances at least and perhaps in reality—toyed with Clarissa's affections.

But Arthur wasn't married either, and securing the succession was his first, last, and primary duty.

"You would not lead Eunice to develop expectations," I said carefully, "because that would be dishonorable. A duke isn't about to marry a squire's daughter."

He sat forward and scrubbed his hands over his face, then rested his elbows on his knees and stared at my boots. Arthur was in great good health as far as I knew. He was in the prime of life and well aware of his responsibilities.

"In point of fact, I could marry Eunice. Society would pretend to be aghast, but nothing in law prevents it. You are right, though, that such a union would be dishonorable."

We were dancing around some truth, some revelation that eluded me. "Arthur, what the hell are you saying?" Or not saying.

"Such a union," he went on, "would be unfair to Eunice. Unfair to any woman, for that matter. I am not... I cannot... I do not fancy women."

This claim contradicted my experience of Arthur. He was a sought-after escort, the dinner guest every woman wanted to be seated next to. A young lady who turned down the room with him was sure to *take*, and a woman he refused to acknowledge became a social outcast—not that he'd wreak that fate on the undeserving.

"You like women. You like Hyperia."

He looked up at me. "Rather a lot. You should marry her, Julian. She's up to your weight."

"I am not up to hers. Left my manly humors in France, or Belgium, or some-damned-where."

Arthur considered me for an uncomfortable moment. "In the King's English, Julian. What's wrong with you, in addition to white hair, wrecked eyes, and a dodgy memory?"

I could huff and sniff and inform His Grace that I was not the fellow who'd been threatened with charges of dereliction of duty, I was the fellow doing the interrogating, but sooner or later, Arthur and I needed to have this talk.

"I cannot... function. With women."

"Could you ever?"

What sort of question was that? "Between the ages of about seventeen and twenty, I *functioned* unceasingly. Soldiering reduced my opportunities, but not my abilities."

"Then captivity is to blame?" The question was clinical in its detachment.

"I hope so, and I hope to recover, but I could not ask Hyperia to wed a eunuch, could I?"

Arthur rose, hands in his pockets, and leaned on the doorjamb. "Our situation is hilarious, viewed from a certain perspective."

"Then why is nobody laughing?" Why did I instead feel an increasing sense of foreboding? With his back to me, silhouetted against the painfully bright morning sunshine, Arthur looked sad and alone, if not tragic.

"We will be laughing. *Forsan et haec olim meminisse iuvabit.*"

From "The Aeneid." *Someday it will be pleasant to remember even these things, perhaps.* More often rendered as: We will look back on this and smile, though Aeneas and his men had endured a bloody lot of wrath of Olympus, violence, and misfortune before landing on Rome's shores.

"Arthur, what judgment of the gods are you enduring?" I rose as well, because if Arthur tried to march off on some press-of-business errand, I would tackle him to the ground, ducal dignity be damned.

He faced me. "That you have to hear this from me is a back-handed comfort. I prefer men, Julian. If you'd like to decamp for Town, I will understand, but I ask that you exercise discretion on my behalf. A felony conviction will see the title attainted, and that... I'd rather avoid that."

A thousand memories assailed me at once, of Arthur bringing a dance partner back to her chaperone and the lady casting a longing, resigned look at his retreating back.

Arthur keeping his distance from all the venues where social barriers slipped—the hunt field, the clubs of St. James's, Tattersalls—and rusticating with a vengeance that left the matchmakers weeping.

Arthur holding our sister Ginny's newborn, his expression both awed and hopeless.

"You prefer men. Entirely? You can't even... for a wedding night?"

"Not even for a wedding night, Julian. Others have broader tastes in partners, but..." He shook his head. "I could not do it." He'd apparently tried, and what a curious undertaking that must have been.

"Well, if you cannot marry, and I cannot,"—I waved a hand in a manner intended to allude to procreation—"and Harry is dead, then who the hell is left to see to the succession?"

"I confess to tendencies that most regard as depraved, and all you're worried about is the succession?"

"What am I supposed to worry about? The fact that I am now the spare was all that stopped me from indulging in a bit of mortal self-injury, if you take my meaning. I failed to rescue Harry from the French. I believed for a time that I might have committed treason into the bargain. What right did I have to draw breath?" I'd begun to pace the confines of the gazebo, my boots drumming on the floorboards.

"I'll tell you what right," I went on. "I was the lone spare. I could take up Harry's responsibility in that regard. I am at least legally a legitimate son of the old duke, and thus I had redeeming value. One day, I hoped to be able to fulfill that office, but I could not ask or expect Hyperia to wait for that fine day—or night, as it were—and then you announce that you're of as little use as I am, and that..."

"Yes?" Arthur loaded a wagonful of caution into one word.

I studied him, my only extant brother, the fellow who'd taught me how to tie my shoes and explained to me that women cried sometimes because men were too weak to admit their feelings, so the ladies did the hard, courageous work of honest emotion for us.

I was still puzzling over that bit of fraternal wisdom.

"Your news comes as a bit of a relief," I said, "now that I study on the matter. My perfect brother acquires a smidgeon of humanity. Something needs doing that neither one of us is up to. Who would have thought? The succession doesn't matter to me, but to be of use to my family... I want to be of use, Your Grace. I need to be of use."

"Arthur will do."

He sounded as if he were conferring a knighthood on me, but I knew better. He'd feared my judgment as badly as I'd feared his. The day when I'd find that amusing was far off indeed.

I tossed myself back on the bench, mind awhirl. "Sit your ducal ass down, *Arthur*, and finish whatever revelations you have to share. I am under the dread assumption that I'll be traveling back to Surrey, and in this heat."

"I haven't any more revelations. You'll keep this to yourself?"

I glowered at him, but my remonstration died unspoken. My brother had put *his life* in my hands—the same hands that had been unable to save Harry—and the question was appropriate.

"I will keep this to myself, though Hyperia is wickedly observant, also utterly trustworthy."

"She seems to like me. One isn't certain whether to be flattered or alarmed."

"Both."

The ensuing silence was different. In the past five minutes, our world had changed, and while the shift meant we both had adjusting to do, the change was also an improvement.

"Tell me about Lord Reardon," I said. "Were you to meet him on your morning rambles?"

"I was. He doubtless wanted to harangue me about my portrait, and I was willing to hear him out—again—and yet, he never showed up."

"He wanted to include your portrait in the exhibition?"

"Nearly begged me to allow it, but I refused. Family pictures are not for public display. I was firm on that point."

And Arthur could be more fixed in his opinions than any cathedral was fixed on its foundations. "Reardon must have mentioned to Huber that he meant to brace you again. This meeting had to be quite early."

"I never saw him, I tell you. I waited by the quarry at the appointed hour for naught. No Lord Reardon, no slobbering hound, no meeting. I'm inclined to let him remain disappeared, Julian."

As was I. "We can't allow that."

Arthur shoved to his feet. "For Miss Eunice's sake?"

"Arthur, *you* were to meet Reardon by the quarry." I followed him down the gazebo steps. "For all Huber knows, that meeting took place after Reardon stopped by the squire's house. Hence Huber's accusation that you were the last to see Reardon alive."

"But I wasn't. I never saw him at all that day."

"I know that, and you know that, but Huber insists otherwise. Huber wants you disgraced, and if he involves the county authorities..."

Arthur set off for the stable. "I cannot have that lot mucking about in my business, Julian. I sent Wellington's best reconnaissance officer to track Lord Reardon down, and you did, and there's an end to Huber's nonsense."

"I was not Wellington's best reconnaissance officer."

"Harry's letters claimed you were. You had the facility with languages, the quick thinking, the sense of the land, the tracking skills... You were the best. So I sent the best, and Huber is an ass."

"That ass apparently suspects you of the proclivities that could see you hanged. Did he see something untoward? Has he any proof?"

Arthur slowed his pace. "He has no proof. *Nobody* has proof. Huber believes any man who hasn't yet lived his three score and ten should be preoccupied with rutting and procreation. That I am not married rouses his suspicions, and his own venal imagination does the rest."

"Venal imaginations abound, Arthur. I used to have one myself. You might be inclined to let sleeping viscounts lie, but Huber's threats mean Lord Reardon cannot remain least in sight."

Arthur waved a hand. "His threats are ridiculous. I'm not simply a peer, I'm a duke. Nobody prosecutes dukes for anything. If we aren't immune by law—and most of the time, we are—we're immune by custom."

The urge to tackle him assailed me again. "You are not immune to *scandal,* you dolt. Huber would allege that Reardon was trying to blackmail you, that you concealed relevant evidence from me because you didn't want me to find Reardon. That you were pressuring Reardon into an untoward relationship. He can paint you in a very suspicious light, and believe me, the court of public opinion never offers exoneration to the innocent."

Arthur had marched us to the stable yard, though the morning was growing too hot for an enjoyable hack.

"You were convicted in that court?" he asked.

"Of treason, fratricide, dishonor... I did not betray my country, and that knowledge consoles me mightily, but my assumed disgrace is another reason why I will not yoke Hyperia's name to mine."

"Does she know that?"

"I have no secrets from her."

"That should tell you something." Arthur strolled off into the blessed shadows of the barn. "Find Reardon, then, and let's hope to God he's still extant to be found."

He disappeared into a saddle room, and I let him make his dignified retreat. For Lady Clarissa's sake, for Eunice Huber's sake, and now for the sake of my brother, I had best find the missing viscount.

And soon.

~

"I thought you should have these." I passed Mrs. Probinger three of Lord Reardon's sketchbooks. We were once again enjoying her back terrace at midmorning, the creek burbling along at the foot of the garden, the maples keeping us in shade.

She opened the volume, then closed it quickly. "Thank you. May I ask...?"

"I had occasion to look through every volume of sketches the missing viscount kept in his studio. Those were the only ones I found with likenesses of you. He drew Eunice Huber in the same style, and I will return those drawings to her when the occasion permits."

Only as I'd ridden Atlas through the lime alley had it occurred to me that Huber might know or suspect Reardon had used Eunice as a model. If so, then the squire had indeed been a father sorely affronted. I'd collected all of the relevant volumes on yesterday's sortie to Valmond House, and I had them with me now.

"Thank you," Mrs. Probinger said again, setting the sketchbooks aside. "I don't know whether to burn them or keep them for a time when I'll be more flattered by those drawings than infuriated."

"Lord Reardon was an utter dolt for immortalizing you in the altogether without your permission."

She took a sip from a sweating glass of lavender lemonade. "Will you venture a *but* for the sake of male pride?"

"I will venture a speculation. Had he attended the Royal Academy or been financed well enough to bide in Town, he'd have had access to life-model classes and the accompanying instruction. No artist considers his education complete without a course in nudes."

She ran her finger around the edge of the glass. "Reardon talked about Town as a Promised Land, the place where all dreams come true and art is valued appropriately. He was an earl's heir, he belonged in Town, and if Lady Clarissa hadn't clung to his arm so relentlessly, he might have gone."

I liked Mrs. Probinger, and more to the point, I trusted her. She had the courage to dance near the edge of the conduct Society tolerated from widows, and she made no apologies for asserting her freedom.

"I doubt Lord Reardon's rusticating was purely for the sake of Clarissa's vanity. She is an earl's daughter. She belonged in Town, too, if that's where she chose to be."

"Then why...?" Mrs. Probinger set down her glass. "They could go anywhere they pleased—Paris, Lisbon, Edinburgh, and yet, the Valmond offspring are nearly fixtures in the neighborhood in recent years. I'm told Lady Clarissa was fond of your late brother, but other than that... Do you suspect something unnatural between them?"

Merciful intercessors. "Military life exposed you to rather a lot, didn't it?"

A robin lighted about two yards from Mrs. Probinger's feet. She broke up a piece of shortbread and tossed the crumbs to her avian caller.

"My husband was no saint, but he wasn't a prude. He suspected a pair of his cousins... Everybody hoped they'd outgrow their inordinate fondness for one another. I haven't kept up with that side of the family."

A day for learning more than I wanted to know, apparently. "I don't suspect any unnatural connection between Lady Clarissa and her brother. I suspect a far more mundane source of scandal stalks them."

Mrs. Probinger took about two seconds to come up with the solution. "Debt? The house is going a bit seedy around the edges, isn't it? I assumed that was a result of the earl and his countess being so often from home, but perhaps they are from home of necessity. And there's Reardon, who longs for Town life, Lady Clarissa, who rejected three proposals in her first Season... I concluded she was fussy, but now... I suppose even then she needed a rich cit looking for any titled wife, not an heir looking for fat settlements?"

Another robin joined the first, and the shortbread was soon gobbled up.

"I missed that telling bit of history, but otherwise, I note the same symptoms you do. The land is tired, the house is fading, the regular trips to Town have stopped, and the lord and lady never seem to be in residence. I'm told the countess is also in poor health, and in our enlightened times, medical care can be a very expensive proposition."

"I am a very bad person, but on many occasions, I've given thanks that my husband didn't linger. He'd have hated being an invalid."

"As would I." *As had I.* "Do as you wish with the sketchbooks. Nobody saw me take them." I'd secreted them in Reardon's knapsack, along with the volume that immortalized Eunice's abundant charms. Excellent art, and prime evidence of both arrogance and stupidity on Reardon's part.

"Why would he leave such indiscreet work where anybody could find it?" Mrs. Probinger asked as the robins flitted away.

"Two reasons," I said, finishing my lemonade. "First, his studio was sacrosanct. Not even his sister intruded there lightly. He assumed nobody would see those sketches. Second, I hope his casual attitude toward the privacy those works should have enjoyed means he expects to be home again soon."

That insight had also occurred to me in the depths of the lime alley, a slender and much-needed reed of support for the notion that

Reardon was having a tantrum rather than decomposing on the banks of a Surrey river.

"Then he's alive and well? I've heard all manner of conflicting speculation. Mrs. Heller came by after breakfast and said we're to fear the worst."

"She wanted to see your reaction to that news?"

"The doctor's wife is not so petty. She wanted to warn me, but said that's only servants' gossip at this point. The news is that Reardon shot himself at some inn in Surrey."

"Not quite." I acquainted her with what I'd found at The King's Man. "But we have no body, and Clarissa confirms that Reardon had planned to stage a mysterious disappearance shortly before the exhibition." Clarissa had done the planning, but her stock was already low enough in the village.

"Have some more lemonade, my lord. Your day will likely be long, hot, and frustrating. I gather whatever scheme Lady Clarissa hatched, Reardon's disappearance wasn't supposed to be *this* mysterious?"

She poured me half a glass from the pitcher.

"Precisely. Her ladyship claims, and I believe her, that Reardon has forgotten his lines. We know not why he's writing himself a new script, and we don't know where he's biding."

"I'm to rack my brain for possibilities?"

"Any suggestions will be helpful. The exhibition grows closer by the day." To say nothing of the tempest Huber's unchecked bloviations could cause for Arthur.

Mrs. Probinger rose, produced a small pair of secateurs from a pocket, and began trimming a rose vine twining through a trellis on the far end of the terrace.

"I think best when I'm gardening," she said, "but all Reardon ever talked about was his art. In Paris, this wonder is to be seen. In Rome, that. Vienna, Prague... He longed to see the splendors of the ancient world, to expand his artistic horizons and shake the dust of Sussex from his feet."

Bad news. Potentially awful news for Clarissa, Eunice, and Arthur. "Did he mention any destination more often than the others?"

"Rome, because it was cheap and full of ex-patriot aristocrats as well as artists. One could learn to paint frescoes in Italy and bring that lucrative expertise back to England, but I doubt he went there."

"Why?"

Snip, snip, snip. "He doesn't speak the language. He has schoolboy Latin and a few phrases of polite French, but Reardon was educated at home. He didn't go up to university. He was spared public school. His tutors were never very impressed with him, save when it came to his art, or so he told me."

I was struck by the difference between poverty for the poor, which was resulting in increasingly crowded and dangerous urban slums, and poverty for the peerage, which had all but isolated Lord Reardon from his natural sources of friendship.

Two different kinds of misery, both awful in their way.

"Did he mention any friends or fellow artists whose company he enjoyed?"

"Hold these, please." She held out the secateurs to me. While I obliged, she threaded a vine through the outermost lattice of the trellis. "I cannot recall Reardon ever mentioning friends, drinking companions, fellows from the club. He was doubtless eligible for membership in his father's clubs, but if a man cannot afford to buy his colors, he's not likely to waste coin on memberships for form's sake. I'll have those back."

I passed over the shears, and she snipped a trailing piece of greenery and tossed it into the lavender border.

"That makes sense." I'd never attributed Reardon's failure to serve in the military to financial barriers, but those were many and steep. An officer was hard-pressed to live on his pay, and to gain his post, he had to buy the commission, then outfit himself from hats to horses and maintain his whole kit on campaign. The quartermasters were technically there for resupply purposes, but the needs of the enlisted men came first.

And rightly so.

"He had to be lonely," Mrs. Probinger said. "You will think me daft, but I swear, most men expect swiving to do the work of friendship, when it rarely can."

What a delight she was. "Did Huber hold those expectations?"

A few more snips before she answered. "The squire meant to present me with an honorable offer of marriage, I'm sure, and he'd be a good provider."

"But?"

"But he is a lonely, bitter man, and I don't need his coin badly enough to take on the challenge of being his wife. Thank God and my father's solicitors." Mrs. Probinger snipped off a pink bloom and threaded it through my lapel. "I wish I could tell you where Reardon is, but I cannot. He was sick to death of Sussex, and yet, other than cousins somewhere up north, I don't know who'd put him up for an extended stay."

"You have been helpful nonetheless."

She gave me an unreadable, very female look. "Finish your lemonade, my lord."

I did—lovely, refreshing potation—and I took my leave, because Mrs. Probinger had been right—my day was bound to be long, hot, and frustrating.

And yet, I'd spoken honestly too: She'd been helpful. Had my manly humors been present at full strength, I'd doubtless have been speculating about her other partners. My gaze would have lingered where a gentleman does not look, and my appraisal of her would have been clouded with...

Call it masculine appreciation, but the honest term would be *casual lust*. Even loyalty to Hyperia would not have completely cured me of speculations and imaginings. But captivity had quieted those longings, in all but a theoretical sense. Instead, I could appreciate Mrs. Probinger for the shrewd, practical, honest, and pretty person she was.

Prior to my ordeal in France, I feared my assessment might have begun and ended with *pretty*. Manly humors would have rendered me blind in a sense. A surprising insight, but given how the morning had begun, perhaps this was the day for surprising insights too.

CHAPTER TWELVE

My next stop was Valmond House, because in all my haring about, I had yet to interview the staff regarding the viscount's possible whereabouts. Servants keep their employers under surveillance of necessity, and somebody might have seen or overheard something of significance without realizing it.

I found the Valmond family seat in an uproar, and the day was growing far too hot for such nonsense.

"Mrs. Aimes is leaving," Blaylock told me as he took my hat and spurs. "Piking off, abandoning a sinking ship, according to the kitchen, and the kitchen is usually right."

The kitchen, meaning Mrs. Felders, upon whom I'd yet to call. I started up the curving main staircase, Blaylock trotting at my side. "Where is Mrs. Aimes now?"

"Packing. Lady Clarissa forbade the maids to assist her. Odds favor her ladyship forbidding the stable from bringing the coach around, but the lads might do it anyway just to give us some peace."

We gained the first floor, and Blaylock gestured to the corridor on the right.

I struck out in that direction. "And where is Lady Clarissa?"

"Gone to ground. Slipped out the door when she finished ringing a peal over Mrs. Aimes's head—through a closed door—and Mrs. Aimes was giving as good as she got. I'm sorry, my lord. I could not exactly march after her ladyship."

"No, you could not. Mrs. Aimes won't be leaving just yet. Blaylock, when was the last time you were paid?"

He didn't hesitate, which was more disloyalty and bad form. Good form had never kept a fellow in comfortable boots, though.

"Wages were regular until this week, my lord. The first of the month came and went, and no pay packets. We're still getting our beer and candles, but her ladyship says Lord Reardon handled the ledgers, and she has no idea how to go on with them."

That might just possibly be true. "Tell the staff not to worry. I am more than competent to make entries in a wage book, and I'll see to it before the day is over. Summon a groom to the kitchen, because I'll need to send a message to Caldicott Hall to explain why I'm tarrying here." And to get Arthur to open his safe and make me a small loan.

The relief in Blaylock's eyes was pathetic. "I'll fetch a groom straightaway, my lord. This is Mrs. Aimes's apartment."

"Thank you. If I don't come down within the hour, best go at the door with an ax. Away with you to set the kitchen straight."

"Aye, sir." He scampered off, an enlisted man only too happy to take orders.

I rapped on the door. "Mrs. Aimes, Lord Julian Caldicott has come to call, and I'm on the king's business, so you'd best admit me. Lady Clarissa is taking a constitutional by the lake, if I'm not mistaken."

The door whooshed open. "Sulking and pouting, no doubt. The Valmond offspring excel at sulking and pouting, with the exception of poor Susan. Do come in."

She was in an old high-waisted morning gown, the sort of dress worn when no company was expected and last night's entertainments had run too late.

"Why now?" I asked, surveying an open trunk half full of dresses, shawls, slippers, and gloves. "Why leave now?"

"The better question is why stay as long as I have? Do sit down. I'd ring for a tray, but the servants are likely following my example and gathering up their effects."

Her cheeks were flushed with heat or ire or both. She subsided onto a chaise, and I took a wing chair. Her sitting room was pretty—blue, gold, and cream appointments, a pleasant prospect of the lake beneath her balcony—but the rug was worn, and the curtains were faded to periwinkle, while the sofa was still azure.

"Have you any idea," Mrs. Aimes said, patting at her forehead with a handkerchief, "any notion whatsoever, how exhausting it is living in this house? Reardon up at all hours, coming and going with that wretched dog. Clarissa fuming at every meal, when she deigns to come to the table at all. My sister is unwell—seriously, perhaps mortally, unwell—and I'm supposed to bide here, playing lady-in-waiting to those scheming brats. I'm sick of it."

She appeared in roaring good health to me and giving Clarissa a run for her money in the dramatics department.

I tugged the bell-pull twice and resumed my seat. "The staff isn't going anywhere, though, I grant you, Reardon is absent without leave."

She worried a nail. "I know. I warned Clarissa he'd slip the leash. He's not as experienced as other fellows his age. No public school scrapping, no wild oats at university, no sobering realities seen in uniform. I don't blame him for the present situation."

"You blame Clarissa?"

"She's the older sibling. She pushed him and pushed him. All he wanted to do was paint."

I, for one, was done blaming Clarissa. "All he *did* was paint, and wander the countryside sketching, and frolic with unsuspecting women who ended up becoming scandal fodder in his sketchbooks. Now an entire exhibition has been planned for his benefit, and he's betrayed Clarissa's trust. Yet, somehow, Clarissa is to blame?"

"The exhibition was her idea."

Blaylock arrived bearing a tray of what smelled like meadow tea—mint and chamomile—accompanied by a small pot of honey and some ginger biscuits.

"All quiet belowstairs?" I asked as he set the tray on the table beside my wing chair.

"Calming down. Groom awaits your orders, my lord."

I withdrew my ever-present pencil and paper and scribbled a few words in French. "For His Grace." I folded the note and printed *His Grace of Waltham* on the outside. "No need to gallop, but to be delivered directly."

"Very good, sir." Blaylock took the note, bowed, and withdrew.

I considered Mrs. Aimes, who still claimed a full complement of beauty, albeit of the mature variety. "Where will you go?" I passed her a cool glass and took a sip from my own.

Heaven. Absolute heaven. If there was a God, and He failed to reward Mrs. Felders for her skill with mere meadow tea, I'd have stern words with Him, assuming Saint Peter admitted me to the celestial realm.

"Where will I go?"

"Yes, when you storm off in high dudgeon from perfectly acceptable accommodations, where will you go?"

"Town, I suppose. Or perhaps I will make an extended visit to Lady Ophelia? She's always amenable to good company in the summer months."

"Lady Ophelia bides at the Hall for now, and I doubt we'll dislodge her in the immediate future. You are leaving in a panic, Mrs. Aimes. Why?"

She rose and went out to the balcony, the French doors having been left ajar. I followed, glass in hand. I had no intention of letting my interrogation drop. Her decision to leave formed another link in a chain of developments that made no sense.

She was a poor relation, a paid companion, something of that

nature. If she'd had other options, they wouldn't compare to a berth at Valmond House.

"Clarissa really has lost track of her brother," Mrs. Aimes said. "She hasn't a clue where he is. He never arrived in Town, and Clarissa says you yourself brought her that news."

"I did, though for all I know, Reardon is kicking his heels in Mayfair as we speak."

She slanted a look at me. "Or he's on the way to Paris."

"I doubt that. He has little French and less coin, according to some. Where will you go, Enola?"

She tried for heroic silence, and when I did not fill it with apologies and explanations and other placatory offerings, she began to cry. I took her glass from her, passed her a handkerchief, and waited for the storm—or performance—to pass.

"I never meant for any of this to happen," she said. "I never meant..." She heaved a martyred sigh. "It was idle talk. That horrid Squire Huber said something about a man only receiving the respect he's due on the day of his funeral. Reardon took up the chorus, about an artist's works gaining value only upon his death. Clarissa got that look in her eye..."

"And you encouraged her?"

"I didn't think she was serious!"

"You knew they were desperate, but now that the plan you all but dared them to attempt is coming unraveled, you are deserting the ranks."

She sniffed, squared her shoulders, and gazed mournfully at the lake. "The plan might have worked."

"Had not Reardon, in true Reardon fashion, gone off and done as he pleased, leaving the ladies to mop up the mess. You will leave today."

"I ought to stay. My departure will fuel talk."

And that had bothered her not at all a quarter of an hour ago, when she could lay the whole commotion at Clarissa's feet.

"You will go to Town and take a hand in preparations for the exhibition so that Clarissa can bide here in peace while I hunt down her brother. You will call on everybody you know who has ever bought a piece of art and on anybody else who is still in Town, and you will gush about Reardon's talent."

"I leave the gushing to Clarissa."

"Time to brush off your dusty skills, then. The exhibition is going forward, and it's in your interests to ensure it's a success. The Valmonds are your regiment, and their honor is at stake. Do your best for their sake, or find yourself drummed out of the corps."

She took the glass I'd been holding, downed a few swallows, and poured the rest out over a bed of roses two stories beneath us—for which she should have been court-martialed, if she wasn't already facing a dishonorable discharge.

"My good name is all I have left," she said. "I cannot afford to be associated with scandal, and the Valmonds are several kinds of scandal waiting to happen. I've even considered..."

What would a last resort, an otherwise unbearable option, be to her? "Huber?"

She nodded. "He's proposed to every widow in the shire and attempted his flirtations with me in the churchyard. Not what I had planned, but then, he won't live forever."

He'd proposed and been serially refused, apparently. What would that do to a man's self-respect? To his temper?

"For the present, you will go to London. The Caldicott traveling coach will be available for your journey, and I suggest you leave tonight to spare the horses the heat."

I was presuming on Arthur's resources, but solving this whole muddle was to his benefit. Then too, he was a duke, not simply another country squire placidly awaiting the year's harvest. He was supposed to be generous and gracious and all that noble twaddle.

"Town will be wretched," Mrs. Aimes said. "Hotter than perdition and twice as malodorous."

Not as hot as Spain in summer, not as wretched as a forced march in ill-fitting boots. "Where is Reardon, Mrs. Aimes? This whole scheme might just work if I can locate the missing viscount."

Her smile was bitter. "If I knew where he was, if I knew that his remains were not washing out to sea, I might be less upset. Reardon's nerves are delicate. You know how artists are. Painting for three days straight, then sleeping for a week. His days and nights reversed. All his geese are swans one day, and the next... he is covered in despair."

"But then he'd take his dog and sketchbook and go rambling"—or get free of this house of woe—"and his geese turned back into swans."

"I will go to London and ensure all is in readiness for the exhibition, but I would rather take a packet to Calais."

"You can take that packet after the exhibition, and Reardon might join you, assuming he hasn't quit the country already."

I left her on the balcony, trying to look stoic and mostly looking tired. Something Lady Ophelia had said propelled me down the footmen's stairs in search of Blaylock.

The staff knew everything, according to Lady Ophelia, and she had a point. Reardon might not have confided in anybody, but any arrangements—to bide with a friend, head to Scotland, or take a packet—would have been made and confirmed by post. The boot-boy typically retrieved the post from the inn, and while he was unlikely to be literate, the footman who took the day's post up to the library or foyer probably would be.

The maid who'd taken outgoing letters belowstairs might well have been literate too. Somebody in the household had to have picked up a whiff of intrigue, even if they'd done so unaware.

My immediate and increasingly pressing challenge was to figure out who that person was and to shake every pertinent detail loose from their memory.

~

I questioned everybody from Blaylock to the aging butler to the chirrupy little boot-boy. They all claimed to know nothing, to have seen absolutely nothing, and to have heard less than absolutely nothing that would shed light on Lord Reardon's present whereabouts.

I had resigned myself to a chat with the proprietor of our posting inn when I recalled that I'd yet to quiz Clarissa on the same topic. She had professed ignorance the previous day, but she might well have some insight unbeknownst even to her.

The head stable lad told me that her ladyship had stalked off toward the lake more than an hour earlier, and I might try my luck taking the same trail. I donned my tinted spectacles and idly tracked her—she was moving at a good clip, considering she wore heeled slippers—until her steps slowed as she neared the water.

The path was overgrown. At one point, I had to hop over a fallen tree, and at another, the shore had subsided, leaving the trail crumbling three feet above murky water. Neglect on every hand, and I hadn't begun to see it until I'd lost my memory.

The Almighty enjoyed a robust sense of irony.

I came upon Clarissa on the porch of the Valmond fishing cottage, a small stone structure going mossy along its northern exposure. The building itself was still upright, but the padlock on the door showed signs of rust.

"You might want to oil that lock," I said, taking the place on the bench beside her, facing the water. "Wouldn't want to have to get the blacksmith out over a lot of old reels and nets."

"I put the best of the tackle into the gamekeeper's hands and sold the rest. We keep the cottage locked so nobody will know it's empty."

"Do you still have a gamekeeper?"

We were in shade, surrounded by woods, the bright expanse of the lake before us. The scene should have been restful, but I sensed from Clarissa an overwhelming weight of sadness.

"We pensioned the gamekeeper and could not afford to hire a replacement. Old Demming keeps an eye on the woods and waterways out of pity. Somebody has to catch an occasional rabbit or pheasant, else the staff would starve. His Grace overlooks the fact that we haven't taken out a proper shooting certificate for Old Demming for at least three years."

Without cosmetics, silks, and an elaborate coiffure, Clarissa looked like what she was: a weary woman past the dewy years and managing a load of regret. She was also quite pretty, with classic features, good bones, and a fine figure.

Former officers sometimes referred to having had a good war. They had come home with every limb intact, having known great adventure and seen much of the world.

Lady Clarissa Valmond was having a bad war, and I knew how that felt. I knew as well the gnawing ache of a sibling gone missing, though in my wildest imaginings I would never have thought to have so much in common with her ladyship.

"Do you know what the worst part is?" She'd gathered up a pile of clover flowers in her lap and was fashioning them into a chain. "The part I did not anticipate at all?"

"Tell me." Though I could guess.

"They all hate me. I have done everything I can think of to keep scandal from my family's door. I have pawned my jewels to buy Reardon his pigments, swanned about with Lord Harry, made a half-hearted try for you, and now my forlorn hope is to besiege His Grace. My lady's maid hates me because she didn't get my castoff gowns—when I had castoff gowns. I instead sold them on Rosemary Lane."

She paused to thread another flower onto her chain. "The staff thinks I'm frivolous, vain, demanding, and arrogant. All I do is sit about with my needlepoint, harangue Reardon, and make calls. I'm useless in their eyes."

I scooped up some of the hoard in her lap and started my own chain. "And all the needlework," I said, "is to retrim your hems and cuffs so nobody will recognize you in last year's fashions. You are embellishing the bodices on the wardrobe from the year before that and doing the best you can with bonnets from the last century. Most of your work is, in fact, done on Lady Susan's frocks so she won't worry quite as much over her appearance as she approaches her come out."

"If she even makes a come out. I've tried not to let her know how bad things are, but Susan isn't stupid." Clarissa's hands stilled. "Neither am I, despite appearances to the contrary. I am tired of the disrespect, the sniffy looks from people whose every coin has come from the Valmond family coffers. In the village, I am all but a laughing-stock. Our neighbors have one question for me: 'So when will your parents be home, my lady?' Mama and Papa cannot come home. They will risk much biding in London, and Mama is so ill..."

Her burden was not merely sadness, then, but rather, despair. "I find the pity worse," I said, ruining my second blossom and tossing it over the railing into the water. "The looks that say, 'Poor fellow, made such a hash of his military career. Claims he was trying to rescue his brother, but could very well have betrayed his rank. Pistol shot to the head might be the kindest thing. It really might.'"

The current took my clover flower and drew it under.

"Why didn't you? Why not just give up?"

"His Grace forbade it?"

She smiled. "The real answer, Julian. Why not let the despair win? Valmond House has been losing ground for decades. Papa is no sort of manager, and the past twenty years have been challenging even for the lucky and clever among the landed classes. I'm an empty-headed, scheming spinster. Why did I think I could even try to bring the situation right?"

And I was an extra spare with a poor memory, weak eyes, and an endless store of nightmares. But right now, Clarissa didn't care about any of that, and neither did I. The lady was having a low moment, and I was uniquely capable of offering her comfort.

A day for surprises indeed.

"You have gone to these heroic lengths," I said, "because you have honor, and you are not what village gossip makes you out to be. Because you are tenacious and resourceful and determined, and your objective is worthy. The regiment is depending on you, and you are not the first to face a want of coin."

"Honor." She all but sneered the word. "Honor doesn't pay the trades."

I looped an arm around her shoulders and gave her a squeeze. "We'll find him." What I meant was that I would find his lordship, and when I did, I might thrash him silly. "Reardon can't have gone far on his limited means, and Mrs. Aimes tells me he has next to no friends."

Clarissa rested her head on my shoulder for a moment, then sat up straight. "Reardon is ashamed. He should have fought, he should have made his obeisance to the Royal Academy, he should have insisted at least on attending university, though I can't see that three years of drunkenness and debauchery are any sort of accomplishment.

"He is so talented," she went on more softly. "He has so much ability. Landscapes, portraits, miniatures, even caricatures." She wound her clover chain around her forearm. "He got paid for doing some botanical illustrations, and I vow he didn't know whether to rejoice over the coin, or despair because he'd accepted it. He used to do caricatures in the posting inns—penny portraits—but only because Sir Thomas Lawrence got his start in a similar fashion. Reardon signed the caricatures with his old drawing master's initials. He had the idea to copy our collection in the gallery, but said he wouldn't turn himself into a forger outright. Hence no signatures."

"Then Reardon has glimmers of your resourcefulness."

"And enough pride to nearly smother them. His sole gift, he said, was his art. So I talked him into this exhibition, and now I wish I hadn't."

We worked at our little flower craft for a few quiet moments while the water lapped at the bank, and I searched our conversation for any useful insights.

"Where are the posting inns Reardon graced with his sketching?"

"Not the Brighton-to-London route. Too close to home and too much chance he might be recognized. He favored the roads leading to Portsmouth. More likely to be commercial traffic or gentry. Come back to the house with me. I have a few of his old caricatures. You'd hardly know it's the same artist who did such glorious battle scenes."

Hellishly glorious. I collected my floral chain and considered the immense trust Clarissa had placed in me, though I'd all but scorned her when I'd arrived at Caldicott Hall. In my last conversation with Arthur, I'd explained to him that being the spare had given me hope that I might one day serve a purpose.

Clarissa deserved some hope too. I wound my floral chain into a circle and draped it over her hair, like the Queen of the May's crown.

"You will not give in to despair, my lady, because I admire you. I admire your courage and your cool head under fire. You would have made a fine officer, and I know of no higher compliment."

She looked confused, and then her chin began to tremble. My handkerchief was no longer pristine, but I ought not to have underestimated her ladyship.

Her dignity reasserted itself, like an infantry unit forming square despite casualties. "Thank you, my lord. I admire you as well."

A fine officer indeed, capable of aiming return fire so it counted. We left the woods at a leisurely stroll, though when Valmond House came into view, Clarissa quickened her pace.

"Do you know what clover symbolizes, my lord?"

Happy cows? "Haven't a clue."

"Clover wards off evil hexes. It symbolizes luck and good fortune."

"And becomes you wonderfully."

"Does it? Does it really?" She bestowed a smile on me I hadn't seen from her before, one that cast all her previous posturing and flirtation into the shade. Those company smiles were brilliant, as exploding artillery could be visually dazzling. This smile, this warmth in her eyes and benevolence in her expression, was purely *enchanting*. "Thank you, my lord."

She wore her crown into the house and led me straight to the viscount's studio, where she rummaged for a bit.

"Here," she said. "Reardon did these for practice, or so he claimed, but he loved poking artistic fun at a sitter."

He'd immortalized Clarissa with a haughty nose, tiny ears, massive ringlets, and ample feminine endowments. The next image was the Earl of Valloise, as mostly seen through the quizzing glass his lordship held up to his nose. Twigs and leaves adorned his lordship's hair, which stuck out at ridiculous angles. Valloise to the life.

I peered at the bottom right corner. "JT?"

"Jean Traffault. An émigré drawing master hired for his command of Continental technique. Reardon and Monsieur were as thick as thieves. Traffault was the only tutor who ever had anything good to say about Reardon. Then one day, he claimed Reardon had learned all he had to teach him and left."

A true teacher, then. "Where did Traffault go?"

Clarissa looked about the studio as if the answer might be on the silk-hung walls. "Not Chichester, but that direction. Arundel, maybe? I recall Reardon going to visit Traffault and coming home with sketches of the River Arun. Ancient bridges, peaceful water, green meadows. Traffault had a brother in that vicinity, but I don't know what became of him. Let's leave this place, if you don't mind."

She escorted me from the studio. and because she seemed to have a destination in mind, I tagged along without comment. We ended up on the west terrace, and the transition from the shadowed house to midday sunshine had me reaching for my specs.

"I don't believe Reardon spent much time sketching the house," Clarissa said, gaze on the overgrazed park. "He's missed wage day. I hadn't planned for that."

"I'll tend to the wage book. You shouldn't have to do every blessed thing yourself."

She continued down the steps to the base of the slightly uneven terrace and stared up at the family edifice. "Reardon did the actual paying. I scrounged about for coin, but Mama's pin money only goes so far. I don't know how Reardon managed to make up the difference. I didn't ask how."

"Today, you will allow me to see to the pay packets, my lady. Oh, and I directed Mrs. Aimes on to Town to oversee preparations for the exhibit. She will depart at sunset. If Reardon is at the town house, she will send word."

Clarissa sat on the uneven, sun-warmed steps. "Enola was in high dudgeon this morning. Ready to jump ship and swim to any available port. I don't blame her, but she thought the whole notion of sending Reardon into hiding would make for splendid gossip."

"Well, no," I said, passing Clarissa my flask. "That was all your idea, and you couldn't be talked out of it."

She opened the flask, sniffed, and took a few swallows of Mrs. Felders's meadow tea. "Of course it was, and let me guess, the exhibition itself was solely her brilliant notion. I ought not to sit out here in the sun."

"You ought, for once, to do as you damned well please. I'm off to bring the wage book up to date."

She passed back the flask. "Thank you, Julian. Thank you, whether you ever find my addlepated brother or not."

"I will find him." I bowed over her hand and trotted up the steps, prepared to dole out the requisite pence and quid.

I had value as the Caldicott spare, but perhaps that was not the limit of my usefulness. Clarissa had needed a friend, and I had obliged.

And that felt... odd, but good.

Very good, in fact.

When I opened the library door, I found Hyperia passing a few coins to the boot-boy, traditionally the last of the staff to be paid.

"Jules." She rose and smiled.

Seldom had I beheld a more welcome sight. The urge to hug her came over me, unexpected and disconcerting. "I expected Arthur to raid the strongbox, not send me the crack troops."

"I've handled wage day before. Lady Ophelia is taking tea with

Lady Susan, who is worried about her siblings. I am worried about you."

"Because?"

She fisted her hands on her hips, putting me in mind of Atticus. "All this bright sunshine, and you racketing about with only your spectacles to protect your eyes. The miserable heat has to be wearing on you, and you are not exactly in the pink. Haring up to Surrey and back, marching about in the woods... When was the last time you ate?"

"Breakfast." A dim memory, blighted by Huber's histrionics.

She was moving toward the bell-pull when I stepped in front of her. "No need. I will take myself to the kitchen, where I am overdue for a chat with Mrs. Felders. Thank you very much for coming, and please extend my thanks to Lady Ophelia as well."

"You're truly managing? You'd tell me if you needed to rest?"

One did not dissemble with Miss Hyperia West. "I would tell you. I'd never admit it to Arthur, but I'd tell you, and perhaps mutter something to Atlas about needing a nap. As it happens, I'm off to the Hall next, where I will collect my saddlebags and set out for the coast."

"You know where Reardon is?"

"I know of one place where he might always be welcome, and so I will look for him there."

"Away with you, then, but,"—she shook a minatory finger at me—"mind you don't overdo."

I saluted, turned on my heel, and headed for the stairs.

CHAPTER THIRTEEN

"Lord Reardon's a good lad," Mrs. Felders said, rhythmically kneading a pale mass of dough. "Bit too much like his father, though, meaning no disrespect." She punched the dough with a floury fist, and I concluded that disrespect was only the start of her vexation with Lord Valloise.

"The earl is much consumed with natural science, as I recall." I made that observation around a mouthful of ginger biscuit.

"He's much consumed with anything that lets him abandon the countess to her friends and dodge..." Another smack. Gentleman Jackson should set his hopefuls to kneading dough if they aspired to join the Fancy.

"Dodge the creditors?" I suggested.

"The talk." She formed the dough into an oval and draped a damp linen towel over it. "The talk, about the money, about Lady Clarissa, about the countess, about topics decent folk ought not to waste their time on. More tea?"

"Please. If you haven't written the recipe down, I wish you would and share it with His Grace's cook."

Mrs. Felders, who had gone completely gray since last I'd seen her, still moved with brisk dispatch. She washed her hands at the copper sink and dried them with a towel that might at one time have been part of a tablecloth.

"The recipe is Mrs. Gwinnett's, my lord. She starts making it up for the servants' hall as soon as the mint gets going. A dash of honey, spent tea leaves, and a pinch of salt, with a few other spices. Not fit for a duke, but the stable lads prefer it to ale in summer."

She topped up my tankard, poured more for herself, and slid onto the bench across from me at the kitchen table.

"Heat is bound to break tonight," she said. "My hip is talking to me. Nobody warns you that old age turns you into a weather vane."

"You are ready to retire?"

She sipped her drink. "Who'd cook for the house, my lord? More honey? I don't care for too much in my meadow tea, but Lady Clarissa has a sweet tooth, poor thing. She never complains about a cold collation for supper, though I'd best not forget the pudding. The viscount is worse—he'll put honey in his coffee—while Lady Susan turns up her nose at sweets, but adores a dark porter. The earl would eat steak at every meal, while the countess would survive on porridge. Oh, the Quality."

I pushed the plate of ginger biscuits to her side of the table. "What does Mrs. Gwinnett say about our tastes over at Caldicott Hall?"

Mrs. Felders took her time choosing a biscuit. "Says you need to put some meat on your bones, my boy, but you eat like a bird. His Grace is finicky. She tries the fanciest French recipes, the most complicated sauces, and he sends half of it right back to the kitchen, though always with his compliments. If he truly relished his cook's efforts, he'd clean his plate."

How many times had I shown up on the Valmond House kitchen steps as a boy, my knee scraped, my elbow bruised, my rambles along the creek having left me famished? Mrs. Felders had known what to do with a hungry, thirsty, happily bedraggled lad.

"May I tell you a secret?"

"You've always told me your secrets, Master Julian."

"His Grace prefers plain fare, such as you probably put out for the servants' hall. A plate of cheese toast would leave him in raptures. He'd eat every bite of steak and potatoes provided he could pour his gravy on the spuds."

She smiled. "Caldicotts are good size. They need hearty meals. I've told Emily Gwinnett as much, but she says he's a dook, you know? Dooks must eat fancy. Lord Reardon liked to eat fancy, too, poor bugger."

"Where do you think he's gone off to? I've asked the whole staff for their thoughts on the matter."

She chose another biscuit. "Hard to say. With Lady Clarissa, I could venture a few guesses if she turned up missing. Her old governess, some cousins up north, a great-aunt, but Reardon never had time for the family connections, and he has no brothers. A solitary lad. No wonder he took to drawing pictures and rambling with the dog. Dog is getting on, though, and Reardon's not a boy."

"Touchstone is biding with us at the Hall for now. He's well looked after."

Mrs. Felders pushed the biscuits back over to me. "Lord Reardon needs to grow up. He tried running away from home as a lad. Never worked. His pa didn't notice he were missing, and his ma said meals were quieter without him. He mighta been floating facedown in the quarry pond, and that was all she had to say."

"You think he's having a tantrum?"

She nodded, and a look came into her eye that suggested she wasn't above turning a full-grown viscount over her knee.

"How was he supposed to grow up, my lord? If his pa were elderly, we'd call him vague. But there's another word for it when you're rich and titled... Serry-ball? Serry-something."

"Cerebral," I said, tapping my forehead. "Building castles in Spain." Though I'd seen many Spanish castles, and they were far more substantial edifices than Valloise was capable of concocting even mentally.

"Aye, castles in Spain. A useless example for a boy who's supposed to put right decades of neglect on the estate and eventually vote in the Lords. No uncles to step in, unless you count Squire Huber, but Reardon has little patience with that one. Says he's stuck in the past. Well, Reardon is stuck in the clouds."

She drained her tankard. "Reardon needed somebody to show him how to go on, and Lady Clarissa tries, but she has troubles of her own."

"What about you? Any troubles these days?" I'd tried for a light note, but Mrs. Felders turned a tired gaze on me.

"We manage well enough here in the country. The home farm, the spice garden, the kitchen garden, the hives... They are all adequate to feed the household. In London, I can't fill the larders as easily. So much must be bought because we are just a bit too far from the estate. The earl's credit in Town is used up, and I ought not to be telling you this."

No, she shouldn't, but in the past, she'd certainly guarded my confidences. "When Lady Clarissa travels to Town, she'll do so as Lady Ophelia's guest. Mrs. Aimes is leaving for Town tonight in the Caldicott traveling coach, which is sizable. She'll be in London by morning, and you can send along enough provisions to tide her over for a week or so. I'll give her sufficient coin to keep her in butter and eggs."

I made that offer not for Enola Aimes's sake—she would land on her slippered feet—but because Mrs. Felders would fret otherwise. She had worried about me in my misspent youth, and I had taken her welcome and good cheer for granted time after time.

I rose, though I, too, was feeling stiff in the hips and knees. "I'm off to chase down our runaway."

She gestured with a biscuit. "Godspeed, lad. You'll need it."

∾

Through a long, hot, dusty afternoon and into the evening, Atlas and I tracked Lord Reardon along the King's highway. A series of inquiries informed me that he had traveled south, then angled west, changing horses every ten miles or so.

He had eschewed traveling by public coach or post, suggesting he was still attempting a measure of stealth, and his destination was apparently Portsmouth rather than Brighton.

Bad news, that.

Brighton was a still-fashionable seaside haunt of the idle and titled, while Portsmouth bustled with maritime trade. Reardon might well be paying a call on his old tutor, and he might thereafter take a permanent leave from his homeland.

I arrived at the market town of Arundel as the last of the light was fading from the sky. The last of my energies had faded some five miles up the road. I had nonetheless walked Atlas the final leg of our journey. Like many steeds with Iberian blood, he tolerated the dry heat of Spain well. We'd been traveling through the worst of England's humid summer weather, a different and more taxing proposition for man and beast.

The inn, smack along the High Street, boasted the usual archway into a square courtyard, though for the moment, the courtyard was quiet. Arundel Castle, traditional seat of the Dukes of Norfolk, loomed up on its hill in dour granite splendor. The place had taken various drubbings during Cromwell's rise to power, and the late duke —The Drunken Duke to his familiars, number eleven by more formal reckoning—had spent considerable time and money on repairs.

Reardon had probably longed to sketch that stony pile. The place gave me the collywobbles. Too much misery and murder associated with the average castle, and Arundel was no exception.

To my weary delight, I learned from the hostlers that a man answering to Reardon's description had turned in a hired hack two days earlier and decamped from the inn on foot. I decided to celebrate by taking a room, ordering a bath, and consuming a plate of ham-and-cheddar sandwiches.

My quarters were at the back of the inn—quieter—and had a small balcony overlooking the working end of the stable yard. Fragrant, and not with the refreshing tang of the ocean. The River Arun had another dozen miles to go before finding the sea.

I similarly had a mental distance to travel before I found slumber. I made a pallet on my balcony and slept as I often had on campaign, half sitting up, my back propped against the inn's venerable stone wall.

In the distance, lightning flashed, and I even heard a faint rumble of thunder, but no rain fell.

What the hell was Reardon up to? Lying low for a time in preparation for his great exhibition? Why not inform his sister of those plans? Bolting for the Continent ahead of angry creditors? Again, that scheme could and should have been shared with her ladyship.

Eluding marriage to Eunice Huber?

Many a fellow had been enticed into taking the king's shilling by recruiting sergeants who disparaged wives and mothers. How dare those infernal women chain a man to domestic drudgery when he ought to be seeing the world and enjoying the sanguinary adventures all braw, bonnie laddies delighted in?

The recruiters had been sirens of death, but they'd also known how to present knavery toward family in an honorable light. Reardon was young, indulged, and sooner or later, he'd be burdened by the realities of the Valloise title.

Perhaps he'd heard those siren songs and was eluding domesticity without benefit of donning a uniform.

When the first streaks of dawn arrived, I was stiff, hungry, and no closer to understanding my quarry's motivation, but with luck, I'd soon catch up to him, and he could answer my questions in person.

Though when had luck ever taken the side of Lord Julian Caldicott for long?

～

Frenchmen were no oddity in Southern England. Napoleon had disdained prisoner exchanges—why pay to send able-bodied enemy soldiers home to rearm against him when he could instead reduce an opponent's numbers by essentially starving his captives?—and thus English parole towns, garrisons, and merchant communities had absorbed some hundred thousand Frenchmen in the course of the wars.

The Revolution had previously sent forty thousand French émigrés to London alone, while others in great numbers had found refuge with English cousins or in less expensive British surrounds.

Traffault or his brother would not be a rarity in a town the size of Arundel, but Reardon himself had given me an advantage.

"Have you seen this fellow?" I asked the inn's proprietress. She put me in mind of the castle: stolid, gray, weathered, and built to withstand the ages. "I am in search of a drawing master for my sister and hoping he might take her on."

She studied the sketch briefly. Prominent nose, thinning hair, a twinkle in the eyes of an otherwise stern countenance.

"Don't know him, but if he's local, he'll not take his usual pint with us. Try the smaller inns, or..." She studied me, probably looking for signs that I owed allegiance to the Board of Revenue or some other government-imposed nuisance. "We have a teahouse now. I hear they're catching on in London. Don't see why a goodwife can't take tea in my ladies' parlor, but who am I to question fashion? The women at their tea might know the local drawing masters. Betty!" she barked at a girl of perhaps ten years skulking in the direction of the kitchen door behind the common's bar. "The sun's up, and the front steps haven't been scrubbed."

"Aye, ma'am. I'm doing it now, ma'am." Betty bobbed a curtsey and ducked out the front door.

"A teahouse, you say?" I infused my voice with wonder at this bit of market-town sophistication. "I've never heard the like. Where would this teahouse be?"

She tucked an errant graying curl under her mobcap. "You walk along the High until you reach the river. Turn left, and it'll be a few doors down. Might not be open at this hour. We serve good China black in the common, fresh leaves for every pot."

"And I have enjoyed that tea myself this very morning." Not the strongest brew I'd encountered. "I'll nonetheless look in at this tea establishment. Do the Frenchmen in these parts favor any particular pub or tavern?"

"That lot." Her features lost their air of harried hospitality. "Killed my sister's boy."

"The man I'm looking for had the good sense to flee his homeland before the Corsican monster came to power. He would condole you on your loss and likely deserve your sympathy for his many bereavements."

As close as I could come to telling her that the war was over, and many a French mother had lost every son, nephew, brother, and grandson she had. My hostess's grief was real and bitter, and who was I to scold her out of it when my own brother's death haunted me?

"Frenchies around here stick to theirselves," she said. "And well they should. If you're looking for one of them, you're asking the wrong lady."

She bustled off, nose in the air, and I counted the conversation useful. Émigrés had an established neighborhood in Arundel, something I hadn't known before, and if Reardon had any sense—an open question—he'd try to secret himself among them.

I collected my saddlebags and my horse and was on the point of tightening Atlas's girth when I noticed the girl Betty hard at work on the front steps.

"Good morning, Miss Betty."

She dimpled at my use of the honorific. "G'day, sir. That's a fine horse. He's not one of ours."

"His name is Atlas, and he's all mine. Might you answer a question for me about how to find my way in your fair town?"

"Aye. I know where everything is. Hard to get lost in Arundel, because you see the castle from almost anywhere. You don't look lost."

High praise, and the perspective of a natural scout. "I'm not lost, but I'm trying to find a friend. He's French, has lived in these surrounds with his brother for several years. Their name is Traffault."

"Miss-shure Truffles," she said, beaming at me. "They live down along the river. You walk the path on the bank toward the sea—other side, not this side—and come to a thatched cottage with roses growing all the way to the second floor. Not much more than a quarter hour. They might still be blooming. Mr. Truffle is very merry, and he always says, '*Bon-jure, ma pettee,*' to me. He drew a picture of me once, but Ma'am tossed it into the fire. Said I wasn't to get vain notions or speak to Mr. Truffles, but I can't help it if he speaks to me, can I?"

"You certainly cannot. I will give your regards to Mr. Truffles. Please accept a token of my thanks for your assistance." I passed her tuppence. Her eyes got round, and she looked to be winding up for a grand oratory of thanks when I bowed and departed.

Children were often the best informants. Of necessity, they kept a close eye on the larger, more powerful creatures in their environment, while adults barely noticed juvenile surveillance.

Atlas and I ambled along the river as the heat began to build again, and I considered what would happen if Reardon wasn't to be found keeping company with the Traffaults. If he'd traveled on to Portsmouth, he could already have boarded a packet or, worse, a merchantman.

Eunice Huber might well be ruined. The squire would make endless trouble for Arthur. Clarissa would be left to handle an exhibition with no artist to show off. The Valmond parents would come to London, in plain view of their creditors, with no promised artist genius on hand to right the family finances.

And Wellington's best intelligence officer would once again be covered in disgrace.

I didn't care for that notion or for the rest of the misery that would result from Reardon's elopement.

I dismounted at the designated cottage, a tidy edifice that looked to be of about twelve rooms, not counting the half-sunken basement. The roses were still blooming, and they imparted a lovely fragrance to the sunny yard. I loosened Atlas's girth and took off his bridle—even twenty minutes at grass would do him some good—and rapped on the front door.

"Un moment, s'il vous plaît! Un moment!" The voice was French and female and rang with the light, crisp precision of a Parisian accent.

When the dark-haired housekeeper opened the door—no mobcap and no smile either—I announced myself in French.

"Lord Julian Caldicott, at your service. My apologies for calling at such an early hour, but I come on a matter of some urgency. Is Monsieur Jean Traffault in?"

Bill collectors did not, in the typical case, knock on front doors, and my French was that of a native speaker. Those two facts probably accounted for the lady stepping back and gesturing me into a spotless foyer.

"Monsieur Jean is in," she said in her native tongue, "but the light today demands painting. He won't be on hand for long. He'll be off along the river. Sunshine and water, flowers, big white sky. He cannot resist these. Have you a card?"

I passed over one somewhat the worse for my travels.

"Come to the parlor, please, my lord. I will make you some tea, and if your horse eats my flowers, I will put him in the stewpot."

"Atlas will be more than content to trim your grass."

She showed me to a room filled with morning light, so I kept my tinted spectacles upon my nose. The décor was reminiscent of the farmhouses of Provence, with sturdy furniture, a sizable hearth, and a gleaming polished oak mantel. The emphasis was on comfort and durability rather than fussy excesses of style.

The space appealed to me far more than the elegant parlors of

Caldicott Hall. This sitting room was a useful part of a home rather than a testament to titled ostentation. When the housekeeper brought me a tray—hot tea, freshly baked croissants with jam and clotted cream—I expressed enthusiastic appreciation and fell to.

After twenty minutes had gone by, and my host was still not in evidence, I abandoned my third cup of tea and went scouting.

Across the entry hallway was a combination office and family parlor. The desk near the mullioned window was modest in size, tidily organized, and had been recently dusted. The sofa looked comfortable if a bit faded—the fate of most furniture in sunny rooms—and the carpet similarly showed signs of wear.

Nothing about the room suggested recent occupation, but a glance at the desk blotter gave me encouragement. Amid flower doodles and fanciful Latin calligraphy, somebody had started a sketch of Clarissa Valmond.

"You passed this way," I said, "and I am on your trail."

I abandoned the front rooms and worked my way back toward the inevitable kitchen stairs. I was halfway down to the lower reaches when through the window on the landing, Atlas alerted me to activity in the yard. He'd grazed around to the side of the house, munching industriously on the lush grass, but he ceased his depredations to lift his head and prick his ears in the direction of the back garden.

"No, you don't," I muttered, bolting down the steps, through a tidy, spacious kitchen, and into an equally tidy garden. A man was easing through the back gate, not tall enough to be Reardon, but a knapsack such as Reardon favored hanging off one shoulder.

"Monsieur Traffault, I will give chase if necessary."

He paused, turned toward me, and let the gate swing closed behind him. "My lord, good morning."

"Good day to you as well." I'd hailed him in French. He had

spoken English to me in return, so I kept to that language. I wasn't here to antagonize him, and I could state my business as easily in English as French. "Might you spare me a moment before you go off on your day's rambles?"

Before he scarpered on me.

"A moment, yes, of course." He approached me, wreathed in geniality, so I prepared to reciprocate with my cheery Englishman impersonation.

"Good sketching hereabouts, I presume?"

"There is always good sketching, my lord. One must have the eyes to see it." Traffault was spare and jaunty. He wore a battered hat at a rakish angle, and his angular countenance beamed universal benevolence. He would have been a ray of sunshine at Valmond House, and his praise would have drawn a younger Reardon like a lodestone.

"Was it you who taught Lord Reardon to find his subjects in nature?"

"His lordship finds peace in nature." Traffault's English was charmingly accented, but precise and correct. "His art wanders many landscapes, while his feet take him to fresh air and pleasant breezes. I am sorry to say you have just missed him. He caught a ride to Portsmouth with my brother not an hour ago."

Bloody hell. Bloody bedamned hell. "Where is he bound?"

"America. He has wonderful eyes to see, but his ear for French is another matter, and English is not widely spoken in the realms he'd find most interesting on the Continent. I am sorry, my lord. He was determined to go, and Lord Reardon cannot be reasoned with when he makes up his mind."

Before I galloped for Portsmouth, I wanted the answer to at least one question. "Lord Reardon left without any word to his sister, who has gone to the trouble to organize a London exhibition that opens in a week's time. He made it appear as if he'd had a fatal accident, abandoned his dog, and otherwise behaved in a troubling fashion. If he wanted to go to America, why not simply bid the family farewell and go? Why this drama?"

Traffault ambled over to a round wrought-iron table in the shade of a cherry tree heavy with ripening fruit. He slung his knapsack into a chair and gestured for me to have a seat. Breakfast dishes still littered the table, coffee cups, a basket of croissants with evidence of the trimmings the housekeeper had offered me—empty jampot, half-empty cream boat. An empty honeypot also graced the table, one subject to the inspection of an enterprising fly.

A pair of robins flitted about in the cherry tree, doubtless making designs on the crumbs littering the flagstones.

Every particle of my being bellowed at me to hurry, to leap onto my charger and catch Reardon before he took ship. Reason, however, argued that Atlas had both speed and stamina, and two more minutes wasn't likely to make all the difference.

"Lord Reardon is a good fellow," Traffault said, taking a seat opposite me, "a talented fellow, but an unhappy fellow."

"One has heard this. No brothers, no friends, no funds for the usual social diversions enjoyed by young male aristos. A sister with managing tendencies, a distracted father, an ailing mother—a dying mother who will grieve sorely over her son's abandonment."

Traffault winced. "I did not know the countess was truly ill."

"Dying, apparently, and Reardon might be unhappy, but to turn his back on his own mother, he must be miserable indeed. He might also be abandoning the mother of his firstborn child—a child who will be illegitimate—to say nothing of the debts Reardon is leaving his family to resolve."

"You do not come to collect these debts, my lord?"

"I come because his sister fears him dead, and I'd like to correct her misapprehension."

Traffault picked up a mug that held a few swallows of cold coffee, swished the contents about, then set the drink down untasted.

"Then you must retrieve my young friend from his travels. I did not know of these circumstances you describe, not the countess's illness, not the baby. The debts are old news. Reardon said only that he's bored, frustrated, and wasting what few years of freedom he has left. Young men are barely rational on a good day, though, I myself was the soul of good sense at his age."

A disarming smile accompanied that gentle self-derision.

"You abandoned your country and your family to take up a life among the heathen English. You'd have been about Reardon's age at the time?"

"*Oui*, and as it turned out, I made the right decision. I would have been, as the English say, cannon fodder for *l'empereur* had I survived the Terror. I would do the same thing again, given the chance. Do not let me keep you, my lord. Portsmouth is forty miles of hard riding, and the day promises to be hot."

I rose—the day was already hot—and offered my hand. "My thanks for your honesty, and I hope you will consider attending the exhibition. The family has no choice but to go forward with it, though without the artist on hand, success is unlikely."

He shook briefly and offered a bow as well. "Safe travels, my lord, and perhaps we will meet again under happier circumstances, though I cannot manage a journey to London by next week. I will see you off."

I whistled for Atlas, who ambled up to the low wall running along the south side of the garden. He chewed a mouthful of long grass and gave me the sort of look that suggested I was in his bad books for interrupting a fine meal.

"Take some sustenance," Traffault said, folding a pair of croissants into a linen napkin. "Not much, but Celeste's offerings are the best you will sample in England. I will see you to your horse."

I wanted to grab my gracious host—who'd been slinking through the gate five minutes previously—and shake him for form's sake.

Something about the whole encounter was off. Why leave me to feast in solitude in the front parlor for twenty minutes? To give Reardon a head start, of course. Why had Traffault attempted to hare off twenty minutes after my arrival? Why not decamp the instant Celeste warned him of my presence?

Why *two* coffee cups on the table? Perhaps Celeste had been enjoying the morning air with Traffault before my arrival, but Celeste struck me as the sort who'd take dirty dishes into the house with her, not leave them to tempt the birds and bugs.

I untied Atlas's bridle from the saddlebag fastenings, while my mind continued to gnaw on fare that was going down uncomfortably.

"Best of luck, my lord," Traffault said, switching back to French. "Avoid the Black Swan if you're changing horses. They overcharge, and their livestock is not always sound. Two miles on, The Happy Hare is a better choice."

Le Lièvre Heureux. Why speak French to me now?

Why two coffee cups on the table?

I finished buckling Atlas's bridle, took up his girth, and tucked the croissants into a saddlebag. The same mental chorus that had been roaring at me to jump in the saddle was now urging caution.

"I greeted you in French."

"Good French. Excellent French," he said, twinkling jovially. "A story there, I suspect."

"A French grandmother who would only allow émigrés to staff my father's nursery. You declined to reply in French, and you reminded me that Reardon has a poor grasp of that language."

The warmth in Traffault's blue eyes acquired a shade of calculation. "I am in England, I speak English. Most people do not hold my nationality against me, but one does not antagonize..."

I waited for him to realize the futility of that argument. "When we got out of earshot of the house, you switched immediately to French. Reardon puts honey in his coffee if no sugar is available. It's his sweet tooth that emptied that honeypot and consumed all the jam. You realized you'd picked up his cup rather than your own and set it down untasted."

I loosened the girth I'd just taken up. "I have no authority to detain Lord Reardon, but I refuse to leave without getting some answers from him." I tied up Atlas's reins and signaled that he could go back to trimming the grass. Grazing in his bridle was bad form. Letting lush grass go to waste was a mortal sin.

"My young guest is determined to leave, my lord," Traffault said. "Desperate to leave. I tell him that Lady Clarissa will not content herself with that bit of foolishness up in Surrey. He has no head for guile, I tell you, no head for anything but art."

"Art, romping, and self-preservation. I will await Reardon in the garden, if you'd please let him know he has a caller."

"He knows," Traffault said, stalking back through the gate. "I will send him to you. He knows, and he refuses to return to Valmond House. When you arrived, I made one last attempt to reason with him, but I am done trying to change his mind." My host stomped away into the house, muttering about "these ridiculous English," and "Why did nobody listen?" and "A perfectly lovely day must be wasted." Et cetera and so forth.

I took a seat in the shade and pondered a stubborn question: What force had compelled Reardon to surrender every pretense of honor for the sake of this disgraceful, disorderly retreat? He was betraying his mother, his sister, his sweetheart, and his standing as a gentleman, and yet, he was apparently determined on this badly bungled exit.

CHAPTER FOURTEEN

The Viscount Reardon who presented himself in Traffault's sunny garden bore little resemblance to the titled sprig I'd encountered at Valmond House. His lordship had learned some hard truths about fatigue, sadness, and perhaps even bitterness since he'd so eagerly shown me his work.

The evidence of maturation was mostly in his eyes, but also in his posture, which had lost the coltish energy of youth and gained something of a gentleman's self-possession.

Or perhaps something of a prisoner's dignity, about which I knew more than I should.

"I'm not going back," he said, settling into the chair Traffault had vacated. "I will fight you over that, my lord, and I am younger and fitter than you."

He lacked my reach, he'd had no older brothers to hone his reflexes or his strategy, and—may all the angels keep it so—he had no idea what wartime experiences could do to a man's capacity for ruthlessness.

"My fitness is improving," I said, taking one of the three remaining croissants before the birds became too bold. "A slow process, but haring all over the countryside tracking you down has been good exercise." Exhausting, but oddly restorative too.

He sat forward, put his head in his hands, and swept his fingers through hair that no longer bore any hint of fashionable styling. Then he straightened and attempted to glower at me.

"I'm pleased to have provided you some entertainment, my lord."

"Summer maneuvers are hardly entertainment. Have a croissant, or I'll finish them off."

A faint purring of thunder from the south disturbed the morning quiet. The Channel was prone to such grumblings, though Traffault's garden would doubtless be glad of some rain—as would I.

"I don't want another damned croissant, thank you just the same. Were you telling Jean the truth? Eunice is... expecting?"

If he was to ask me only one question, that was the one a gentleman should pose. "Eunice is very concerned for you, and she has reason to suspect she carries your child. Early days don't always tell the tale, but she hopes to marry you."

Reardon shoved out of the chair. "She was having you on, my lord. She never wants to see me again. She's getting back at me because..."

"Because you frolicked with Mrs. Probinger, and you took advantage of the trust both women showed you to sketch them in the altogether without their knowledge or permission."

He charged at me. The simple expedient of tangling my boot between his feet sent him stumbling against the table.

Truly, I owed my older brothers, and Harry in particular, for salient aspects of my education. "Bad form," I said, "to attempt to assault a seated man who has done nothing but recite a few facts. If you want the benefit of my opinions, I will happily provide those, too, and we can go best out of three falls."

I really should not have baited him, but he wasn't the victim here, and I was due some diversion for the past several days' charging about in the heat and dust. Though as to that, a tempting breeze stirred the boughs of the cherry tree and riffled Atlas's mane as he grazed along the garden wall.

"You've violated my privacy if you've seen those sketches, my lord," Reardon said, whipping his hair out of his eyes. "*Bad form.*"

"And you violated Mrs. Probinger's privacy *and her trust* by creating those drawings." I took another bite of Celeste's excellent baking, while Reardon had the grace to look nonplussed. "If you are furious at my presumption, my lord, she's angrier still—and with much better cause—at yours.

"Besides," I went on, "when a peer's only heir of the body disappears, with no clue as to reasons or plans, you should expect the missing man's effects will be thoroughly searched. Clarissa explained that you were supposed to go absent without leave, then turn up in London in time for the exhibition. A stunt to get tongues wagging. Harebrained, though tongues are indeed wagging, I'm sure."

I helped myself to the second croissant. Let the viscount sustain himself on pride and artistic ambitions.

"Aunt Enola promised me that a hint of intrigue would do more to advertise the exhibition than would a notice in the *Times.* Clarissa agreed, though by then, Clarissa was desperate. She would have paraded naked through Hyde Park to draw notice to my art."

He shifted his chair to avoid the rays of the sun as it climbed into the sky, then resumed his seat.

"All you want to do is paint," I suggested, "but the world intrudes on your desires." Paint and swive, apparently. "You hope to make art to your heart's content in America."

He shuddered. "Not America. They have wolves and bears and worse in America, though I asked Jean to tell you that. I'm for Rome. Two years should be enough to learn to paint frescoes. Nip over to Greece, maybe jaunt about in Albania for a time."

Byron had made such journeys into a romantic ideal. War had denied him the traditional grand Continental tour, so—Byron-fashion —he'd made other and more exotic plans.

"They have wolves and bears in Albania, too, Reardon, but the wolves and bears here at home sent you on this flight. Your mother's health is failing."

He took the last croissant as the stiffening breeze twirled little funnels of dust across the garden. "Mama's health has been failing since I was in leading strings. I saw her in the autumn at Lyme Regis or one of the spa towns. She's not young, Papa would exasperate anybody, and her illnesses are her way of going on."

"That's not what Dr. Heller says, and he's a competent physician."

This earned me a peevish look. "Heller never said anything to me, and I'm supposedly the man of the house when Papa's off dodging creditors or chasing butterflies."

Clarissa had doubtless been the man of the house since before her come out. "Your mother is dying. A young lady you walked out with could be carrying your child. Your sister is relying on you to host an exhibition that could be the salvation of your family's fortune, and *now* you decide to pike off to Rome?"

Another rumble of thunder punctuated my question, though I didn't hold out much hope of rain. The morning air was hot, but not with the oppressive, leaden quality that came on as evening approached.

Reardon had spilled crumbs onto his cravat. He brushed them away with a hand that shook slightly. "Mama isn't dying, Eunice wants no part of me—though she wouldn't mind becoming Lady Valloise—and Clarissa is equal to any challenge. I've just disappeared a little more thoroughly than Clarissa planned—or I had until *you* showed up."

"Shame upon me, but letting Clarissa fear you'd taken your own life shames you, and I wasn't about to let her suffer such uncertainty. Why did you send Touchstone home?"

Reardon crossed his legs at the knee, straightened an imaginary crease in his breeches, and fluffed his limp cravat again.

"Touch is too old for a sea journey. No longer the tireless hound of his youth. For every mile I hiked, he used to cover five. Lately, I've had to plan our routes so he has rest, water, and shade."

Credible, but a prevarication, and a theory had formed in the back of my mind as Reardon had been snorting and pawing his way through this discussion.

"How good are you?" I asked. "As a painter?"

"Competent. I've improved with time. I'm not in Traffault's league. Jean should be the president of the Royal Academy, but they aren't keen on Frenchmen at the moment."

That bit of modesty on Reardon's part encouraged me. "Do you know what the hardest part of war was for the average soldier?"

Reardon sent me a curious look as the wind further disordered his hair. "I imagine marching for days on bad rations held no appeal. Sweating and freezing mile after mile on the Spanish plain. Facing the French over fixed bayonets had to be a bit daunting."

I did not want to explain this to Reardon, though somebody had to, or he'd never win the war with his own insecurities.

"You are correct that those ordeals were challenging, but worse yet was the night before battle. The soldiers who were literate wrote letters home and tucked them into their effects. We knew to search for such letters if a fellow didn't survive and to send them on to his loved ones.

"The message was always the same: 'If you are reading this, I've died an honorable death. Please take comfort from that, and remember me fondly.' I wrote hundreds of those letters for men who could not wield a pen themselves. Then I'd cut off a lock of the fellow's hair to include with what might be his final words. A terrible ritual."

I could see Reardon seize on my recitation as inspiration for a painting. A young lady clutching a glossy curl, a single-page missive discarded in her lap.

"Why doesn't anybody speak of this?"

"Too painful, when we can instead speak of victories and adventures. The nights before battle were the worst. We had nothing to do but wait, worry, pray, and write those damned letters. Then we'd tend to our weapons and gear, as if a tidy uniform would make us harder to kill. Very few of us got drunk. We knew we'd need the oblivion if we survived the next day."

Reardon took to studying his boots. "An art exhibition is not a battle to the death."

My faith in his lordship was modestly vindicated. "If the exhibition is not well received, it's the death of your ambitions and the death of Clarissa's hopes. She is not well liked, Reardon, and she has missed the opportunity to make an advantageous match." She was also deuced pretty and damned determined, which had a lot to do with the not-well-liked part.

Some old honorable who'd already buried a wife or two might take a fancy to her, or she might charm a wealthy's cit's son into offering for her, but such terrain would be rough going, given the family's situation, particularly if Reardon scarpered.

And finding a safe harbor for Clarissa would do little to pump the bilges of the family's sinking financial ship.

"The exhibition will be well received." Reardon spoke as if reciting a family motto, not a dearly held conviction. "I'm good enough. Not brilliant, but I chose the subjects that would appeal to those who claim to have refined taste in art. The sort with something to prove and the money to prove it. The paintings will sell."

He probably believed that, and I hoped he was right. Nonetheless, Reardon had gone to neither university nor public school, and he was too young to have frolicked much in Mayfair's matchmaking waters.

A possibility other than success had doubtless occupied his imagination.

"In the alternative," I said, "your exhibition will be an opportunity for polite society to gloat without spending a shilling. They will come to see a portrait of a titled family in ruins, a likeness of an earl's daughter who disdained marriage when it was offered to her and who's on the shelf now.

"The same daughter," I went on, "who failed to bring a ducal spare up to scratch and couldn't win the time of day from the duke himself. As for the son, he's a courtesy lord who avoided military service—even in the militia—just so he, claiming to have weak lungs, could hike all over the shire for hours on end. This is a rendering of scandal many will be eager to see, and half the spectators will have lent your father or your mother money."

Reardon was back to glowering at me. "No, they will not. Papa and Mama are too proud to beg or borrow. If you believe nothing else, believe that."

"But you are not too proud to turn your back on your family in their darkest hour and make a run for the coast."

"Damned right, and that's all there is to say to it. I'm leaving for Rome next week, and I will not be in evidence at the London exhibition. I don't expect you to understand, so please just leave me in peace and..."

"And?"

"And tell Clarissa I'll write."

"She'll return your letters unopened."

This observation earned me a slight, crooked smile. "I know, and I will write them anyway, but I really must be about my life, my lord. You needn't attempt any further persuasion. My mind is made up."

That was my cue to rise and make a few doleful parting comments echoing Lady Ophelia on the subject of Young Men Today.

Though I myself was still a youngish man, and I had a few more questions for his lordship.

$\sim$

Torrential rain prevented my immediate return to Caldicott Hall, but then, I owed Atlas a day of rest. My own health benefited from a respite under Traffault's roof as well. He would not allow me to return to lodgings in Arundel, and he seemed to delight in conversing with another man in his native tongue.

Reardon eluded further questioning in the garden by stomping off into the house, repairing to his room, and shutting the door. He appeared for supper—any schoolboy would choose good food over a protracted sulk—and deigned to join Traffault and me on the front porch for a brandy.

I'd spent the day watching raindrops trickle down windowpanes while I pondered what I knew, what I suspected, and what questions continued to confound me.

By evening, the rain had moderated from a useless downpour to the soft patter that gave the ground a good, nourishing soak. By morning, the clouds would move on, and cooler temperatures would prevail. Good traveling weather when I, for once, wasn't ready to move on.

We took seats around a small wooden table beneath the dripping eaves, Celeste's singing from within the house serenading us as Traffault served the drinks. She'd chosen an old French lullaby about a fellow whose candle had gone out and who could barely see by the light of the moon.

Probably the first lullaby ever sung to me, though as a child I'd never really understood what all that searching about in the darkness with the neighbor lady had been in aid of.

"To peace," Traffault said, lifting his glass.

Reardon and I joined the toast. The brandy was exquisite—also probably illegal.

"My brother would adore a case of this," I said, savoring the nose. Ripe, sweet oranges, a hint of honey, sunshine on old oak, a note of caramel...

"A cousin in Bordeaux provides for my cellar," Traffault said. "Your brother must apply to Chateau Fournier and hope for a favorable reply, for which even a duke will have to be patient."

"I'll apply, and one day I might have the great satisfaction of gifting my brother with a superior vintage."

Reardon remained silent, but then, he was a fellow with much to contemplate. I would leave on the morrow and had reached the forlorn-hope stage of my attempts to return him to his family.

"What shall I tell Lady Clarissa?" I asked Reardon. "In my experience, family can forgive us much if they know why we make the choices we do." I had no idea why Harry had left camp on that fatal night, and the question plagued me without mercy.

"Tell her I want to paint."

"You've been painting," I retorted. "For years, you've done nothing but paint."

"Honing my skill," he muttered. "Creating inventory. If Clarissa can sell half what I left behind..." He tossed back his brandy—an offense against manners and good taste—and shoved to his feet. "I bid you good night. If I'm not up to see you off in the morning, my lord, safe journey, and thanks for your efforts."

He was hanging on to the plan to go to Rome by his fingernails. I delivered one last tromp on his knuckles.

"How can you afford this journey?" I asked, rising, because this was the loosest of the loose ends I'd spent the day pondering. "How could you afford a fresh horse every ten or twelve miles as you've journeyed all over the Home Counties? A sovereign for The King's Man when you'll need lodgings and lessons in Italy—lessons in Italian, if not painting. Passage to Rome isn't cheap, and yet, Valmond House is hoarding sugar, and Clarissa hasn't had a new bonnet in years. Even so, you can apparently afford to buy yourself a new wardrobe on the Continent."

The viscount stopped mid-retreat toward the door, as if I'd jabbed him between the shoulder blades with my bayonet.

"Everything is cheaper on the Continent," he said, turning slowly. "That's why all the remittance men racket about the Mediterranean. I'll manage, and in a couple of years, I will come back with skills nobody in England is teaching. I'll have money and commissions, and by then..."

"Your parents will be dead? Eunice will have been sent away in disgrace to live with an aunt in Derbyshire? Clarissa will marry some gouty old baron in need of a few extra sons? Your own child will be toddling about with a lifetime of whispers and disgrace awaiting him?"

An unkind thrust, but my words had Reardon clutching at a porch post and gazing out into the sodden night. "Eunice would have told me. You have to be making that bit up."

"Eunice only confided in me," I said, "because she needed for me to grasp the seriousness of her situation. You could marry her and take her to Rome with you, but instead, you leave her to face the consequences of your actions alone."

"Listen to him," Traffault said. "Money is important, but the respect of your children should matter more."

"My son can't respect me if I'm rotting with consumption in debtors' prison." A flash of lightning illuminated Reardon's expression of bleak certainty.

Reardon was not expressing a fanciful fear, but rather, a contemplated fate. Debtors' prison was so rife with disease that it amounted to a death sentence for many, and corruption ensured that few who went in ever found the means to earn their way out. The earl could not be jailed for debt, but Reardon, a commoner despite the courtesy title, could.

"You were unable to pay Huber the penny stakes racked up over chess games, but you parted with a sovereign to guarantee Touchstone's safe passage back to Valmond House." The hound had worried me, and the old dog's fate also apparently worried Reardon.

The viscount pressed his forehead against the porch post. "Just leave it, please."

Mrs. Probinger hadn't given him that sovereign. Eunice hadn't given it to him. He hadn't found it stashed under a rock either. I mentally retraced his rambles, from the Valmond House stable yard to the foot of the mill's lane...

"You met *Huber* on your rambles. Your plan was to meet Eunice, but Huber ambushed you first."

"Please stop," Reardon said, straightening. "Nothing can come of your speculations. The day has been long and—"

And finally the puzzle pieces were forming into a logical pattern. "Huber has threatened you with an action for debt collection if you don't quit the country, and he sweetened the pot by paying your travel expenses—or he dug you a bigger hole. Did you sign anything?"

Traffault swore softly in French.

Reardon stared at me, and I could not say whether I saw raindrops or tears on his cheeks. "My lord, you are guessing and I must ask you to stop."

"I am applying reason to facts. The Valmond family's problem is money. Therefore, anybody seeking to control you would do it through money. How much did Huber offer?"

Reardon returned to the table and tossed himself into a chair. Traffault poured him more brandy, though he merely stared at the glass. "This doesn't concern you."

I wanted to smack him, but he was just possibly trying to be honorable. Allowances must be made for young men in the throes of attempted heroics. Though why did nobody make allowances for my attempted heroics where Harry was concerned?

"Huber is a bitter man," I said, propping a hip on the damp porch railing. "The one bright light in his life is Eunice, who appears devoted to him."

"She loves her father, would do anything for him."

"She loves you," I said, though since when was I an expert on women's sentiments? "Huber told you she was only interested in your title, trying to trap you into marriage?"

"Or preparing to make a fool of me. Said I was reading too much into flirtation, and Eunice isn't old enough to marry without her father's permission anyway. She's friendly by nature, but the Huber family has learned never to trust a title in matters of the heart. She was having a lark with me, Huber said, though I don't think he grasped how passionate that larking had become. Huber made sense. When he's not grumbling, he can make a great deal of sense."

"He suggested you merely wait until she's of age?" Another two years, of course.

"More or less. Reminded me that she was his youngest, the best of the lot, and so forth, didn't know her own mind, and needed another couple of years to appreciate what I offered. Then he started talking about debts, implying threats, dangling solutions..."

The squire had doubtless segued smoothly from matrimony to money, though supposedly it was the nobs who took a mercenary view of marriage.

"You accepted a loan?"

Reardon nodded. "Fifty pounds, enough to get set up in Rome. Another fifty pounds. He loaned me the first fifty so I could buy the canvases and whatnot for the exhibition. Clarissa doesn't know that. She thinks canvases and gesso, frames and pigments can all be had for a song. If she knew what a decent set of brushes costs..."

"So you owe him a hundred pounds?" A modest country household could make that much cash last a year.

"It's worse than that. Huber will clear my debts in Town if I remain out of the country for one year. He'll consent to my marrying Eunice if I remain out of the country for two. I will still owe him the hundred pounds, though."

In two years, Huber would have no legal say in who his daughter married. "I thought Eunice didn't truly care for you?"

Reardon sat up a little straighter. "I'll be an earl someday. Huber won't mind having a daughter who's a countess."

Huber could have that pleasure within a fortnight, but he'd decided on another course. Why? Because he was a doting father who truly wanted his daughter's company for another two years? Because he realized that Reardon needed to get out from behind Clarissa's skirts and do some growing up?

I could not attribute such avuncular goodwill to the squire, try though I might. "Will your paintings earn enough to pay off Huber?" I asked.

Reardon merely stared at his brandy, but Traffault answered my question with a shrug. "Any painting earns more if the artist is on hand to flatter the patrons, to accept commissions, to heed suggestions for further works. Who knows what the public will think of the work of a ghost?"

"They will pay more," Reardon said fiercely.

"You are not Gainsborough or Reynolds," Traffault shot back. "I have told you this. You are nobody, another penniless aristo, and I am less than nobody. Yes, you have talent, but anybody with talent has enemies. They will flock to this exhibition and murmur against you, all the little minds from the big Academy. Damn you with faint praise, mutter about talent needing time to mature. You listen to your sister, your aunt, your stupid neighbor, but you do not listen to me."

"Reardon disdains to listen to the woman who may be carrying his child," I said. "Eunice personally implored me to find you, to ensure your safety."

The viscount took another sip of brandy. "When was this?"

"Two days after you turned up missing. She went to pains to talk to me privately, and why would she lie about facts that could see her ruined?"

"Because you will never make those supposed facts public."

Reardon's faith in my discretion was touching, also a bit alarming. "I am a ducal heir," I pointed out. "I could well end up residing for decades at Caldicott Hall. Every Sunday, Eunice will have to face me in the churchyard, knowing that I hold her confidences. She might suspect her father of scheming to get rid of you, though I doubt she'd admit those fears aloud."

"She loves the old boot. Sees the good in him, says he's terribly lonely, but that man... He can have me jailed, my lord. Don't think he won't."

"His daughter won't allow that."

Reardon shook his head. "Eunice won't know her father had anything to do with it. He'll simply round up my London creditors, whisper to them of passage booked for Italy, and turn them loose on me. To the rest of the world, Huber will be the kindly neighbor who tried to prevent my ruin and who hopes I can muddle on somehow."

I listened to that credible prognostication, and at the same time, I recalled Huber threatening Arthur with considerable scandal if Reardon wasn't found.

"Does Huber know how you were getting to Rome?" I asked. "From which port you meant to sail?"

"Dover is fashionable," Reardon said. "London closer. I wanted to see Jean before I left my homeland, though. Huber told me I needed to leave evidence of my possible death—no notes, no directions to loved ones, just enough to raise suspicions, but nothing conclusive—and simply disappear."

"You are not going to Rome," I said. "Not just yet."

"Why not?"

"*Because Huber has changed his mind.* He wanted to be rid of you, but Eunice apparently put her father wise to a few facts. If she learns of his scheme to hound you out of the country, he will lose the regard of the one person who seems to matter to him. Huber will become the butt of such scandal that he won't be able to show his face in public, much less hold a magistrate's duties again. I would go so far as to hazard that Huber will forgive you those hundred pounds if you just come home."

Reardon finished his drink. "It won't be you tossed into prison if you're wrong, my lord."

"I have been in the worst prison imaginable, you ignorant puppy. I survived to rejoin my regiment and do my bit at Waterloo." Traffault's brows shot up, and I moderated my tone. "It won't be my child stigmatized with illegitimacy and dependent on Huber's indifferent charity. It won't be my first born who could by rights have someday been an earl or a lady, but for my pigheadedness."

Reardon peered at me owlishly, as if I'd suggested that a proper artist would paint the Yorkshire hills pink and the sheep orange.

"I saw a way to take my debts out of the family equation," he said, "to leave Clarissa with an inventory to sell, to start over without a woman I care for leading me a dance before the whole shire. Forgive me for following my conscience."

Such righteousness and such youth. I would have howled with laughter at Reardon's self-serving summary of events, except the same hubris had sent me trailing after Harry into the night. I'd honestly believed that I alone could keep Harry safe. I alone had the wit to outfox a whole French garrison.

So noble of me. So arrogant and so bloody stupid.

Though I had, let it be said, *meant well*. "You'll leave with me in the morning?" I asked.

"Go with him," Traffault said. "You shall explain to your sister and your Eunice that you needed to pay your respects to me and gather some courage. A debut exhibition would try the nerves of any artist. I cannot return to France. I'm wanted there for crimes I did not commit. Go home while you still have a home to go to, *mon ami*. If you do not, I fear for your welcome at Celeste's table."

Traffault rose, bowed to me, and slipped into the house.

"He means that," Reardon said, jamming the cork back into the bottle. "Celeste's table is his table. Jean cannot be reasonable once he makes up his mind, and Celeste... Celeste's stubbornness could stop a moving mountain."

I collected my drink. "How fortunate that you are fashioned of more reasonable cloth. I'll want more of Celeste's good cooking before I leave in the morning, but I won't tarry if you're inclined to dither."

I saluted him with my drink and went for a ramble in the damp and darkness. Reardon had much to ponder and half a bottle of excellent spirits for a digestif.

I wanted to say good night to my horse and review the day's events in private. The viscount's revelations had answered many questions, but I still had a few more queries to put to the good Squire Huber.

And if he tried to lie again, I had the means to make him regret any dissembling—any *further* dissembling.

CHAPTER FIFTEEN

Celeste set a typical English table for breakfast—ham, eggs, toast—as well as her signature croissants with all the trimmings. I had awoken to the wonderful aroma of her baking and thanked heaven for such a lovely start to my morning.

Traffault joined me for the first meal of the day just as the sun topped the horizon.

"I heard the viscount all night," he said. "The boy stirred about, doubtless trying to sketch away his troubles. Have you seen his recent paintings?"

"I have." I buttered a croissant and dabbed some jam on it. "His technique is flawless, and he chose subjects that will appeal to a London audience."

"He took no chances?"

I thought back over Reardon's battle scenes. "He took chances. Nothing politically radical, but no clichés either."

"A prudent course. If the viscount were some squire's son, he'd have an easier time of it. Your Polite Society judges their own most harshly."

Celeste had brought in a fresh pot, and as she poured Traffault a second cup, she caught his eye. They exchanged a look full of regrets, acceptance, and deep affection. She was many years his junior, but their mutual regard was substantial and sincere.

"The boy is awake," she said. "Let him eat in peace, you two. He barely picked at his supper last night."

"Of course, *mon ange*," Traffault said. "One does not bring discord to the table."

She scoffed as only a Frenchwoman could scoff. "Lord Julian, you will take good care of young Reardon?"

"I will do my best. Some matters he must put right himself."

"*Oui.* You cannot fight his battles for him." With another significant look at Traffault, she left the room. Entire lectures were wrapped up in her glances, and articulate replies were respectfully conveyed in his.

"Could Celeste return to France if she pleased to?" I asked.

"She could, but she says her home is here now."

"If you could go back...?" I should not have asked, but some part of me wanted to return to France, to the scene of my ruin and Harry's death. The scene of questions without answers.

"Celeste is my home. My family in France is for the most part dead, and those who are left recall me as an arrogant hothead with a big mouth. The winds of misfortune blew at gale force in France for years, and worse, they blew in all directions. Royalists, moderates, republicans, radicals... We slaughtered each other, year after year, until even a despot began to look preferable to the chaos. My best memories are here. My house is here, my Celeste is here. I have found peace in England. I hope the same can soon be said of you." He took a sip of rich black coffee. "The prison you mentioned—a French prison, *non*?"

"A fortified chateau serving as a mountain garrison. I was held captive for a time."

"Aren't we all held captive at some point in this life?"

As Traffault offered that bit of philosophy, Reardon joined us.

The viscount was freshly scrubbed and combed, if a bit pale. He took the plate from the setting at Traffault's right hand.

"Good morning, all. Jean, if you'll loan me a horse, I'll pick up a hired hack in Arundel. His lordship and I have many miles to cover today."

Thank the merciful powers.

"You are going home?" Traffault asked in the same tone he might have asked for the salt cellar or jampot.

Reardon busied himself at the sideboard. "I must at least speak with Eunice. I promised Huber I'd not explain my plans to her in any detail, but Huber and I might not have been in possession of all the relevant facts when we struck our bargain."

I finished the last of my eggs. "Keep those plans to yourself—those former plans—when you speak to her. Do as Traffault suggests, claim you needed time to gather your wits. An artistic temperament benefits from quiet reflection, and you did leave her with some general reassurances."

Reardon set down a heaping plate and grimaced. "Do you make a habit of prying confidences from the unsuspecting?"

"I make a habit of dealing in truth whenever possible."

Traffault passed Reardon the coffeepot and the honey. "Squabbling will help pass the time on your journey. No need to exercise manners on my behalf. You will give my regards to Lady Clarissa?"

The amount of honey Reardon drizzled into his coffee was disgusting. "If she's speaking to me. Clarissa won't buy that business about me needing a few days to myself."

"She will." I'd parsed a few questions in the night, too, finally, so I gave Reardon the benefit of my thinking. "You hiked to the scenic overlook at The King's Man, took in the view, then simply turned around and walked back the way you'd come. Touchstone was notably incompetent in the hunt field, according to what you've told the duke. The hound could trail your scent, but not your direction. The confusion thereafter was mine. On the strength of an old boot I noticed on the riverbank, I feared you might have come to a bad end."

Traffault buttered himself a croissant. "You wanted your family to think you dead? For shame, young man."

"I wanted to satisfy Huber's requirement that I create ambiguous circumstances. Failure to do so would have broken our bargain. Any coaching inn has a store of forgotten or misdirected luggage. Heaving a boot over the precipice was the work of a moment."

"But what to do with Touchstone?" I murmured. "You love that dog."

"He was the companion of my youth. Told him all my troubles, which were legion, and shared with him all my adventures, which were largely imaginary. Somewhere along the way, he grew old, though. When I set out on my rambles last week, I had no idea Huber would... confront me."

"Ambush you. And you might well have that scheming dragon for a father-in-law."

Reardon stirred the sludge that filled his cup. "If my discussion with Eunice goes well, Huber and I must negotiate the terms of the wedding settlements. I don't relish that thought."

"Neither does Huber," I pointed out. "You can put him in Eunice's bad books."

"He can put me in Eunice's bad books."

Traffault saluted with his mug. "A reason for everybody to behave civilly. The English pride themselves on civility, I'm told."

"We do," I said. "If we can't pride ourselves on common sense, civility will have to do." Traffault had come to a reasonable conclusion: Huber and Reardon, out of mutual unwillingness to court Eunice's disfavor, ought to strike adequate terms in their settlement negotiations.

Something Mrs. Probinger had mentioned, though, sent unease prickling across my nape. That and the wonderful domesticity Traffault and Celeste enjoyed.

"Finish up, Reardon," I said, downing the last of my tea. "You are right that we have hard riding ahead of us."

He took another leisurely sip of coffee. "We're in a hurry now?

The exhibition is still days away. We could, in fact, go straight to London, and—"

"We cannot go straight to London. I've been wrong about this whole situation, and if you don't get your lordly arse into the saddle within a quarter hour, Eunice's bad books will be just the start of your troubles."

Reardon set down his cup. "What on earth are you going on about?"

I smacked him on the back of the head. "Your sister. This whole scheme hasn't been about you, but rather, about Lady Clarissa."

I bolted from the breakfast parlor, sending up a prayer for her ladyship's wellbeing and Lord Reardon's ability to ride like hell.

~

"You treat this horse," I panted, "as if he's just brought news of Wellington's victory at Waterloo. You walk him out—in shade—until he's cool. You rinse him off with tepid water until the water runs clear, rub him down until his coat shines. A mash with applesauce and half a handful of salt. Tepid water on his back, tepid water in his bucket. Don't let him drink from the creek until he's cool. Do you understand me?"

While I delivered this exhortation, Atlas stood at the Valmond House front steps, his coat a mural of dust and sweat, sides heaving. My boy had come through for me, pounding along for mile after mile. We'd lost Reardon at the last change, while Atlas had hit his stride two miles from Arundel and never relented.

"This horse," I went on, "means the world to me, and he has saved the honor of the House of Valloise. If he colics..."

The groom, who might well have served his apprenticeship under Xenophon, took the reins over Atlas's head. "He'll not colic on my watch, my lord. I've worked with post ponies, and I'll cool him out proper. Ye could stand to use some of that tepid water yourself."

I needed a gallon of Mrs. Felders's meadow tea, a bath, and two days of uninterrupted sleep, but first I needed to speak with Clarissa.

"Lord Reardon is perhaps two hours behind me, unless he decides to break his journey. He's on a hired hack. You can spread the word of his homecoming to the staff."

The wizened old face split into a grin. "Ye found our prodigal! Somebody should send word to Caldicott Hall, my lord. The hound will want to know."

"Good thought, and let the duke know too." The sun had set—finally—and I jogged through lengthening shadows to Valmond House's front door. Rather than knock, I admitted myself.

"Greetings to the house!" I bellowed. "Lady Clarissa! Blaylock! Anybody!"

Blaylock hustled down the main staircase. "My lord, what's amiss? Lady Clarissa is at supper, and she has guests."

"I'll just bet she does." I trotted up the steps, every joint protesting the exertion. I was parched, my eyes had passed from stinging to throbbing miles ago, and I'd sustained myself on what fare Celeste had stashed in my saddlebags.

I was a mess, about which I did not care. I burst into the formal dining room and found not only Squire Huber, but also Lady Ophelia, Hyperia, and Arthur.

"Oh, lovely," Lady Ophelia said. "Julian has arrived, a bit late and the worse for travel, but now the numbers match. Perhaps you ought to freshen up a bit before joining us, my lord?" Her tone was cheerful, while Hyperia looked relieved.

Before I could reply, Huber was on his feet. "Young man, how dare you present yourself in all your dirt? You disrespect our hostess with this display." Even as Huber fired that broadside, his gaze held worry.

Had I found Reardon in time? How much did I know?

"I apologize for a lack of formal attire," I said, closing the door behind me, "but I assume Lady Clarissa would rather have news of her brother as soon as may be. Lord Reardon is well, and he's on his way home. He should be here before moonrise. He and Miss Eunice Huber have unfinished business."

Huber sank back into his seat. "You found him?" Was that hope or dread in his voice?

"I found him, and I came to an understanding with his lordship about various financial matters. If the ladies will excuse us, I'd like to speak to the squire and His Grace on the terrace."

Hyperia rose, a glass of water in her hand. "You will drink this first, my lord, and when the kitchen sends a tray to the terrace, you will do it justice." She pressed the glass into my hand and leaned close enough to murmur in my ear. "You cut it close, Jules, but not too close."

Good God, how I adored Hyperia West. I longed to wrap my arms around her and simply hold her. She'd been fighting the rearguard action and without anybody having to give an order.

"A tray will be appreciated." I knew better than to gulp the water, but I'd never tasted anything so ambrosial. "To the terrace, gentlemen, and yes, Huber, that is an order, so march. Ladies, the gents will join you shortly in the parlor for tea."

Arthur looked amused and came along like the good, quiet duke he was, and also like a brother prepared to defend my flank if need be.

"What the hell are you about?" Huber began before we were even out of the house. "Charging in with no manners whatsoever? You stink, my lord. You are nobody to be giving orders, and you had better have a good explanation for your very eccentric behavior."

I was no longer the small boy who feared Squire Huber would send me to the assizes for scrumping a few apples from my neighbor's orchard.

"Sorry to disappoint you," I said, sailing out onto the shadowed terrace. "The only explanation I can find for the past week's nonsense is a lonely old man's bitter determination to make the world repay him for a life that's held remarkably few disappointments."

"I will not be insulted by the likes of you," Huber retorted. "A traitor to the crown, if the talk is to be believed. A poor soldier who got himself captured by the enemy and betrayed his rank and possibly his own brother."

Old business. Old, boring business. I crossed my arms and leaned against a cool marble pillar. "Do go on."

"I won't call you out," Huber said, "lest your dear mother suffer another bereavement. So you found Lord Reardon. Good and well. He apparently chose to be found. A number of impatient creditors will want to know his specific whereabouts."

"My lord," Arthur drawled, "don't neglect your water."

I took another few sips of heaven, though I ought to have dashed my drink in Huber's face. "You all but blackmailed Reardon into leaving. Told him you would not approve a match with Eunice, that Eunice was simply toying with him. You further got him in debt to you and threatened to set the blacklegs on him if he remained in England."

I pushed away from the pillar and strode a slow circle around Huber. "You wielded the stick of financial disgrace and romantic failure with one hand. With the other, you dangled a few carrots—a fresh start in Rome, homecoming in a mere two years, an implication that Eunice wouldn't be permitted to marry anybody else in those two years. Relief from personal debts if the two years were served without mentioning anything of your schemes to Eunice."

Arthur propped a hip on the balustrade, arms crossed.

"The viscount is a spendthrift," Huber snapped. "Not fit for marriage. He thought to paint his family into solvency, and his sister had to goad him into it. I should not be blamed for trying to protect my daughter from developing expectations that could only end in heartache."

"But then your daughter informed you that she'd developed more than expectations." I faced him, and though I was exhausted and famished, if Arthur hadn't been present, I might well have found the energy to pummel the old windbag. "And you had to modify your schemes."

"Eunice is blameless, and you had best not imply otherwise."

"Eunice, like her father, is determined. She knows who and what she wants, and she will have him. You, on the other hand, will not have Lady Clarissa for your wife."

"Ah." Arthur put a world of comprehension into a single syllable.

Huber tried for more bluster. "What has Lady Clarissa to do with her rackety brother disappearing just when she most needs him?"

"She was relying on him to disappear—temporarily—and you turned her scheme on its head. His temporary absence became a desertion, leaving the lady in a panic, without means, and without allies. Then Mrs. Aimes quit the regiment, meaning not even a chaperone stood between Lady Clarissa and scandal. Would you whisper a promise in Lady Clarissa's ear to pay off Reardon's creditors? Offer to give him some funds for a fresh start in Rome? Make one loan do the work of several?"

Arthur had risen to stand beside me. He said nothing, but he was the duke and the Lord Lieutenant. He needn't utter a word.

"You saw to it that Clarissa was cut adrift on a sea of looming scandal," I went on, "without even an escort for Sunday services. By the end of tonight's meal, you would have informed her—reluctantly, of course—that Reardon had skipped off to the Continent to avoid debtors' prison. In a touching display of gallantry, you would atone for your failure to talk Reardon out of bolting by offering Lady Clarissa the refuge of a mutually respectful marriage."

Huber limped off to prop his bulk against the balustrade. "Are you quite finished?"

"No. How many of your old military friends would you recruit to attend Reardon's showing, provided Lady Clarissa agreed to make you the happiest of schemers?"

He scooched around like a broody hen on her nesting box. "I might have sent a few letters. Unlike some, I support my neighbors in their difficulties."

Arthur took up lounging on the balustrade too, close enough that he could apprehend Huber if the squire took a notion to sprint for the stable.

"You support your neighbors," I replied, "by forcing them to choose between disaster and domestic misery. Before you leave tonight, you will accept my note of hand for the sum of one hundred pounds, and you will return to me first thing tomorrow Lord Reardon's vowels, legibly signed by you and marked 'paid in full.'"

Huber looked me up and down. "A young man toward whom I was generously supportive, one who presumed on my daughter's trust and who will one day become a member of the peerage, now has all your sympathy and support?"

"My sympathy is for Lady Clarissa and for Eunice. Reardon might well become your son-in-law, so I'd advise a negotiated cease-fire. Then too, just as Clarissa has been managing the family's situation as best she can, Reardon has come of age without a commanding officer to show him how to go on. You might have fulfilled that role."

Huber's sigh should have rattled the shutters. "I tried to, you prosy, meddling, pimple on the arse of polite society. What do you think all that bad chess was about? Reardon is too much like the earl. He's either making sheep's eyes at Eunice, or he's maundering on about light and perspective and symbolism, for God's sake. What sort of guidance can be offered to a fellow whose highest aspiration is to find the perfect metaphor for justice?"

True bewilderment colored Huber's question.

"And you used to be just like him," I said, joining the other two lounging against the balustrade. "How the mighty are fallen."

The silence that formed was almost companionable. Huber tippled from his flask. Arthur watched as the stars emerged against the deepening darkness.

"I suppose you'll want to see me charged with blackmail?" Huber groused.

Arthur rose and brushed at his trousers. "I want to, of course. You all but entrapped Lord Reardon, then failed to assist in efforts to find him. You lied, schemed, and connived against an innocent young woman. Had Eunice not intervened, Reardon might even now be sailing off to distant ports, and your grandson—a potential earl—would be born into scandal instead. You should be bound over for the assizes and tried for multiple felonies."

His Grace shot his cuffs and scanned the night sky. "Lucky for you, I am notoriously lenient regarding judicial matters. I see no reason to turn up vindictive just because you are the offending party."

Arthur sauntered into the house, then turned in the doorway. "Don't leave me alone with the ladies for too long, Huber, or I might revisit my decision. Julian, good work. My thanks. See you at the Hall."

"Good God, he puts me in mind of your father," Huber said, taking another pull on the flask. "Such condescension, and we're supposed to admire him for it."

Huber would soon be attending a very public London wedding, else I would have fed him to the roses, face first.

"Do not insult my brother. He could have made you a laughing-stock, or seen you prosecuted for your stupid schemes. Instead, you get the benefit of the very restraint and moderation you've so bitterly criticized him for."

Huber jammed the cork into the top of his flask. "I don't like him. Don't care for the company he keeps, though I'll not say more on that matter. I respect the consideration Waltham has just shown an elder, though, and that will have to suffice."

I was exhausted, hungry, thirsty, and I reeked of hours on the road. On some other day, I could follow my brother's example of noble forgiveness. Tonight, I had had enough.

"Say one more word against His Grace—ever—to the neighbors, to your old military chums, to the fencepost at the foot of the drive, and I will explain to Eunice your role in Reardon's disappearance. The viscount won't tell her. Waltham will never say a word. I, on the other hand, am a traitor and a bad soldier and a pimple on the arse of polite society. If you want to see the love die in your daughter's eyes, merely give me reason to suspect that you've disparaged Waltham in any regard. I am not threatening you, Huber. I am reciting a solemn vow."

Huber let me have the last word.

Prudent of him.

I remained alone on the darkened terrace, with Arthur's parting resounding in my heart and Harry's ghost, for once, silent.

Julian, good work. My thanks.

~

"Wake up." A gentle hand shook my shoulder. "Jules, I've brought food. Wake up."

A whiff of honeysuckle came to me. "Hyperia." I swam up from dreamless depths and opened my aching eyes, grateful for the darkness of Valmond House's back terrace.

"Of course it's me." She pulled two chairs up and used the balustrade as a table. "Can you rise?"

Upon Huber's departure, I'd slid to the flagstones, my back to the porch railing, and promptly surrendered to the arms of Morpheus.

"You want me to stand?" For her, I would make the effort, but my dignity would suffer.

"On second thought, no. I'll join you." Before I could protest, Hyperia was sitting cross-legged beside me, the skirts of her evening dress pooled around her, her shawl a pale patch against the night. "Lovely how the stones hold the sun's heat. Did you finish the water?"

I spied an empty glass on an unused chair. "Yes."

"Good, then you can have more. I left Lady Ophelia to manage Huber." She passed me another cool, sweating glass of water, and I spied yet a third on the tray.

"I wanted to hurt him, Perry. Badly wanted to hurt him."

She handed me a sandwich. "Beef and cheddar, slightly melted. Mrs. Felders says you used to favor them as a boy."

"God bless Mrs. Felders."

"So why is Huber still walking more or less upright? He threatened your only surviving brother, dealt unfairly with Reardon, and had dishonorable designs on Lady Clarissa."

"Care for a bite?" I held out the sandwich to her, and she took a nibble.

"Scrumptious. Answer the question."

"Huber was spared a trouncing because he failed," I said slowly. "Then too, had he not behaved so badly, Arthur would never have confided in me regarding certain burdens he's been carrying. I would not have apprised Arthur of some details bearing on my own situation. I would never have pushed myself to feats of stamina for which I will pay, but that also fortified me. My eyes aren't what they used to be, but my wind is coming back." Was that a metaphor? "I don't understand the whole of what's happened in the past week, Perry, but Huber's failure was my success."

Julian, good work. The most wonderful benediction I'd ever heard.

We were sitting side by side, backs to the railing, the tray on one of the chairs. I sipped my water and demolished Mrs. Felders's fare, while off to the east, the horizon acquired a glow.

"Huber has been circling Valmond House for some time." Hyperia scooted closer and took a sip of my water. "I had a word with Mrs. Aimes before she blew retreat to London. Huber called here regularly. His visits consisted of protracted laments about the increasing cost of everything. Then he'd aim disparaging remarks at the duke and drop roguish hints about the mystifying stupidity of London bachelors for allowing Lady Clarissa to elude matrimony for so long."

"While he patted her knee and gazed upon her with adoring speculation. Clarissa doubtless saw no harm in humoring him—she's good at humoring clueless men—particularly when nobody else was on hand to flatter her. He was acting neighborly, he's some sort of distant family, and he and Reardon might have even talked art from time to time."

Had I not located Reardon, Huber's scheme would have succeeded—he would have backed Clarissa into that tight of a corner —particularly if he'd taken measures to ensure the London exhibition was poorly received.

Hyperia yawned. "Mrs. Aimes kept her suspicions to herself because Huber might have become Clarissa's last resort."

"Clarissa has weathered many battles. Surrender can loom like a solution after a few too many forced marches."

Harry had surrendered willingly, at least to appearances. Maybe he'd been tired of the fight. I was certainly tired of fighting his memory. My sainted brother had been something of a cad toward Clarissa, not because he'd paid her to be his escort, but because he'd lied to me about the nature of the relationship.

"Stop thinking matters to death, Jules. Drink some more water and promise me you'll keep a carafe by your bed tonight."

I could not envision rising, much less remaining awake long enough to make the journey to Caldicott Hall. "I am about to fall asleep again, Perry. Beg pardon in advance."

She passed me the third glass. "Get comfortable, then." She patted her thigh, an invitation. "Lady Ophelia will keep everybody chatting amiably over the teapot for another hour or so. You might as well nap."

I downed about half the contents, shifted to my side, and pillowed my head against Hyperia's muscular thigh. She draped her shawl over me, and I fell asleep to the exquisite pleasure of her fingers winnowing through my hair.

My last coherent thought before surrendering to bliss was a question: Harry had lied about his dealings with Clarissa. What else had he lied about?

CHAPTER SIXTEEN

"Hyperia was beside herself with worry for you," Lady Ophelia said, rattling cups, saucers, and silverware fit to rouse the hundred. "Riding hellbent in the heat, haring all over the county, neglecting meals."

Arthur sent me a commiserating glance across the breakfast table. We were once again dining al fresco. The storm I'd weathered at Traffault's had passed through this corner of the shire as well, and the morning air was pleasant rather than oppressive.

I wore my glasses, though we sat in shade. I'd be keeping my specs handy for some time, given the state of my eyes. Damned dust took a toll in addition to the harm done by bright sunshine.

"I was merely on reconnaissance," I said. "No bandits lurking in the hedgerows, no French patrols waiting to pounce when I stopped to water my horse. The English countryside is a lark compared to—"

"I despair of you." Lady Ophelia tossed a balled-up table napkin at me. "You will be the ruin of my nerves, young man. The very ruin." She flounced off into the house, leaving me alone with Arthur and the doves cooing at us from the eaves.

Hyperia and Clarissa—our guest for the nonce—had left the table earlier, claiming a need to pack for the trip to London.

I removed the napkin from my lap and laid it in an empty chair. "The feeling is mutual, Godmama. When did Lady Ophelia develop such a flare for drama?"

Arthur stirred his tea. "You excel at giving us bad turns, Julian. You went missing and were presumed dead. Then you were listed as a captive. Then dead again, then missing again. Then I got word you'd escaped but might have fallen prey to the elements. If you weathered all that merely to come home and break your head in some Sussex ditch, Lady Ophelia would take it very much amiss." He lifted his cup and saucer. "As would I."

He sipped placidly, while I pretended a fascination with my eggs. "Atlas would never toss me into a ditch."

"He'd best not. More meadow tea? It's Mrs. Felders's recipe." Arthur filled my glass before I could reply. He'd also let me have first crack at the jam.

"Why are we enjoying a mere omelet this morning?" I asked, grasping at any conversational straw. "No fanciful designs rendered in basil leaves, no spun sugar artwork. Have you sacked Cook?"

Arthur set down his tea cup and buttered a slice of lemon bread. "I had a word with her. Explained that your digestion has not yet returned to full duty. Still a trifle delicate."

"You told a falsehood. Shame on you, though the eggs are luscious."

"I did not tell a falsehood. When you first came home, you could barely manage beef tea and dry toast, Julian. You didn't eat enough to keep a finch in good fettle. You still limit your spirits, and all you managed last night was cheese toast and water."

Beef and cheese toast, and a lovely dose of affection and protectiveness from Hyperia, though I wasn't in the mood to think too hard about that last bit.

"Harry told a falsehood," I said, rather than argue the finer points of my own digestion with a duke new to the art of cosseting. "Led me to believe Clarissa was his mistress, when she was, in fact, nothing more than his hired matchmaker repellant."

"I miss Harry," Arthur said. "But I don't miss everything about him. He had a gift for complicating what should have remained simple."

I had never thought to hear His Grace disparage our departed sibling, but then, Arthur wasn't disparaging Harry, exactly. What he offered was more in the nature of confession of his own frustrations.

"Well put," I said, "but I've been thinking about Harry's treatment of Clarissa. Because she was squiring him about, none of the other eligibles made a try for her. They all assumed Harry had won the field. We owe her, Your Grace."

Arthur gave me an inscrutable look. "I'm not marrying her, and neither are you, Julian."

"I'm not?"

"If you had seen the way Hyperia West looked at me when I suggested the time had come to waken you... You have a very fierce friend in Miss West."

"As she has in me. But who was Clarissa's friend? We are so accustomed to Valloise and his countess racketing about that we didn't notice that they'd abandoned their own children. We consign the little ones to nurserymaids and governesses, but when offspring leave the schoolroom and take on the greater world, they truly need their parents and their friends."

"Does this peroration have a point?"

"We need to be better neighbors, Your Grace. You are a fine duke, staying the hand of the law when an excess of hares is going to waste, keeping the local house of worship in good trim, paying the miller timely so he can be more patient with the rest of the shire. That's all wonderful and commendable and worthy."

"Good manners prevent me from either falling asleep or citing the press of business. Do try to be succinct, though. I have my own packing to tend to."

His valet wouldn't allow him within ten feet of a trunk or valise, poor sod. "Clarissa and Reardon have been in trouble for years. They lack funds, but more to the point, *they lack friends.* Huber could prey on them because we never took the time to see how hard Valmond House was listing to port."

"Naval analogies. Charming."

Enough of the duke. I needed to talk to my brother. "Arthur, have you never borne a weight on your soul, a worry, a despair, that grew heavier and heavier as all hope faded? A burden on the spirit that made you think awful, ugly thoughts until those thoughts began to develop a certain seductive appeal?"

I rose and stared hard at the home wood, the playground of my youth, sheltering and wondrous but also dark and mysterious.

"I was so lost in France. I can't tell you how long I wandered in the mountains, freezing and starving, wondering what I'd imagined in that chamber of horrors and what I'd truly experienced. The Valmonds aren't freezing and starving—yet—but I'm sure they've had nightmares similar to my own. Harry had a flare for unnecessary complications, and you and I must have a flare for honorable behavior."

Arthur came to stand beside me. "I'm sure you will elucidate the particulars for me, new as I am to the concept of honor."

"You will bid loudly and often on Reardon's bucolic landscapes."

He nodded. "I can do that."

"You will direct Lady Ophelia to talk up this exhibition as if the Regent's legendary banquet were a mere picnic by comparison."

"She's already sent a dozen dispatches to her familiars, Julian. I can still frank mail, whatever my other shortcomings."

"Then she needs to send three dozen more. I want Wellington to comment favorably on Reardon's work, Arthur, while London's biggest gossips hang on his every word."

His Grace was quiet for a moment. "As it happens, Wellington owes me a favor. I'll call it in, and he'll be relieved to even the score."

Emboldened by my success, I tossed out the final challenge. "You will retrieve your portrait from the person you've lent it to and allow that likeness to play a prominent role in the exhibition."

Arthur ambled down the steps at a deceptively relaxed pace, and I followed. When we'd reached the privacy of the gazebo, he treated me to one of his arctic stares.

"Have you been snooping, Julian? Spying on your own brother?"

"I have been *thinking,* sorting facts and observations. I'm good at it, according to some. Osgood Banter acknowledges that his friendship with you goes back years. When I was in trouble at the Makepeace house party, he alerted you to my problems—something only a true friend would dare to do. When I quit that gathering, he alone of all the guests apologized to me for the treatment I'd received. The Banter family seat is ten miles west of here."

The arctic stare acquired a hint of sorrow. "Hence our acquaintance. He and I are of an age. We were in the same form, the same year at university. England is supposed to rule the world on the strength of such associations. What of it?"

Traffault's words came back to me, about everybody having to do a stint in some sort of captivity.

"If I were to explore the route between here and Banter's estate, I'd find, about midway between your household and his, a vacant tenant house, a fishing cottage, a secluded hunting lodge. Your extensive morning hacks mean you can trot thirty minutes west, while Banter trots thirty minutes east, and—"

Arthur held up a hand as if to ward off a blow. "Allow me a scintilla of dignity."

Since when did a scintilla rival the dimensions of Gibraltar? "Dignity is all well and good, but I'd also allow you some damned joy."

Arthur sank onto one of the benches. "I am content. I have so much more than most."

And so much less than many. A few hours a week of the domestic joy that Traffault and Celeste could revel in for decades.

"You are wealthy, and you have influence." I took the place beside him. "Tell Banter you need the loan of the portrait for a few weeks. If he's truly an appreciator of fine art, get him to the exhibition and involve him in a few bidding wars."

"He knows his art," Arthur said, looking wistful. "Proses on about it at the oddest times. Said Reardon had true talent. Said only a real artist could put a *twinkle* in my eye and make it look... ducal. My eyes do not and never shall *twinkle*."

That sad pronouncement broke my heart. I'd lost Harry in a matter of hours, Harry who'd delighted in giving Society grist for the gossip mill. And here was Arthur, who risked his life even speaking of his deepest longings.

If I didn't give Arthur a push toward his heart's desire, I'd lose him all the more painfully year by year. He'd be less and less my brother and more and more the duke, the automaton clicking and whirling whenever duty wound his key.

Forget twinkling. He'd never smile, never laugh, never indulge in a spontaneous hug.

He deserved better than that. I was a better brother than that. Not just the spare, but rather, the only brother Arthur had left and one determined to be worthy of my office.

"This autumn," I said, "you will make your postwar tour through the Low Countries and spend some time in Paris. Everybody who is anybody has already been. Take Banter as your traveling companion. God knows, Devonshire takes a whole entourage when he's on the Continent. Byron met up with traveling companions. Be fashionable for once."

Arthur's gaze went to the Hall, so majestic and staid. "What of harvest? I make it a point to be on hand for harvest."

Oh, for God's sake. "I will lounge about the Hall looking lordly until the crops are in. London is too damned noisy, and Atlas prefers country life anyway."

Arthur resumed studying the home wood. "Atlas prefers country life?"

"He's a horse of particulars, an epicurean among equines. He claims the autumn grass at Caldicott Hall is not to be missed. You, on the other hand, will get yourself to the Continent before the weather turns."

Arthur sniffed. He scanned the landscape, then his gaze settled on me. "Do I hear somebody presuming to give His Grace of Waltham orders?"

"You assuredly do, though first you have to pack for London and pass along a few orders to Banter."

"What of the dog, Touchstone? He seems quite comfortable here at the Hall."

Said the man who'd never been permitted to have a pet. "I will coddle him until he bays with contentment. Go see to the press of business, Your Grace. I'm for a nap here in the shade."

"You're sure?"

"I have given you a direct order. Don't be insubordinate. Away with you."

Arthur touched my shoulder. "I'm gone. Sweet dreams, Julian, and my compliments to your horse on his excellent good taste."

He bounded down the steps and trotted quick time for the house. I settled on the bench, prepared to catch another much-needed forty winks.

Julian, good work. This time, the voice in my head sounded very much like Harry.

～

"Bleedin' lot o' people hereabouts," Atticus said, peering out the parlor window at the relatively uncrowded streets of Mayfair. He cut a dash in his new jacket and boots, and I vow the child had gained two inches of height in a fortnight.

"Language," Hyperia chided. "And the more people who attend Lord Reardon's exhibition, the better."

"Blee—bloomin' Wellington were there," Atticus said, letting the curtain drop. "He truly do have a splendid beak."

Atticus, decked out in a sober Sunday jacket, had lurked among the throng at the opening earlier in the day. He'd goggled, he'd muttered, and he'd even taken an interest in the art, but he was for the most part keeping his impressions to himself.

"Wellington was there," Hyperia said. "Moreland, Quimbey, our own Waltham. An embarrassment of dukes. A heavenly visitation couldn't do more to earn Lord Reardon favorable notice."

"Good food too," Atticus said, wandering away from the window. "Pretty food."

Arthur had turned Cook loose on the challenge of a summer buffet to offer the exhibition's guests, and the kitchen had exceeded all bounds. Ice sculptures, canapes, flowers, sweets...

"Get out of your Sunday best," I said. "You were enjoying a half day at the exhibition, but if we're to see Miss West home, you'll need to be in uniform."

Atticus, who'd loudly disdained livery, wore his striped yellow jacket with more pride than the Royal Household Guards wore their scarlet tunics. He studied maps of Town by the hour, and I'd heard him in close conversation with Arthur's valet on the subject of boot polish.

He scampered for the door but paused on the threshold. "Old Hookey had a proper chat with you. He didn't just give you the nod."

Wellington had turned the casual nod into a high art. His nod could say, "Lovely to see you," while also conveying, "That will be close enough." I didn't precisely like him—as a commanding officer, he'd insisted on managing every aspect of an engagement on the day of battle, with occasionally disastrous results—but I respected him, and as Atticus noted, Wellington had acknowledged me.

At length.

"Go," I said, pointing to the door. "Half day is over. Back on the job, my lad. Have the stable bring the curricle around in thirty minutes."

He sketched a jaunty bow and pelted off.

"How does Waltham abide having such a lively young fellow underfoot?" Hyperia asked.

"Arthur is a bad influence on Atticus, or the other way about. They take turns trying to stare each other into submission. Atticus always bursts out laughing first, and then Arthur permits himself to relent." Not quite smile, but relent.

Hyperia closed the remaining curtains. "You're waiting for the sun to wane before you take me to Lady Ophelia's, aren't you?"

"Yes. Also giving Atticus a chance to crow belowstairs and change into his preferred plumage."

"And to eat. That child's appetite would shame the devil." She closed the last pair of curtains, casting the duke's family parlor into cozy gloom. I had elected to bide with Arthur rather than at my own London residence. Most of my staff were off seeing family in the shires, and all too soon, Arthur would be larking about on the Continent.

And whose fault was that?

"I don't know who was more pleased with today's crowd," Hyperia said. "Lady Clarissa, Lady Ophelia, or Lord Reardon."

"Eunice Huber was the most pleased. Reardon and Clarissa were relieved." As I had been. Reardon and I had had a quiet discussion regarding his finances and the possibility of various commissions coming his way. Osgood Banter had allowed as he'd have time to sit to Reardon before autumn, and Lady Ophelia had also claimed a pressing need to be immortalized on canvas. Quimbey, who qualified as a dear old soul at large, had made similar noises, while Huber had stood around looking as if Reardon were his personal artistic discovery.

"Have you considered having your portrait done?" Hyperia asked, taking the end of the sofa, toeing off her slippers, and tucking her feet up.

I took the place beside her. "Not yet. Why does it feel so good to simply sit?"

"Because you overtaxed yourself last week, and we aren't children who can be restored to full vigor in a single nap. Will you let Reardon paint you when you've regained your glorious manly tresses?"

"I'm likely to end up blond, but it's not my hair that makes me hesitate to join Reardon's throng of sitters."

She glossed her fingers over my locks, which I wore tied back in an old-fashioned queue. "You are the ducal heir now. Your portrait would reflect that, unless you were very firm with Reardon. You aren't Harry, Julian, and I'm glad of it."

"You didn't care for Harry?"

"Harry cared too much for Harry. He would never have told Waltham to go admire great art on the Continent, would never have ridden over hill and dale in search of a prodigal painter, unless he could make hay with the tale at his clubs. Harry was shrewd."

"He was a good reconnaissance officer and a good brother."

"You were too, Jules. You are too. What did Wellington have to say?"

Trust Hyperia to see to the heart of the matter. "He was quiet for a time, studying Reardon's painting of victory, then he said something about nothing being half so melancholy as a battle won, save for a battle lost. I didn't catch his precise words, but he went on to note how glad he was that the battles were behind us. I am certain I was supposed to agree and feel a sense of absolution. The great man himself was treating me as a fellow soldier, and in public. If you'd told me three months ago..."

Hyperia shifted to sit hip to hip with me. "Maybe Wellington sought absolution from you?"

I examined that extraordinary notion and found it... not outlandish. "I never did learn why Harry sneaked out of camp. He might well have been under orders of some sort, but I can't imagine his orders included surrendering to the nearest French commandant."

That French commandant, now an English baron, was available for questioning, though such a challenge daunted me. Harry's halo had taken on a hint of tarnish in recent weeks, and I wasn't ready to learn anything that might further jeopardize his sainthood.

"Whatever Wellington was about," Hyperia said, "half the gossips in London saw him reminiscing with you. When the Little Season starts, you'll receive invitations, Jules. Lots of them."

"When the Little Season starts, I'll be down at Caldicott Hall, supervising the last of the harvest and explaining to Cook that my ducal brother has the alimentary preferences of a yeoman, while I like the occasional fancy pastry or artful sweet."

"Wherever you bide, expect Lady Ophelia to keep an eye on you."

"Will you keep an eye on me too?"

Hyperia rose just when I might have reached for her hand. Something lovely had passed between us beneath the stars on the Valmond House back terrace. Not romantic, but intimate.

Reassuring and sweet.

"You don't need a minder, Julian. You mutter about not having the fitness you enjoyed in Spain, and your eyes pain you, but you are not the walking shade who came home from Waterloo."

"I have made progress," I said slowly. "I hope to make more."

She studied me, and I was on the point of admitting that I had not made enough progress—no manly stirrings to start my day, no ribald thoughts erupting at inopportune moments—when Arthur joined us.

"I thought you were taking Miss West back to Lady Ophelia's?"

"Soon," Hyperia said. "When Atticus has donned his professional attire. Today went well, don't you think?"

"Today," Arthur replied, "went splendidly. Lady Ophelia takes all the credit, of course, when Huber isn't trying to snatch it from her. Those two share a certain turn of mind. Gives one the shudders. Take a look at this."

He passed over a single folded sheet of foolscap, the broken wax seal—purple—bore the scent of rosemary. The hand was tidy and feminine.

My Lord Duke,

A child, whom I believe to be the offspring of the late Lord Harold Caldicott, has come to bide temporarily under my roof. The boy's mother succumbed to illness a fortnight past, and I am not in a position to see to the boy's upbringing.

Please excuse my presumption, and do advise...

Mrs. Charles Danforth

I passed the note to Hyperia. If Arthur had wanted me to hold the matter in confidence, he should have kept it to himself for a few more hours.

"Do you know what that is?" Arthur said, gesturing to the letter. "That is a complication and possibly a blackmail scheme in the offing when I have travel plans to make. Harry has been gone for some time, and this... this... situation is brought to my notice only now?"

"The mother has only recently passed on," I pointed out. "Perhaps she wanted nothing to do with Caldicotts of any stripe, and Mrs. Danforth refuses to take on the rearing of a complication. Besides, if the boy is legitimate, he's not only a complication. He's also a potential solution."

That was the sort of thing Harry would have said—true and relevant, but needlessly blunt.

"A solution indeed," Arthur replied. "If he's legitimate."

Hyperia shoved the letter back at me. "He's a bereaved child, an orphan, and apparently a Caldicott. Waltham, what will you do about him?"

Arthur's pleased expression made me uneasy. "I will send my best, most discreet, most noticing brother to look the situation over and gather other and further particulars. Legitimate or not, the boy could well be a Caldicott. We look after our own. I'm off to dine at the club. Miss West, good day."

In grand good spirits, His Grace of Waltham jaunted off, leaving me with a puzzle to solve. Another puzzle, and one that led me from bedrooms to brothels to barracks, at no little risk to my humble person, though that, as they say, is a tale for another time!

Made in the USA
Middletown, DE
22 November 2023

43272952R00136